Daughter
of Light and
Shadows

Daughter of Light and Shadows

ANNA McKERROW

Bookouture

Published by Bookouture in 2018

An imprint of StoryFire Ltd.

Carmelite House
50 Victoria Embankment
London EC4Y 0DZ

www.bookouture.com

ISBN: 978-1-78681-465-4
eBook ISBN: 978-1-78681-464-7

For Laura

When thowes dissolve the snawy hoord
An' float the jinglin' icy boord
Then, water-kelpies haunt the foord
By your direction
An' nighted trav'llers are allur'd
To their destruction.

Robert Burns, 'Address to the Deil'

Prologue

1590, North Berwick, Scotland

Grainne Morgan stood on the rough wooden stage at the edge of the stinking harbour. She was exhausted; she had been made to stand inside a dank, dripping cell with no room to sit down for three days until she was hallucinating from lack of sleep; dirt streaked her torn grey dress. Still, she would not confess that she had done anything wrong.

Today, the sun – usually the source of joyful wisdom in her gentle worship of the wild landscape – was her enemy for the first time. It was Midsummer, usually a day for feasting and celebration, but today the heat was oppressive; she had a harsh red burn across her nose and across her bare white shoulders.

Tears streaked her muddy face; her long black hair had come undone from its neat plait and was plastered to her neck with panicky sweat. Next to her, five other women from local villages stood lashed to the same rough-hewn poles. Three of them were unconscious, hanging forward from the pole by their wrists. One of the unconscious was only a child: nine years old and there to implicate her mother.

In the crowd that jostled to get a better view, the friends and family that had known Grainne since she was a babe held each other's hands tight and looked away, grimacing. Not to attend might mean that they condoned Grainne's actions, and the minister had made it very clear that there was no shortage of stakes for those who communed with the faeries.

Confess! Confess that ye are a witch and receive God's absolution! The local sheriff was a barrel-chested, bearded, thick-set man wearing the colours of King James, who believed that Grainne and the others were responsible for raising winds to shipwreck him at sea.

Grainne shook her head. She knew she was close to death; she could see her faerie guides waiting for her, forming a line from the wooden stage over and out to the sea to the distant faerie city of Murias. They held out their hands to her as the sheriff's hot grasp encircled her neck. *Confess, and ye shall go to your death godly. Not as the Devil's whore*, he muttered in her ear; she felt him harden as he pressed up against her from behind. Bile rose up into her throat but she choked it down. She would not be disgraced any further.

'I am no whore. I am Grainne Morgan, Beloved of the Fair Folk!' she spoke into the jeering crowd before the sheriff's thick fingers could cut off her speech. She called upon all her remaining strength and reached her hand out for the faerie closest to her – a green shimmer in the air, tall and ancient – feeling its spectral touch on her fingertips. The faerie energy entered her, just as it had done so many times before, and she felt warmed and enlivened by it.

'You do evil today by taking the name of the Fair Ones in vain! They are no devils; they are our own angels, the light ones that are a part of our lands. That have always been in the streams and rocks and trees and moss, since before there was Man, and certainly before there was this village.

'They wait for me, though you cannot see them. Aye, I do not go to my death. I go to live in the hills for ever; in the far castles of the Fae that are sweet mead and fresh bread and dancing for all eternity.'

Startled, the sheriff's hands loosened; Grainne watched the faerie that now stood next to her uncurl his fingers from her skin. She had seen this moment; she knew it, had known it in dreams, and she knew that she would suffer no more in this world of pain. Just moments stood between the end of her life in the worldly realm and her life in the faerie one. But she had one more task before the faeries would take her away for ever. She raised her chin and drew in a deep breath, summoning all her power.

'But they will curse you, you men that bring pain to this land of magic! I curse you! In the name of the Kings and Queens of Falias, Gorias, Finias, Murias and the Shining Castle of the Moon! In the names of earth and stone, air and winds, fire and hearth, water and sea, I curse you! Let no more the Fair Folk help you. Let a blight be on this land!'

Grainne watched as the waves outside the harbour walls rose and roiled higher and higher. The breath had almost left her, and her eyes blinked shut. Her body slumped against the ropes that held her upright to the stake. But the water rose higher and higher, and the crowd turned and ran from the impossibly high tide which rolled and crashed over the boats and the walls towards them.

As she died, Grainne was no longer aware of the flood that came over the harbour, or the screams of the villagers who had come to watch her burn as they now ran for their lives.

And as she left her body, she held out her hand for the faerie in the water, who had gills like a fish, and whose blue skin was slick like an eel. Its eyes were not human and held no compassion for the drowning around them, but it grasped Grainne Morgan who felt herself become fluid like water, too. She knew that the other women – and Joan, who had been denied the years to grow into one – would be taken by the

Fair Folk, as reward for their faithful honouring of the Fae. The Fair Folk would not let their favoured humans be strangled and burnt.

She went willingly and, as the faerie took her hand, the Fair Folk of Murias, the Faerie Realm of Water, led her in their dance over the waves to the distant castle, and she was at peace.

Chapter 1

The shop was called Mistress of Magic, and Faye Morgan ran it like her mother had before her.

As Faye turned the sign to 'open', she watched as, across the other side of the small road in the Scottish village she'd lived in all her life, the elderly minister cast her a baleful glance and refused to return her friendly wave. Ignoring his response – or lack of it – she kept the polite smile plastered on her face and turned back to look at her inheritance.

The tall stone hearth, blackened on the inside and topped with the original stone mantle, remained from the days when the shop had been a house. Generations of Morgans had sat in the same tin bath before the fire of a night time, watching the sprites in the fire dance, listening to stories of the faeries; of the kelpies and selkies, and of women that fell in love with beautiful faerie kings and bore their half-fae children.

The hearth was also where grandmother, and her mother before her, had sat and received the villagers with all their ailments and worries: had dispensed medicines, wisdom and fortunes for those that preferred the old ways. Faye still did.

Her mum, Moddie, had made the downstairs of the house into the shop in the 70s. Flower power had made its way even up here to a tiny village in Fife; stubbornly, despite some of the villagers telling her that no-one would come, Moddie had filled the windows and wooden shelves with crystals, her homemade incenses, books and tarot packs. Faye remembered being a child, standing behind the glass counter, her nose just over its top, watching Moddie – Modron, an old name for such a young soul – talking to her customers about astrology, spell casting, runes in the full moon.

Perhaps it was the magic that made Faye a shy child; the fact that she could see the wind, could smell a storm coming, and watched the different colours of the customers' auras fluctuate as they had their palms read or picked up the crystals that sat in little baskets along a table by the window. Though Moddie was not shy at all; before she died, grandmother sometimes took Faye's hand and told her she had more of her father in her blood than her mother. But that was all anyone ever told her about her dad.

She never knew him; he had disappeared just before she was born, and Moddie never spoke of him. She said nothing at all but, sometimes, if Faye asked, she got a haunted look on her face. All Moddie would say was that he had had to leave Abercolme: no more than that… except once. Once, Faye remembered catching Moddie unawares; she'd been a little tipsy, maybe, and Faye had come downstairs, woken by a bad dream. Moddie had been sitting at the kitchen table with a friend of hers, a woman from the little coven she ran at the shop – Faye couldn't remember her name, they'd moved away quite soon afterwards. There was a half-full bottle of wine on the table between them, and Moddie's cheeks were flushed.

Faye had dreamed of her father; only, in the dream, all she could see of him was a looming shadow. She described the dream, held in Moddie's warm embrace, sniffling into her mother's comforting soft flannel shirt.

Ah, well, that's all he'll ever be, sweetheart, Moddie had replied, stroking her hair. *A shadow. He didn't want us, child, so don't waste another tear on him.* And, to her friend, she had said, *That's one mistake I'm never making again. Almost killed me.*

Almost killed me. When Faye had gone back to bed, she had stared at the ceiling for what felt like hours with the phrase turning around and around in her head. What did Moddie mean? Had her father tried to *kill* her mother? Was she the daughter of a murderer? A picture began to form in her eight-year-old mind: a tall man, made of shadow; a scowling man, a man who wanted to hurt Moddie.

The next day Faye asked Moddie what she had meant, but her mother shook her head impatiently. *Nothing, little goose. Turn of phrase.* There was no more explanation than that, except being told not to worry. He wasn't ever coming back.

Now that she was an adult, Faye suspected that her father had been one of Moddie's hippie friends: too irresponsible to be a father; someone here and gone on the wind. Perhaps it had been drugs; perhaps things had got violent. Either way, the Morgan women kept their own surname and their own counsel.

Faye watched as the elderly minister made his way down the street. Grandmother had been quite good friends with the minister in her day; Moddie said that he was often invited in for tea and cake, and a talk about God and angels in front of the fire.

Faye sighed, and looked up at the old blackboard behind the counter which read *Support Your Local Witches.* She smiled to herself. She remembered Moddie drawing the message in chalk when Faye had been perhaps five or six. Minister Fraser had taken offence to Moddie conscripting some members of his congregation to her witchcraft group which had started meeting at the shop on Friday nights. He'd written a rather nasty piece about Moddie and the evil she was apparently wreaking at the shop, and published it in the village newsletter, entitled *Support Your Local Church.*

Grandmother, who was still alive then, had rolled her eyes dramatically.

'Such an impertinent fellow. Not like Minister Crowley,' she had sighed. 'Now, there was a learned man. Do you know what the wisest people in the world know, Faye?'

'No, Grandmother.' Faye remembered her excitement at the prospect of learning what only the wisest people in the world knew. To Faye, her grandmother was absolutely one of the most knowledgeable people in the universe.

'The wisest people in the world know one thing, my darling girl: that they know nothing,' she had sighed, and got up to make a pot of tea. 'Always remember that, Faye. There are more things in heaven and earth than can be dreamed of. And many of them are stranger than you can ever imagine.'

Faye reached for the piece of chalk she kept next to the counter and traced over her mother's words, then, remembering grandmother, added: *There are more things in Heaven and earth than can be dreamed of.* She smiled at the memory.

An hour after she'd opened for the day, Annie swept in regally. Faye looked at her watch in slight irritation, but only slight. A struggling actress, Annie's work came and went, hence her job in the shop, which Faye could be flexible about if Annie had to disappear at a moment's notice.

'Morning,' Faye said, only a little pointedly, as Annie unwound her rainbow-striped scarf and unbuttoned her long orange coat. She wore vintage designer pirate-style boots on top of some black PVC leggings, with a sweatshirt covered in sewn-on patches of toadstools, frogs and elves. Her ears were pierced several times over and she wore one long skeleton earring that grazed her collarbone. Her hair was short and, this week, bright blue.

'Early voice class, my sweet dahhh-ling,' Annie trilled in her actress-y accent; it was almost perfect, but there was a rumble of Scots underneath. Faye smiled, she found it impossible to be angry with her oldest friend for long. 'Tea? Let's have a tea. It's absolutely Baltic out.'

'Just made one. Kettle's still hot.'

'Mahh-vellous. God, that voice teacher's a lunatic, aye. Spent two hours lying on ma back, just doin' vowel sounds.' Annie slipped back into her usual accent. 'Sorry, sweetheart. Won't be late tomorra.'

'That's okay.' Faye waited for Annie to come back to the shop floor, tea in a multi-ringed hand. 'I've got to go and pour some candles. Can you mind the shop?'

'Aye, nae worries. Pour some love ones for me.'

Faye smiled. Annie's constant search for Ms Right had become an obsession long ago. She described herself as a hopeless romantic, but in Faye's opinion she was far from needing any help at all.

'Is that wise?'

'Aye, well. I need somethin'. Feel like I'm gettin' to the bottom of the pool. Not like there's that many lesbians in Abercolme.'

Faye grinned.

'If there were any new ones, I'm sure you'd know about it,' she said, pulling out a bag of organic soy wax flakes from the store room. 'I'm going to do these in the kitchen, so you can't come in for another cuppa for a while.'

'Aye, fine. The healing and protection ones have been popular too recently. Mind ye make more of those.' Annie sat down behind the counter, set her tea on it and picked up Faye's tarot cards, shuffling them absently. She started laying them out and Faye peered over her shoulder as she walked past, going to the store cupboard for her stock of essential oils for the candles.

'Love reading?'

'Aye. No brainer.'

'Yeah, well.' Faye frowned at the cards. 'Not much there though.' Annie had laid out the centre of a Celtic cross formation, the most common kind of layout for an overall picture. As she laid the final four cards in a column alongside the central cross, Faye laughed. 'Oh. Spoke too soon,' she said, as one of the Kings came out, followed by The Lovers. 'Not one for you, though. A King? You going straight after all these years?'

Annie sighed, picked up the cards and stuck them back into the deck. 'Reshuffle,' she said, cutting the pack three times and halving and sliding the cards into each other repeatedly. 'Obviously they were still tuned into your energy. I'm not in the market for a man. Dunno what ye see in them, sweetheart.'

'No, neither do I, most of the time.' Faye sighed and opened the store cupboard, selecting rose, lavender and neroli oils. She closed the cupboard again and started to clear space in the kitchen for her work. She was well aware of the fact that to make a good love-drawing candle, she had to create the atmosphere of love as best she could as she made them, but it was difficult when she'd never truly been in love herself. Not like Annie, who fell in love every other week.

Faye put a CD into the player and the haunting and otherworldly music filled the room. She lit some rose and benzoin incense in a heart-shaped earthenware holder and shook the wax flakes into the big heatproof glass bowl she'd placed on top of a large casserole pot with boiling water in the bottom. As they melted, she closed her eyes and sang to the music; to the heart-filling and heart-breaking melodies that spoke of love so brilliant it was difficult to look at directly; at passion so intense it could crack foundations: a house, a tower, a mind…

As she stirred in the oils to the wax, making hearts and pentagram shapes with the spoon, nine times each, she concentrated as hard as she could on the feeling of love that was in the music. *Is that what love is?* Not for the first time, she wondered if she wanted something so destructive in her life. Wasn't it better to be undisturbed by the storms that raged in the battle for love? And yet her heart yearned for it, and she poured her heart's longing into the wax.

As Faye watched the candles cool in the pretty pink glass holders she had sourced, and inhaled the scent of rose, she placed seven dried rosebuds into the half-melted wax of each candle. With each rosebud, she made a wish for the user of the candle – for romance, passion, mutual love, appreciation, kindness, longevity and healing. Last, she traced a heart in the top of the almost-set wax of each one. She would trim the wicks tomorrow and restock the shelves in time for Valentine's Day.

She sat down on the kitchen stool, closed her eyes and focused on the music, feeling the longing for all the things it spoke of and all the things she never let herself believe – love at first sight, that special knowing people talked about when they met the love of their lives. The magic of meeting your soulmate, the person who knew you without being told. It was a fairytale, wasn't it? Those people were deluded; hypnotised with lust and illusion. People weren't perfect. Lovers left. Moddie's lover – her father, whoever he was – had left. She wanted to believe, but she didn't.

Someone would get the benefit of her creations, but she didn't believe it would be her.

Chapter 2

'Annie, you can't drink all the wine. It's an offering for the sunrise.' Faye hugged the foil blanket around herself and pulled her scarf back over her nose. It was December and they were camping out on Black Sands Beach, waiting for the cold sun to break over the black night horizon for the winter solstice.

Annie drained the insulated travel mug of the home-made raspberry wine they'd brought. Faye made it from the raspberry bushes in the garden behind the shop; like any good witch, she had maintained the garden that had always been there as far as she knew. Scabious, comfrey, lavender, dandelion, mugwort and nettles grew along the stone-walled edges of the long garden behind the house. Two apple trees stood like guardians at the end, and the raspberry and bramble bushes dominated the east side of the garden, drinking the sun into their ripe fruit every summer. On the west side of the garden, wild white and yellow roses clutched their wall like possessive lovers, not allowing anything else to grow there.

'Cannae let these good offerings go unappreciated.' Annie burped. She did the same thing every year. In a way, it was part of their tradition now. She and Annie usually came to the beach late on the night of the 21st December, the shortest day, and camped on the beach, ready to watch the sunrise and welcome in the new solar year. Faye liked presents and turkey dinners as much as the next person, but she had always celebrated the old ways in private – when Moddie and Grandmother had been alive, they had too. Now Annie had become her solstice companion.

Grandmother had died of a heart attack when Faye was twelve, and Moddie had passed, suddenly and without warning, from a stroke when Faye was eighteen. The local doctor was surprised as Moddie was young still, having had Faye when she was in her early twenties, and in generally good health. She had steered Faye away from where Moddie had been laid peacefully in the spare room and made her a cup of tea. *Strokes can happen at any time,* she'd said, handing Faye a mug with a generous amount of sugar stirred into it. *I mean, it's something that happens in your brain, as you know. But it's like a lightning strike. Something as fast and savage as heartbreak. Or, falling in love in the first place.*

Faye, who suspected Moddie had been heartbroken over something in her past for some time, hadn't answered. A stroke was medical; it was mercurial, exactly like lightning. It was just one of those things; she suspected the doctor of trying to make her feel better. But death was a door that seemed to swing open easily for some as soon as they walked near it, and was slowly, creakingly pushed open for others, after a long struggle. For some, it seemed that they danced with one hand forever on the door, daring it to open, until one day, it acquiesced. Moddie, for some reason, had prompted the door into the next life to swing open suddenly and gather her into its velvety blackness at the first hint of her passing by.

Because Faye was eighteen already and an adult in the eyes of the law, no arrangements had to be made to look after her; she continued running the shop almost without a break. But she was still young, and Annie had taken to dropping in more to help and staying over at the house a few

nights a week. Neither of them ever talked about it, but Faye knew that
Annie was substituting herself for Moddie in all the little spaces she had
used to inhabit in Faye's life. And that included the solstices.

Every year, Faye and Annie brought Grandmother's grimoire with
them and recorded their thoughts and impressions of the solstice in
it. The grimoire was a book of old Scottish folk magic, added to by
generations of Morgans. In the blank pages at the back, after the pages
of remedies, rituals and strange sigils, there was a handwritten section
which was a cross between a diary, recipe book and magical journal,
where Grandmother and the Morgans before her had observed the moon,
the seasons, recorded the magic they did and how well it worked. That
aspect of the book was what people called a Book of Shadows, nowadays:
a kind of reflective journal of magic which was always a work in progress.
Faye had found it a few years ago when she needed more stock space for
the shop and had finally set to clearing out Grandmother's room which
was downstairs at the back of the cottage. It had been convenient for
the formidable woman to be on the ground floor when she'd started to
find the stairs difficult. Not that she gave up her mobility easily, Faye
had remembered with a smile as she'd packed boxes with the blankets,
throws and nightdresses that had stayed in Grandmother's wardrobe
after she died, as if she'd just been away on holiday. And after walking
became tough she'd taken up residence in the easy chair by the fire in
the shop, which had been the sitting room when she was a bairn, telling
stories, reading palms and dispensing advice. Sometimes Moddie had
rolled her eyes, not wanting her mother in the shop all the time, but
Grandmother wasn't going anywhere.

At the bottom of a drawer containing woollen socks, scarves and
various hairbrushes – Grandmother had kept her white hair long,
and still brushed it a hundred times every night, just like she had

done with Faye and Moddie's deep red auburn curls when they were children – Faye had found a large, brown leather-bound notebook. It was plain on the cover and wrapped with a leather thong. When she opened it, she found Grandmother's neat, copperplate handwriting. *The Magical Record of Alice Morgan*, it read.

It started with some passages that concerned local faerie lore.

At Midwinter one of the faerie kingdoms of Murias, Falias, Gorias or Finias take a child and, at Midsummer, a willing woman. The child must be under a year old, so that it can be raised in the Glass Castle with no memory of its mortal parents, and the woman must be fair, and willing to join the Faerie Dance forever more. In thanks, the faerie king and faerie queen will bless the land and grant boons to the villagers of Abercolme for their generous offerings.

There was a song that Faye remembered from childhood:

Midsummer, Midsummer, Midsummer delight; go to the faeries on Midsummer night
Take thee a maiden, take thee a wife –
Take thee a bairn for the rest of its life –
Midsummer, Midsummer, Midsummer delight; go to the faeries on Midsummer night.

Grandmother had taught it to her, and they'd sing it together at Midsummer on the 21st June every year, when Grandmother insisted that they take a picnic to the beach. They'd sing and dance and have all of Faye's favourite things to eat, and lemonade to drink, but Grandmother would always insist they were home by teatime.

Faye looked out at the black sea and sky, smiling at the memory. Grandmother said that the faeries were the reason that Abercolme seemed to have always been blighted – at least, for as long as anyone could remember. According to Grandmother, the frequent storms, flooding and subsequent loss of crops on the farmers' lands were because the villagers no longer observed the old ways. Moddie had rolled her eyes when Grandmother started on that particular topic. *It's nothing to do with the faeries, Mother,* she had said. *It's just bad luck. Sometimes bad things happen.*

However, a lot of bad things had happened in Abercolme: there was no denying that. In the 80s and 90s, the local fishing community had been hit hard by the effects of overfishing in the Scottish coastal waters, and many old local family businesses – bakeries, butchers, blacksmiths – had not survived the financial struggles of a national recession, leaving Abercolme a ghost of what it had once been. Before that, though, there were worse things. Strange tragedies: unexplained house fires that had killed whole families; a busload of children from the village school, killed in a crash on a road across the local moors. Broken families, drug-taking, alcoholism. There had been a number of murders, more than a small coastal community should have had. There was a dark side to Abercolme, and even though the locals might have got used to it, Faye still felt it, like an icy wave underneath a warm summer tide. She had stayed, though: *where else could she go?* All Faye had was the shop, and Annie. Leaving Abercolme, as dark as it could sometimes be, would be to leave her heritage. Her ancestors had trod this sand; Faye at least had the comfort that the rising Midwinter sun might cast her shadow on the same place it had theirs.

She had showed the book to Annie, and together they'd leafed through the thick pages. Grandmother had written down her dreams in it as well as spells, healing she'd performed for various villagers, and accounts of her rituals at the new, full and dark moon.

Annie had always been fascinated by Faye's witch heritage: the fact that she could trace her family back to Grainne Morgan, hundreds of years ago, and further before that. But Faye didn't like to think about it; every time she did, it was as if she could feel the fire licking up her own skin. The ancestral trauma from such a thing, she had read, lived on in the generations following. She could well believe it. She had had nightmares as a child: of being shut in a dark, smelly room with no light or air. She would wake up from those dreams crying and with a sensation around her wrists as if they had been chafed by rope.

How to explain the crackling panic that engulfed her when she thought about those women? The great-grandmother Morgans, who had, perhaps, if this legend was to be believed, overseen the sacrifice of babies and women to the faeries? And what did that really mean, if it was true? Faye knew of the old beliefs that if a baby was sick, you could leave it out for the faeries who might take it and leave a changeling in its place – a faerie baby to be brought up as human in the place of the ailing human child which would be spirited away to be faerie for ever more. But that was an old belief, and the world had moved beyond leaving sickly children in the wild to die.

'There's all kind of things in here. Look – spells for health, luck...' Annie said, interrupting Faye's thoughts. She was flicking through the thick, handwritten pages, absorbed, until she exclaimed and jabbed her finger down on the paper. 'Ha! Knew it. Spell for love. To summon passionate love, aye, that's what we want! Good on ye, Grandmother Morgan.' She pulled out her glasses and slid them onto her nose. 'We're gonna do this.'

'I don't want to,' Faye replied.

'Why not? Bet it's good. Your grandmother was brilliant, aye. Every year I find something new in this book. I don't know why you don't have it out in the shop all the time. People would love to see it.'

The thought filled Faye with a worried panic.

'Oh no. I couldn't do that. This is her grimoire. It's so personal.'

'But, Faye… she's passed, sweetheart. Can't hurt.' Annie held her torch up to the book again. 'Says here that the first step is to make dolls. *The object of your desire is to be rendered as dutifully as possible, with the hair and fingernails if it is to represent one person in particular.*' Annie read it aloud in her actress-y voice, as if she were a television announcer from the 1950s. 'Wow. D'ye think Grandmother Morgan was out and about, picking toenails out of people's bins, aye? Not for me. But it says here ye can just make one up that represents your ideal partner. I'd be well up for that. Why not? We could ask Aisha to do it with us, she's single.'

'I don't know. I'm not sure I want that. It's… I dunno. More trouble than it's worth.'

'Course ye do. You're always moonin' around like some kind a lost faerie, Faye. Look at ye. Made for romantic hair-whippin' in the wind, moonlit seaside rendezvous.' Annie shone her torch into Faye's face. 'Look at that face, aye. If no-one takes ye soon I'm going to try and convert ye to a lesbian.'

Faye shrugged. 'No offence, but I don't think I'd be a very good one.'

'Aye well, don't rule it out. But the ceremony? Come on, Faye. What d'you have to lose? I know you're shy. I know ye don't want to get hurt. You're afraid. But it doesn't have to be earth-shattering, okay? Ye could just have a little fun. Ye need some fun, sweetheart.' Annie put her gloved hand on Faye's shoulder and looked into her eyes in the dim light of the torch. They had a campfire but it was burning low and the coals were only a dim glow in the dark.

'I am having fun. I'm here with you on a sub-zero beach, waiting for the sunrise. Honestly. Who else is doing this?' Faye argued, but she knew Annie was right. And that Annie normally got what she wanted, one way or another.

'Promise me, sweetheart. You need this. I bloody need it too.'

'You get a new girlfriend every other week.' Faye rolled her eyes. Annie wasn't usually this earnest, and it felt strange.

'I know, I know. But I want someone I really like. That I can trust.' Annie looked at Faye out of the corner of her eye. 'Not just to sleep with. I want someone to love.'

'Are you being serious?'

'Aye. Why not?' Annie looked away wistfully at the black sea. 'I've only been in love once, and that was a long time ago.'

Faye narrowed her eyes at her friend; she was an actress, after all, so she could roll out the drama if she wanted to. But Faye knew her well enough to know when she was being real or not, and she thought that in this case she was.

'Fine, fine. We'll do it. Anything to stop this emotional blackmail.' Faye grinned and took the grimoire from her friend. Grandmother's handwriting was so familiar; neat copperplate, spidery with time. She felt the tears spring to her eyes as the memory of the woman she had loved so much came back, breathing and vivid. 'Let's see what we'll need.'

She was still peering at the book with the torch in her hand an hour or so later when she noticed the light had changed, and she could see the page better. She looked up and saw the first faint rays of the sunrise reaching out over the horizon, and nudged Annie, who had dozed off inside the tent.

They walked down the beach a little together, foil blankets tied around their shoulders like magicians' capes, passing a flask of mulled wine between them.

'Happy solstice.' Annie hugged her and they stared up at the sun, blanketed by dawn-pink clouds, glinting on the grey-green sea. 'May all our wishes come true this year. Make a wish on the new sun.' She raised her thermal cup to the sun and closed her eyes. Perhaps Annie really was wishing for someone she could love.

Faye held the Thermos up and made her own wish on the new sun, before taking a drink and pouring a small libation of the wine into the sand by her feet. She had, in previous years, wished for her health and for the shop to be successful. She was about to do the same again, but as she closed her eyes and felt the faraway warmth of the new sun caress her skin, a sense of bravery overtook her. *I wish for love. True love to come to me*, she said, and was surprised at how much she found that she truly meant it.

Chapter 3

'So. Are we all ready?'

Faye looked at the other women in turn. Annie, her many-ringed hands folded in her lap, sat cross-legged on the old black sheepskin rug in front of the hearth, the firelight flickering on a pair of oversized reading glasses. Next to her was Aisha, wearing a vest top that said *Witch, Please* in bright pink on stretchy black fabric, grinning excitedly.

'I can't wait!' Annie looked around her at the candles that flickered around the shop: on the shelves, on the counter and in lamps around them as they sat in a circle on the rug. 'This is awesome. We shoulda done this years ago.'

It was past closing time and Faye, Annie and Aisha sat on the sheepskin rugs in front of the hearth fire in the shop; a sweet incense burnt in the air.

'Let's do it,' Aisha muttered. 'I have needs, ladies.' Aisha had been working part time in the shop alongside doing her PhD at Edinburgh Uni for the past year, job-sharing with Annie. It worked well, as neither Annie or Aisha could commit to full-time hours and, anyway, Faye couldn't afford to pay them both to always be there. Aisha was a huge music fan and had slowly been trying to educate Faye, bringing in CDs for her to try every week. Usually she came to work in jeans and scruffy band T shirts, although she couldn't ever quite disguise her small waist, delicious curves and glossy black hair, which she usually tied up in a knot. Tonight, though, it was loose; Annie gave her a long look as she came in and took off her coat, hat and gloves.

'Scrubs up well, this one, aye.' She raised her eyebrow at Faye. 'Seems like my troubles might be over.' She winked theatrically at Aisha.

'I wouldn't stop your search just yet.' Aisha grinned. 'Faye said to come in the mood for love, so I thought putting a bit of lippy on wouldn't hurt.'

'Your hair *is* lovely, though, Aish. You should wear it down more often.' Faye motioned to them both to sit down. Aisha blushed, but looked pleased.

'Thanks,' she said shyly as she joined them on the rug.

'Come on! Let's do this. The night's auspicious. Look at that moon!' Annie wriggled her shoulders in excitement and they all looked up through the plate-glass shop windows at the huge yellow-gold moon that seemed to hang pregnant in the black sky. 'It's a Friday, the best day for love spells. And it's a full moon. Ach, I'm horny. Bring me someone, moon! I'm not even fussy by now.'

'Hey. I thought you wanted your next great love?' Faye raised her eyebrow at Annie, who sat opposite Aisha so that the three of them made a triangle within the circle.

'I do. Just saying, nothin's off the table. Or floor, in this case. Shall we get started, then? You going to clear the space, call the powers in?'

Annie knew more or less as much as Faye about witchcraft; Moddie and Grandmother had taught Faye, and Faye had taught her friend. Later, when Grandmother had passed on but Moddie was still alive, she had treated both of them as her daughters. *Ah, my witchlings, come in and learn,* she'd say sometimes when they tiptoed into the kitchen, trying to get a glimpse of Moddie's spell-making.

Moddie had relied more on the modern witchcraft books that she stocked in the shop than Grandmother's family wisdom, though Faye never knew why; perhaps she found the old traditions too familiar. A lot was similar, but much was different. When they were teens, Moddie had taught them how to cast a circle according to modern witchcraft; Grandmother sniffed at what she considered her daughter's modern notions. *No point calling in the powers like you're in the theatre, standing there, waving your arms like an idiot. The powers would be there all the time if ye were living rightly with them,* she'd say, glaring at the purple and blue-covered paperbacks that featured elegant women's profiles against crescent moons. *Hell mend ye if ye conjure some kind of foreign spirit in the house…*

But Moddie would roll her eyes. *Ma, come on now. Times are changing,* she said, and so Faye learned a combination of Grandmother's old ways and Moddie's newer ones, which served her well now that she ran the shop.

Faye picked up a rose crystal wand – the stone for love – and walked around her friends, imagining drawing down moon and starlight from the clear black Scottish sky. When it was cloudless like tonight, the night sky reminded her of the freezing, eerily flat water at Loch Lomond, further inland to the west of Abercolme. She had visited a few times; it was an eerily beautiful place at night, with water that appeared black in daylight because of its great depth, but was as clear and sharp as diamonds.

She felt the power fill her from above, then brought the power up through her from the earth; the rich black earth under the worn flagstone floor; the wet green of the woodland, and the dark, rained-on sand of the beach that she had felt between her toes so many times that she almost missed it when it was gone. The power of earth and stars filled her and met in her middle, spiralling into each other and building heat through her body.

Faye felt the power of earth and sky flow through her, through the wand and, with her eyes half-closed, she saw it light up the stone-flagged floor, making a circle of light that glowed in the same pink as the crystal wand.

Next, Faye called in the elements: north for earth, east for air, south for fire, west for water. Going to each point in the circle where she had already placed the candles inside their glass lamps, she spread her arms wide and called out to the spirits of each element to protect them in their work.

When she turned to west to invoke the power of water, she envisaged a wall of water, like a waterfall, flowing to her; to the south, a wall of fire that crackled and spat. When she faced the east and opened her arms to connect with the power of air, she imagined standing on top of a mountain with the wind pushing at her from against the drop below. And when she turned to the north, she felt the steadfast power of earth spiralling around them; envisioned mountains in front of her, felt the lushness of the earth under her feet, even though she stood on the stone-flagged floor of the shop that was worn smooth in places and dipped with the wear of feet over hundreds of years.

The women gripped each other's hands. In the middle of their circle Faye had set up an altar for their love spell. In the centre she had placed two deities: the horned god Pan representing nature on one side, representing all things masculine and virile; a statuette of the goddess of love, Aphrodite, on the other, standing in her seashell with her hair wreathed about her naked body, representing the energy of love. Around the deity figures she had scattered shells and pebbles collected from the local beach; a vase of red and pink roses stood behind them.

She had lit pink and red candles, two of each, and benzoin, rose petal and jasmine incense burnt fragrant smoke around them from where it smouldered on top of a charcoal disc in an earthenware holder. In preparation for their ritual, Faye had also filled a blue-painted pottery chalice with a pentagram on the front with half of a mini bottle of champagne. *A lover's drink to entice a lover*, she thought as she watched the bubbles burst on the surface of the golden fizz. *Why not.*

'Let us first set our clear intention in our work. That we will attract romantic love to ourselves in the best way possible for us, individually; that we trust the gods to bring us exactly what we need,' she said, opening Grandmother's book. The ritual additions were hers, to set the mood and create the space; the spell itself noted only the bare bones of what was needed: desire, and a poppet doll.

'They should be sexy. The men. And women,' Aisha added.

'Okay, okay. We'll attract romantic love and great sex to ourselves, and we trust the gods to bring us what we need.' Faye smiled and raised her eyebrow at her friend. 'Good enough?'

'Aye.' Annie wriggled on the rug. 'What? It isn't that comfortable sitting on a stone floor, ye know.'

'Let's get started, then. Get out your poppets.'

Each woman laid a doll onto the rug in front of them. In preparation for the spell, Faye had told them to each make a poppet of their ideal partner as a focus in the spell. Aisha put hers in front of her shyly.

She had drawn a big red heart in marker pen on the white t-shirt material she'd made her poppet of. 'He's got a good heart,' she explained. 'And I stuffed him with cut-up copies of *Rolling Stone*. So he'll be intelligent and into music.'

'Okay, well, that makes sense. Annie?' Faye turned to her shop assistant. 'What have you got?'

Annie placed a Barbie in front of her.

'This is her.'

'Barbie?'

'She's got big tits, she's blonde, she's into fashion and she's, like, had about a million professional careers. What's not to love?'

Aisha laughed. 'That's so cool. I love it.'

Annie picked up the Barbie and smoothed out its little t-shirt, on which she'd written GIRLS RULE.

'So. I gave her a kind of activist t-shirt because I want someone who cares about politics. And I gave her this miniskirt and cowboy boots because she still needs to be hot. And she's carrying some little books I made because she's intelligent and she likes reading. And, look, I coloured in all her chakras.' Annie pulled up the doll's t-shirt to show exploding stars in the colours of the rainbow going from red at the Barbie's groin to dark blue on her third eye. 'So she'll be spiritual. Into yoga or something, at least.'

'Of course. However you do it is fine.' Faye nodded. 'Okay. So, we present these poppets to the gods and ask them to bring these qualities to us, or something better.' She placed hers next to the other dolls.

'Faye, that's beautiful!' Aisha gasped. 'How long did it take you?' She picked it up and turned it over gently in her hands.

'Oh, not long,' Faye murmured, and looked away, embarrassed. Her poppet had actually taken a week to make; she'd neglected restocking the shop because she'd been sitting at the shop counter, stitching it for days.

She had made a man's shape; tall, long-legged, strong in the shoulders, but not too meaty a figure. It had dark-blond hair made of a golden wool with a dark copper fleck in it that she'd found in Moddie's old mending basket, which she'd woven into braids. She had embroidered blue eyes and, as it had turned out, quite a pouty mouth. On the body she had sewn her wishes in blue and gold. The stitching was fine and delicate; as a child, Moddie had taught her how to embroider: chain-stitch, cross-stitch, open-leaf, fishbone.

In a fine running stitch she'd written a long line of rhyming words, wrapping the doll's body. *Let him be kind, beautiful, magical, free; let him be loving, gentle, and in love with me.*

Aisha read out the words; the fire crackled as her voice wove the magic that had already begun with the stitching.

'That's lovely, Faye.' Annie smiled gently and took her friend's hand. 'I hope he comes for ye, I really do,' she said.

'Thanks,' Faye blushed, and placed all three on the altar. 'Right. So, now we've created our poppets, we charge them with the elemental energy to give them life. Starting with air in the east, go clockwise and imagine all four elements flowing into your poppet.' Faye closed her eyes and saw each element immediately, flowing and combining into a golden-white light that surrounded and filled her little doll. 'Now! Say with me:

Bring love to me; so mote it be.
Fill my heart; so let it start.
Satisfy my desire; by earth, air, water and fire.
Blessed faerie realm, bring love to me.
Blessed Fair Folk, bring me the satisfaction of my desire.

She had learned the chant from Grandmother's book and repeated it, wondering if Grandmother had ever cast this spell, and what the outcome was if she had.

The women chanted after her, three times: *Blessed faerie realm, bring love to me. Blessed Fair Folk, bring me the satisfaction of my desire.* Faye took each poppet and wafted it through the incense smoke, then replaced them on the altar; she took up the blue chalice of champagne and gulped. She focused as hard as she could on the desired outcome, but her mind shifted every time. It was like trying to look through bevelled glass. She knew she wanted someone. A lover, someone that would pull her heart open and deserve the love that lay there, dormant, waiting. But, though she could see a vague figure in her mind's eye, it wouldn't come clear. Still, she had made the doll, at least. That would do its work if Grandmother's book was to be believed.

'So mote it be,' she intoned, and passed the cup to Aisha.

'So mote it be,' Aisha repeated, and passed the cup to Annie, who sipped twice before passing it back to Faye. 'What now?' She looked at the door as if she expected someone to walk through it immediately.

'Now, we close the circle and wait,' Faye said quietly, feeling the magic spiralling around her, big and powerful. Something would come of this. She knew it, deeply, inside herself.

'Do you think they'll come?' Aisha whispered. 'Like, together? In a group?'

'That seems highly unlikely.' Annie stretched out her legs and knelt, preparing to get up. 'But, you know. Magic works in its own weird way.'

'It will be what it's supposed to be,' Faye said, as she banished the elements from the circle, imagining each one disappearing: the fire dying and going back to ground, the water drying away, the mountains receding, the strong breeze dropping to a light breath. Closing the circle by walking around the outside of the space and smudging at the circle of light with her foot, she took care not to disturb the rose petals. 'The altar can stay up overnight. I'll take it down before we open in the morning,' she said. 'Let it have as much time in the moon as it can.'

'Will it work?' Aisha murmured to Faye. 'Will it really, do you think?' Her wide, long-lashed brown eyes searched Faye for reassurance and, for the first time, Faye saw something she hadn't seen before in Aisha's eyes; a raw need, a yearning. Perhaps Aisha needed this more than Faye had expected.

'I'm sure it will.' Faye reached out shyly and touched Aisha's soft cheek. 'Have faith,' she murmured, and Aisha nodded.

Annie knelt in front of the altar and bent her head for a moment, no doubt adding an extra prayer to the gods. Faye watched her friend trace her fingertips over the words of the spell in the book. If Grandmother had cast this spell, had it brought her Moddie's father? Had Moddie cast it to summon Faye's own father? And, if so, how good was a spell that summoned lovers who would try to kill you, then desert you?

Suddenly, the door swung open and an icy winter blast of wind blew in from the outside. The bells next to the door jangled in alarm, and the old charm of pebbles strung together with string that hung there, made by Grandmother as protection, shook violently.

'What the...?' Aisha was the closest to the door, instinctively stepping out into the street. As soon as she did, the gusting wind died away and the full yellow moonlight painted shining streaks on Aisha's long black hair. She looked up in confusion at the moon which seemed to fill the sky.

Faye ran to close the door, goosebumps prickling her skin. She had been so sure she'd locked it. As she did so, she felt a kind of presence pass her and go out through the door. The incense smoke which had built up in the room billowed out into the night air, but it was more than that. As if the spell had been truly released into the world.

Faye's heart beat in a panic as she pulled Aisha inside and closed the door again hurriedly behind them both. The door banging open had coincided with feeling as though the stone-flagged floor had dissolved under her, and now she was falling.

Aisha's face wore an odd expression; her wide eyes dreamy and staring. Her cheeks were flushed and hot, even though it was cold outside.

'Aisha! Aisha! What's up?' Faye shook her friend gently, realising that she was also hanging on to Aisha to stop the disorienting feeling of the floor slipping away under her. The roses faded from Aisha's light brown skin. Her eyes cleared, and she met Faye's gaze. Faye felt the room right itself and her feet firmly back on the stone.

'Nothing… I…' Aisha gazed through the glass door outside onto the street, which was almost as bright as daylight, and smiled quietly, as if she had a pleasurable secret. 'I'm fine. You should see the moon out there, Faye. I don't know why you locked the door in the first place.'

But Faye felt something other than pleasure at the languid yellow moonlight outside. It felt odd; she couldn't remember a time when the full moon had ever felt strange to her before. Yet there was a strange atmosphere out there, like the heavy warmth before a storm.

Faye pulled the blind down on the door, blew out the remaining candles in the shop and turned on the harsh electric light.

'Back to real life,' she said as cheerily as she could, but her voice wavered.

Chapter 4

There were two routes Faye usually took across the beach, depending on whether it was high or low tide.

At low tide, she walked across the wet brown sand, as close to the water as she could. If it was at all warm, she took off her shoes and let the water wash her feet. If it really was too cold – the icy water in winter was too much to bear, really – she kept her boots on, but bent down to trail her fingers in the water from time to time, looking out to sea.

At high tide the short beach was almost totally submerged, apart from the rocks right at the edge that bordered an area which was half-sand, half-grass. If Faye came to the beach at that time then she balanced across the rocks in bare feet or with boots until she got to her favourite rock; high up, the tide hardly ever reached it and she sat up there like a mermaid, watching the waves roll in and out.

Despite loving the sea, having practically grown up at the beach, Faye had a deep fear of what was in its depths. The clear, cool wavelets that stroked the shore were one thing; even going up to her knees was fine. Sometimes she even swam along the shoreline, but no further than a few metres out into the deeper water, where the sea floor dropped away sharply in steep banks, and only when the sea was flat and calm. She had seen many sea storms from up in the village when no-one dared to go anywhere near Black Sands; where the waves rose high and lashed buildings furiously. She had seen, once, a dolphin washed up dead on the beach, swept in a storm from deeper waters. And, like everyone in the village, she remembered fishermen – when she was a child and people still fished the waters here – whose boats had capsized in a storm, or the poor souls who had gone swimming too far out and never came home. The dark sea was capricious and terrible; Faye both feared and loved it. Most of all, she respected it. It did not do to disrespect the sea.

It was a scramble to get to her favourite spot, but when she was sitting there, the rocks were arranged in such a way that she was hidden from anyone on the beach. Faye was pretty sure it was only her that used it; she tested it by leaving strands of seaweed trailing over different areas in the rock. When she returned, no-one had ever moved them.

The only thing that overlooked her rocky perch on the beach was a house, but it had been closed up for as long as Faye could remember, though it was kept in good repair by whatever property company owned it. It had been built in the sixties by some rich architect who was drawn to Abercolme for the coastline; Moddie had told her he had unknowingly built the house on a ley line, or some other sacred ground. Either way, once it was built, Grandmother had said that the local faeries were displeased, and had cast a curse on anyone who lived there. Whatever the reason, it had been bought a few times but always sold soon after, so had been empty for as long as Faye could remember.

Often, she came to the beach with a spell ready to cast into the waves; sometimes, she came just to be with the sea, loving its strong, elemental force. The air at the beach was always bright and clear. She didn't mind if it was cold. She loved the salt spray on her face; she loved the wildness of the water and the way it changed colour, from grey to dull green to blue-black and turquoise, occasionally, in the summer.

Today, the tide was almost out. Faye had to open the shop soon, not that anyone would ever hold her to opening exactly on the stroke of ten. She'd brought a thermal cup of coffee with her and a roll fresh from the village bakery.

She walked across the sand as usual, listening to the seagulls call to each other, feeling the spring sun on her face. The sea was calm today, and when the sun came out from behind the clouds, it glittered on the water as if it were glass.

A flash of light made her look up, surprised. One of the windows on the house facing the beach was open at just the right angle that it was reflecting sunlight into her eyes exactly at that moment. The house was all steel and glass, that ultra-modern look that had been popular when it was built. Most of the villagers hated it; it didn't fit in with the rest of the village, which was full of the old-style Scottish stone houses. But Faye had always thought it belonged there, somehow. The glass reflected the sea and the sky in all its changing moods and colours, and on full moon nights when Faye had been at the beach, the house, dark and uninhabited, had caught the moon like a glass temple.

She stared for a moment, shielding her eyes from the bright glare. She saw that a few of the windows were open, in fact, and when she looked harder, she could see the blinds that were usually closed had been opened, meaning she could see into the house.

She walked up the beach towards the rocks and closer to the house. Inside, people were moving furniture; she watched as two men carried some kind of desk up a set of stairs. Someone was moving in for the first time in years; Faye was perhaps six or seven when there had been someone there last. It was when Grandmother had still been fit enough to accompany her to the beach on a scavenging trip, anyway – that was when Grandmother had told her that the house had been cursed by the faeries.

I wonder how long this one will last, she smiled to herself, pulling the tartan wool shawl around her shoulders to keep out the cold. *And if there really is a curse on it.* Moddie hadn't given her a direct answer when Faye had asked her about it after being on the beach with Grandmother, when her mother was plaiting her hair for school. *But IS there a faerie curse, Mummy?* She had watched as Moddie's deft hands braided the three hanks of the deep auburn hair that fell in natural – but often wild and knotted – ringlets around Faye's shoulders. But when she gazed up to her mother's face from the edge of her bed, mirrored in the glass of the dressing table opposite, Moddie had a strange expression. *Just Grandmother's tales. Go on and get dressed for school now, little one*, was all she had said, but she had hugged Faye fiercely before she let her go.

'Great view out here!' a voice called from behind her, and she looked around in surprise.

A man with longish black hair was walking up the beach towards her; tall, slim, brown-skinned and unshaven with probably a week or more of beard. He was wearing a black knitted hat and a blue duffel coat over black jeans; his trainers were wet already.

'It certainly is!' she called back, watching him approach. He was holding a sheaf of papers, but as he got a few feet from Faye, the wind came up unexpectedly hard and blew them out of his hand.

'Oh, shit!' he shouted, and started running after the paper, which had turned the quiet beach into a sudden storm. There was no way he was going to get them all; instinctively, Faye collected up the ones nearest to her, watching him as he ran around, trying to catch the others. It was as though there were sprites in the wind, pulling the paper away from him right at the last minute, curling and parading them around him like cruel puppet masters. She started laughing; first, politely, into her hand, and then louder, as he jumped into the wavelets at the edge of the tide, splashing himself in the process. He made such a comical figure, and it was such a sudden change of events from her expected quiet beach meditation, that the mirth overtook her and she felt herself laughing hysterically like she hadn't done in years.

The man came up the beach to where Faye was holding on to the rock and wiping at her eyes.

'Having a good laugh at my expense, I see.' He was rueful, but a smile played on his lips. 'You're going to have to help me clean this up, you know. Bystander responsibility or something.'

'Sorry.' She took in a deep breath.

He handed her a wet flyer. 'Here. You might as well have the last salvageable one.'

ABERCOLME ROCKS, Faye read at the top of the pink paper. Underneath, there was a list of what she assumed were band names, then MIDSUMMER EVE written at the bottom. *Midsummer, Midsummer, Midsummer delight; go to the faeries on Midsummer night* – the old rhyme played in her mind.

'What's this?' She looked back up at him. Close up, his eyes were such a dark brown they were almost black; his eyelashes were long and soft.

'Abercolme's first music festival. That I know of, anyway. Hi. I'm Rav Malik.' He held out his hand; Faye shook it, politely. 'I'm promoting a festival up here. I was supposed to be plastering these all over town.'

'You managed the beach.' She looked around them; the wind had died again.

'Yeah. Not quite the plan, but maybe a few snails will buy tickets.'

'Snails don't live on beaches. The salt would kill them,' Faye laughed. 'You're not from around here?'

'You got me.' He looked shyly at his shoes and then back at her.

'Sorry for laughing just now. But you did make a bit of a meal of it.' She couldn't help teasing him, just a little; there was something about him that made her feel it was all right.

'Aye, well.' He shrugged.

Faye pushed her hair out of her eyes where it was tangled from the sudden wind. 'Who's moving into the glass house? Do you know?' She didn't know how much the house was worth exactly, but it was always bought by wealthy, older people before they moved on. This guy didn't look more than thirty, and wasn't exactly dressed like a millionaire.

'Me.' He smiled at her. He had a nice smile. 'Just moved my company up from London to Edinburgh. Amazed it's been empty so long.' He looked mournfully at the paper-strewn beach. 'That wind came out of nowhere.' He shook his head, looking around at the beach. 'I guess the weather here's temperamental. I haven't lived by the sea before.'

'You get used to it.' Faye smiled.

'And you are?'

'Faye Morgan.'

He nodded, smiling.

'I'm going to have to pick this lot up, aren't I, Faye Morgan? Or the village elders will curse me.'

She laughed. 'The village elders would tell you it's not them you have to worry about.'

'Oh. Who do I have to appease with burnt offerings?'

She started picking up the stray flyers, mostly wet with seawater. 'Me, probably,' she said, over her shoulder.

He stood up and stared at her. 'You? Why?'

'I'm the local witch, you could say. My family's been here for generations.'

'Witch? What, eye of newt and toe of frog?' he gazed at her now, the sea making a shushing sound behind them. Overhead, the seagulls circled and squawked.

'No. Herbs, plants, the moon, magic… that kind of thing.'

'Right.' He smiled, crinkling his eyes against the hard spring sun. 'I don't think I've ever met a real witch before.'

'You probably have. You just didn't know it.' Faye ran for three flyers that the wind was buffeting along the tideline. Rav followed, picking up more. Faye caught them, and stopped to face the wind coming in off the sea. It was cold but beautiful.

'So you're local? D'you know anything more about the history of the house? The agent was pretty clueless.' Rav appeared next to her and stuffed another handful of mulched flyers in his pockets, rubbing his hands together. 'Crikey. Colder than it looks, eh?'

'I run a shop in the village – Mistress of Magic. Yeah, that house has a history. My grandmother used to tell me stories about it.' She didn't break her gaze away from the water. Part of her felt resentful that he was here; she was used to this being her space, most of the time. Even in the summer when there were tourists, most of them went to the Silver Sands Beach which was connected to this one – Black Sands – by a small coastal link. Black Sands wasn't as conventionally pretty, but it was much better for magic.

'I'd love to hear them sometime.' Rav's eyes met hers, and held her gaze. *He's probably nice to everyone,* Faye thought, reflexively. *He's not flirting with me.*

'Well, pop into the shop. I'm open every day except Sunday,' she said, looking away hastily. 'Anyway, I've got to go and open up. Good luck with your festival.' She bent and picked up a dry flyer from a few feet away. 'I'll put one up in the window if you like?'

'I do like. Thanks.' He caught her eye again and his eyes twinkled. 'I'll look forward to seeing you again soon, Faye Morgan. Or should I call you *Morgan Le Fay*?'

'Just Faye will do,' she said, picking up her forgotten coffee which had no doubt gone cold now. She made her way back to the footpath, feeling him watch her go. Once she was far enough away, she waved, and he waved back.

I can't believe I waved, she thought. *Still, he won't be here long. They never are, in that house.*

She was surprised to feel sad at the idea. *Ah well. He knows where to find me,* she thought.

Chapter 5

It was raining; the *driech* weather typical for late March. She'd still walked the beach in the rain, though, before opening up; she didn't mind a drenching, and she was curious to see Rav again. But there had been no sign of him today, or any of the days in the past week her walk had taken her to Black Sands. Usually, she walked the beach, or sat on her rock, a couple of times a week; she admitted to herself that perhaps she had gone there a little more regularly than usual on the off-chance she might see him again.

When she came back from her walk, she saw that Aisha had taken down Grandmother's old hagstone charm – nine pebbles with natural holes in them, strung together with string – and left them on the shop counter. Puzzled, she picked it up and inspected it; it was dusty; she supposed that Aisha might have intended to clean it at the end of the day before, and forgotten. Aisha closed the shop on Wednesday afternoons; it was Faye's afternoon off in the week, as the shop was open on Saturdays.

When she had dried her hair, hung up her coat and made a cup of coffee, she sat down at the counter and held the charm carefully. Grandmother had knotted the twine between the stones, and dust had made its careful way into the creases; Faye carefully loosened the knots and cleaned the dust away. She dusted the stones themselves, and smiled as she thought of Grandmother, whose clever fingers had made this once.

The bells tinkled as the glass door pushed open, but Faye kept polishing. Incense smoke filled the air; her coffee was half-drunk and mostly cold in a faerie mug next to her. The face in the rough clay, handmade by a local supplier, gurned in a ridiculous expression. Gentle Celtic music played in the background.

After a few minutes she looked up, an automatic smile on her lips. This time of day, it'd be a local, though not anyone she knew that well, otherwise they'd have said something by now. Even so, at the edge of her awareness, there was a feeling of strangeness. An unknown presence. The faint smell of the sea in the rain, even over the incense smoke.

He stood in the doorway, looking at her. Smiling at her in such a way that made it feel that he knew her.

'Oh! Morning.' Faye pulled her glasses onto her nose from where they held her auburn hair back from her face; without them, her long fringe feathered her eyes. Irritated, she pushed the hair away, only for it to fall straight back again. She peered through the glasses at him. 'Come in.'

The man gave her an odd look, and gazed around him before stepping through the doorway into the shop. Faye shivered as he did so, but it was cold outside, still raining. It occurred to her that he was taking his time to come in, but sometimes people who hadn't been to the shop before were a little unsure about it, on account of it being a witchy shop, even though it was warm and welcoming inside.

'Welcome,' she added, with a smile, to reassure him.

'Thank you,' he said.

Tall. That was her first thought. His face was slightly long, high-cheekboned. Afterwards she couldn't say what he wore; something nondescript, perhaps dark coloured, which didn't matter anyway. It was his blue-green eyes that transfixed her; and when he spoke, his mouth, which had a slight sulky fullness. Lips that wanted to be kissed; a bottom lip that deserved biting.

He had asked a question, and she had no idea what it was. Without thinking, she stood up, turned away and put the charm down in an open box behind her, then turned back to him.

'I'm sorry?' she asked, suddenly and completely befuddled and appalled at herself for thinking about kissing this man at the first time of seeing him. This never happened.

'I said, nice shop you've got here.' His voice was slightly accented; she half-frowned, trying to place it.

'Oh. Thanks.' She smiled, her heart racing. Faye was suddenly very aware of her own breathing; it was as if she was back in the school play that she still had nightmares about now and again. It had been her turn to say two lines in *The Lion King*, but when the time came, she'd gone completely blank and stared out at the smiling crowd of parents, sweating in fear. Afterwards, Moddie had hugged her, said it was no bother. *Nobody even noticed, sweetheart*, she'd laughed; mussed Faye's hair. But Faye had felt like a failure. In times of stress she still dreamed of being onstage with nothing to say.

'How long has it been here?' He smiled down at her again, and his eyes lit up with an odd glow when he did. They were strange, luminous: exactly like the sea on a cloudy day, when the sun came through the clouds and the colour of the sea changed from grey-green to jewelled blue.

'Oh. It opened in the seventies. It's always been our house, though. Belonging to my family, that is.' She felt as though she was jabbering. Faye took a deep breath while pretending to take a sip of coffee. 'You're not local. What brings you here?' she managed to ask over the rim of her faerie mug.

'Adventure.' The stranger ran two long fingers along the glass top of the shop counter, looking down at the pendants and rings showcased underneath. Faye stared; he was rough-shaven, and his slight beard was a dark blonde like his shoulder-length dirty blonde hair. He leaned in closer to her. He didn't have the air of a young man – he was too centred, too present for that, and she got no sense of that pressing need so many men under thirty had to impress, to demand her attention as a child would with their arrogance and showiness. Yet he had few lines on his face; no grey hair that she could see.

'This one is beautiful.' His voice was low; his face was inches from hers. Ordinarily, it would have been an invasion of personal space, but the idea didn't even cross her mind; she was spellbound.

He looked up, and time seemed to slow. Faye felt his gaze on hers and it was as though a mist descended, obscuring the shop, leaving only her and the stranger in the middle, like the eye of a storm; the quiet inside a tornado. She felt a sense of shifting, as if she was not secure on the ground at all, but instead had her feet in wet sand as the tide washed in and out, pulling her in, burying her feet deeper and deeper. Dimly she remembered a similar sensation after the love spell, when the door had flown open in the wind. But while that had been fear and disorientation, this was a kind of pleasant fugue.

She didn't know what he was pointing to; she couldn't look away from his eyes. It was exactly how she'd felt before, in the seconds before kissing someone for the first time: a sweet anticipation, a sense of an incredible longing filling the tiny inch of air between their lips.

How would it feel to kiss that full-lipped mouth? The hint of a smile played at its corner; Faye's own soft lips parted involuntarily. Even though she'd kissed her share of men before, there had been no-one with this sense of immediate attraction; no other sweet, hot crackling energy as this was, making her lightheaded. It wasn't necessarily just him, but in her too. A heat that lit her up from the tips of her toes to her forehead.

She noticed part of a tattoo, half-hidden by the collar on his t-shirt. She couldn't make out what it was, but the part she could see against his tanned neck was blue; the top edge of an animal head, perhaps. From his neck, her gaze dropped to his well-muscled chest which was obvious even under his t-shirt, which wasn't especially fitted. He was rangy but strong; athletic, healthy, like he spent a lot of time outdoors.

Without meaning to, Faye sighed. Somehow, the introduction of her breath into the small space between them blew away the mist that had hidden the rest of the world. She felt her return to the mundane hard and unwelcome, like a change in the temperature. As if someone had opened the door to her cosy shop again and the icy draught had swept in.

Faye jumped and dropped her cup; coffee spilled over her laptop keyboard which was open on the counter. She had been meaning to start the quarterly accounts but hadn't been able to bring herself to focus on it yet.

'Oh, no. Oh, god. Sorry. I…' Hurriedly she picked up the mug and looked around for a rag to soak up the coffee from the computer. 'No, no, no!' she muttered. Not finding anything to hand, she tore off her plain green long-sleeved t-shirt, thankful she had a top on underneath, and dabbed the laptop keyboard.

'Here.' He held out the cleaning cloth she'd been using.

'Oh. Thanks. Sorry,' she repeated, feeling stupid and annoyed at herself. *This is what you get for mooning over the first good-looking man that comes in since the bloody shop opened*, she chastised herself, thinking also that she was glad Annie wasn't here. She'd take great pleasure in teasing her about this for years to come. *Faye, remember when that gorgeous blonde guy came in? Ye can't be trusted with a hot drink. Faye, we're gonna need to get ye oven gloves for when the fellas are around!*

'Don't apologise. Accidents happen.' He smiled as she took it and wiped the keyboard. She tested the open spreadsheet, saved it and reopened it. 'Is it all right?' He leaned over as Faye frowned at the flickering screen.

'I think it's gone…' She stopped mid-sentence as the tall stranger reached over and touched the keyboard gently. The screen went black. 'Oh no!' she wailed. She couldn't afford a new laptop right now; takings were steady, but Mistress of Magic wasn't exactly a multimillion-pound business.

'It'll be all right. Give it a minute,' the man said, moving around the counter. Despite the situation, Faye was vividly aware of him next to her; she was standing now, and, being a tall woman, she found satisfaction in realising that he was taller. She found herself gauging where her head would rest perfectly on his chest if she lay next to him, or if she melted into his lean body in an embrace…

In the strange way that happens in times of crisis, she felt in that moment that somehow they had already moved on from being strangers to something more like friends. But later, when she looked back at their first meeting, she would know that it was in fact something else entirely that had made her feel that way.

He touched the laptop again, and Faye thought for a second that she saw a flash of electricity between his finger and the computer, but she rationalised it away. An electric shock, if anything. And then the laptop screen flashed blue, and the usual starting screen appeared.

'Oh, thank god,' she breathed as the spreadsheet reappeared, apparently unharmed. She checked through the usual functions; it all seemed fine.

'There you are. The way they make these things now, it's hard to break them,' he said, that twinkle in his eyes again. She knew that was absolutely wrong, but she smiled along with him nonetheless. Her gaze shifted to the shop window.

'Oh, the sun's out!' she exclaimed, and went to the door. Opening it, she stood in the sun as it blazed down unexpectedly between the grey clouds. She could see that it was still raining on the beach just a few minutes' walk away, but here, at least, there was a brief interlude in the weather.

He stood next to her and looked up in pleasure at the early spring sun; Faye breathed in its warmth, a smile spreading on her cheeks. A similar warmth emanated from him, next to her, as they stood together in a moment of silence, as if they had always been standing there together. She wanted to lean into him; wanted to feel his body against hers.

'See?' his warm voice caressed her like the sun itself. 'Things have a way of working out, even when you don't expect them to, Mistress of Magic.'

He gave her an intense, long look, and turned to go. 'Goodbye, Faye Morgan. I'll see you again soon,' he smiled, and bowed theatrically while walking backwards.

She was back inside the shop when she realised that she had never told him her name.

Chapter 6

'Did you *hear*? The whole village's talking about it!' Aisha burst into the shop and startled Faye, who was stacking new books onto the shelves: two new spell books from an American publisher, a guide to psychic self-defence, Scottish faerie lore. Mistress of Magic was a destination in itself for witchy folk across Scotland, and even wider; last week she'd had American tourists in who had chosen Abercolme for a stop on their holiday just because of the shop. *All thanks to you, Moddie*, she smiled to herself.

'Did I hear *what*? You're the second one to startle me today. I'm going to need some sort of herbal remedy on a drip at this rate,' Faye slowly slid the books onto the wooden unit and noticed it needed dusting. She was still half enchanted by her mysterious visitor – she felt strangely floaty, as if half of her was somewhere else.

'Dal Riada! They're coming!' Aisha danced around the faded-blue high-backed chair by the hearth. 'I'm so excited! I've got both their albums. They're going to play at the festival!'

'You're saying that like I'm supposed to know who they are.' Faye raised an eyebrow at her friend, who was scrolling her phone screen.

'You do know. Dal Riada. You've got one of their albums somewhere. Here, listen.' Aisha's phone played a fast, folky Celtic tune.

'Oh, that.' Faye went to the counter and rummaged in the drawer where she kept CDs for the shop's sound system. Aisha had given her a couple more a few weeks ago and she'd slung them in without much thought. 'I haven't played it yet.'

'Oh, Faye! All you listen to is harp music and Brahms. There's a world of new music out there, you know.'

Faye listened to the tune for a minute.

'Celtic folk isn't new. Moddie used to play it when I was a child,' she replied, though she liked the fevered drumming and the fluted voice of the singer. It did remind her of Moddie: of being swung around in her mother's arms, Moddie's red hair flowing around both of them like flames; of Moddie singing along with the fast lyrics, of her feet drumming on the stone floor after they'd shut up shop and the moon glinted through the windows.

'You know what I mean. Thank the goddess for Abercolme finally making it into the twenty-first century!' Aisha was beaming ear to ear. 'And who knows, eh? Maybe that's how we meet our new lovers!'

'Maybe.' Faye smiled, thinking of the tall man and blushing at how easily she thought again of kissing him.

'Any progress on the spell, anyway?' Aisha picked up the rose quartz crystal wand Faye had used in the ritual. 'Has something happened? You look... I don't know. You're blushing.'

'No... nothing.' Faye knew that she sounded completely unconvincing. Had it been Annie asking, she wouldn't have been able to lie, but she didn't know Aisha as well. Yet Aisha gave her a perplexed smile.

'Are you sure, Faye?' Aisha had returned to her usual look: hair tied up, no makeup, ripped jeans and a Pink Floyd t-shirt. Yet Faye noticed her beauty more today; her long lashes, dewy skin. Either Aisha had always had this just-been-kissed look, or something had changed with her, too.

'No. Well...' Faye considered telling her friend about the tall blond man that had come in earlier, but he wasn't exactly the outcome of a love spell – nothing had happened; she'd just spilt her coffee on her laptop, looked like a moron, then he'd left.

'What?' Aisha looked up. 'Something's up. I can tell. It's been two weeks since we did the spell. Surely something's going to happen soon?'

'Not that quickly. Minimum one month until the next full moon. Probably longer.' Faye wrote on a tiny price label and stuck it on the carved wooden part of a wooden wand, picking up another from a box to price.

'Months? Really?' Aisha sighed.

'Take some rose quartz home. It draws love to you,' Faye looked up from the labelling.

'I've already got some.' Aisha sighed. 'So. What's up? I can tell it's something. What?'

'Oh, nothing. It's just… I met a man on the beach last week.'

Aisha smiled and put the rose quartz wand down. 'What man?'

'Just some guy. He's bought the glass house on the beach.'

'I know the one. So what's he like?'

Faye considered what she remembered of Rav. Soft brown eyes, self-deprecating sense of humour.

'Nice. Our age, I guess. He has his own business of some kind. Just moved up from London.'

'Excellent. And when're you going out with him?' Aisha raised her eyebrow archly.

'We're not going out. We just met on the beach, that's all. Oh. He's organising that music festival your favourite band are playing at.' She pointed to the same flyer in the window as Aisha was still clutching in one hand.

'You had that there all the time?' Aisha rolled her eyes. 'And you didn't tell me?'

'As we've already mentioned, I've no idea who these people are.'

'Dal Riada. Only the best band I've ever heard. And the absolute sexiest, too. Look.' She pulled out her phone again and tapped the screen. 'Here. You can't tell me they aren't supernaturally good-looking.' She sighed again, and passed the phone to Faye.

There were four of them: three men, one woman. Aisha was right: they were all remarkably beautiful. The men were well-muscled, fit, tattooed; the woman stood like a faerie queen among them.

And the one standing on the left and looking unsmilingly into the camera was the same tall, blond man Faye had daydreamed about kissing earlier in the day.

Chapter 7

'You're gonna love them!' Aisha shouted over her shoulder as they made their way into the crowded bar. Faye held her arms as close to her sides as she could, trying to get jostled as little as possible, but the bar was so full that they could barely make it inside at all. Taking her hand, Aisha snaked her way expertly through the bubbles of space that opened and closed between people like the tiny slivers of sunlight through clouds over the beach at Abercolme.

Faye stayed as close to Aisha as she could. She was cautious in crowds, though she never really knew why. Perhaps it was the knowledge of what a crowd could do; the witch trials were never far from her mind, and there was a kind of ancestral echo that resonated through the ages from Grainne Morgan's death to Faye; a line of pain braided with fear. Fear of being who she was; fear of being a woman with any kind of power.

Being the child of a family of witches as well as a single mother wasn't easy in a small village where everyone else had a mum and dad at home and no magic in them whatsoever. Most people had been kind, but not everyone. Faye had learned to blend into the background as much as she could, though Moddie had disapproved. *Witches and women have been persecuted for long enough,* she told Faye as a child. *Take up space, otherwise it's taken from you.*

But Faye preferred not to take up space, particularly. She learned what Moddie and grandmother taught her: the old ways, passed down through the generations. About herbs and ailments, about healing and astrology and how to appease the fae spirits that lived in the house and in the wild, leaving them small offerings, asking for their help. Abercolme was coastal, so it had the connection to the sea sprites, the kelpies, too. But this was a crowded bar in Edinburgh, and there was no room for any spirits... unless they were disguised as humans.

Aisha pushed her way to the bar and waved frantically at the barman until he craned forward; she shouted for two beers over the noise and handed one to Faye.

'It's so busy!' Faye shouted, even though Aisha was standing right next to her.

'I know! They've got such a following. No-one even knew anything about them a year ago. They just came out of nowhere,' Aisha yelled back. 'Just look at the lassies in here. Obsessed. Just like us.' She grinned and took a long drink from her bottled lager.

'You're the one obsessed,' Faye shot back, smiling at Aisha's excited face, but she was intrigued to see the tall blond man again. Aisha had told her all about him, and the rest of the band, on the way here on the train as it rolled over the iconic red bridge over the Firth of Forth.

He was Finn Beatha, who sang and played the flute. The drummer was French, according to Aisha; his name was Paul. There was a girl in the band who played the harp and also sang, Aoife, and there was another man, a Scot, Angus, who played guitar and piano and a variety of other instruments as needed.

'Nobody knows much about about any of them,' Aisha shouted as she swayed to the background music that was coming from the speakers. 'Just that they do these amazing gigs. The one I went to before was an out-of-body experience. I'm not even kidding, Faye. It was like a religious thing.'

'Well, that's some build-up. I hope they live up to it,' Faye shouted back. She noticed that she was getting stared at by some of the guys in the bar; one or two smiled at her. She looked away. Everyone knew that nobody ever met the love of their life in a crowded bar. Anyway, they were probably smiling at any woman who caught their eye.

The lights in the bar switched off and the band walked onto the small stage. There was a deafening roar from the crowd as the stage lights came up and bathed all four in a shifting green, gold and white light. Faye stared up at Finn Beatha, her heart quickening as the drummer, Paul, in a kilt and wearing what looked like a wolf pelt around his shoulders, started pounding out a fast rhythm with his hands on two large drums.

Finn cried out; a kind of animal whoop, his silver flute in hand, and put it to his mouth. He started playing a kind of fast jig, following the quick drumbeat; Faye felt herself going into a kind of trance as the other instruments joined in and Aoife began singing over the top; Faye thought the words were Scots Gaelic, but she couldn't be sure. She was tall, with long black hair in convoluted braids arranged on her head and cascading down her back. The plaits were ornamented with silver clasps in the way the Celts had worn their hair, and tattoos wove their way down her arms; it looked like they had been done in blue woad. All of them had spirals and other symbols painted on their faces in the same style.

On stage, Finn was no longer wearing the nondescript dark clothes he'd worn at the shop that day. Now, he was stripped to the waist and Faye could see the whole of the tattoo she'd glimpsed at his neck. It was a horse, appearing to ride up his body from the right side of his waist, up under his arm and with its head resting on his shoulder. She couldn't quite make it out from where she stood, but the part she had seen was the eye of the horse, which was designed as a well of spiralling water.

He was well-muscled; Faye took in the lines of definition on his stomach and chest. A kilt sat on his hips, and he was barefoot under that. His eyes were closed as he played; the music swirled into the audience like a spell itself, weaving the people together. The trancelike feeling intensified; Faye closed her eyes and let the tune come into her space. She had no fear of swaying and falling over, because she was so tightly packed in there was nowhere else to go.

As soon as she closed her eyes, the whole place changed. She was immediately somewhere else, with the same feeling as when she was doing magic: it had the same vividness, the same sense of almost-reality.

She was on Black Sands Beach, sitting on her rock, and Finn Beatha was playing the flute on the beach. There was no-one else there. It was night and a full moon sat pregnant and heavy in the clear black sky above; it was reflected in the black water.

Finn took the flute away from his lips and looked straight up at her. She felt her whole body come alive, like a pleasurable fire engulfed it. He started singing, and she knew he was singing to her. To summon her to him.

She didn't speak much Gaelic so she couldn't exactly tell what the song was about, but she didn't need to know: the call in her blood was unmistakable.

In the dream-vision, she rose from the rock and walked along a stony trail to the black sand. He continued to sing, never looking away from her, and she came to him, as if she were attached to Finn Beatha by a silver rope and he was pulling it in, closer and closer.

Finally she stood in front of him, dressed in a flowing white dress and wearing an elaborate rose-gold necklace of some kind. She was aware that she was naked under the gauzy material, but not cold; a light, warm breeze blew the dress against her skin.

Finn stopped singing, pulled her to him and kissed her.

His lips were as soft as she had imagined. There was a strange sense of falling when their lips met; a sweetness and an underlying sense of longing, as if he was in some way a faraway home she had never imagined she would find. One of his hands was on her cheek, the other, softly, on her neck, and his touch made her feel dizzy. She was no longer aware of her feet on the black sand; only of him; his smell, like smoke and seawater, and the feel of her hands in his hair.

Someone nudged Faye hard and she opened her eyes, returning to her body in a sudden shock of weight and heaviness. She gasped and reached out for Aisha, who was still next to her. For a minute she didn't know where she was or how she had got to this noisy place from Black Sands, and she felt faint.

'Hey. Faye! You all right?' Aisha held her by the shoulder and looked into Faye's eyes. 'Ach. It's too hot in here. Let's get some water and go somewhere to cool off,' she said, and guided Faye out of the bar.

Outside, Faye sat on one of the outside tables for smokers and Aisha bought two bottles of water from the shop next door. She uncapped them and handed one to Faye.

'You okay? You went peely-wally there for a second.'

Faye took a long drink of the cold water and felt herself come back a little more to normal.

'Yeah. Thanks. I don't know what happened. I went into a kind of trance.'

'It's that kind of fast drumming. Like a rave. I was somewhere else myself.' Aisha drained the rest of her bottle of water.

'Maybe.' Faye looked back inside the bar which was full of jumping shadows; she saw other people with the same glassy stares as she knew she'd had. It was as though the band were enchanting everyone there. 'It was strange. I went... somewhere. That man, the one singing...?' She closed her eyes and saw him again in her mind's eye.

'Finn?'

'Yeah. I saw him on Black Sands Beach. Singing to me.'

'Lucky you.' Aisha smiled tightly, but then looked away; she probably didn't want to admit that she too had been enchanted by the band. Perhaps she had had some kind of erotic daydream as well. If Faye had been with Annie, she would have said more. But Annie was away on an acting job, though she had been uncharacteristically vague about what it was. 'I wish I could find myself on a beach with Finn Beatha. He's... he's like a dream, isn't he?' Aisha looked wistfully through the open door back at the band.

'You'll find someone real,' Faye reassured her. 'He's coming. I'm sure of it.'

Aisha sighed and fiddled with the label on her water bottle.

'I guess. It's just that...' She trailed off, looking embarrassed.

'What? You can tell me.' Faye smiled confidentially. Aisha had worked in the shop for a year now, but still Faye knew very little about her; only that she was studying at the university and that she was interested in magic and music. She had sought the shop out and asked Faye if she was looking for help one day the previous summer; said she'd heard of it as one of the best places in Scotland to get supplies. Impressed with her knowledge, Faye had taken her on. But Aisha had never spoken about her personal life, and Faye hadn't pried further. Annie had, but with little success.

Aisha looked uncomfortable.

'I… I haven't ever been with anyone. In that way. You know?' She inclined her head to the stage.

'With a man? Or woman? I mean, you made your doll a man, so I'm guessing…?' Faye asked gently. 'You're a virgin? Aisha. That's nothing to be worried about.' She smiled and took the younger girl's hand. 'I haven't had many boyfriends. Or one-night stands, come to that. It's okay. Just because Annie's confident in that way doesn't mean everyone is.'

Aisha blushed; clearly, it was hard for her to talk about this.

'I wanted to go to university. I'm going to be a geneticist. But my parents would rather that I married one and concentrated on popping out babies like my sisters are. And that's cool, y'know? That's fine if that's what you want to do. But I don't.' Her tone was quietly fierce. Faye imagined that it would be pretty difficult to get Aisha to do anything she didn't want to do.

'Of course! I so admire your brains, Aish. There's no way I could do what you do,' she replied. 'God knows we need more women in science.'

'Well, sure. Though there always have been women doing important work; it's hard for you to get to the top, is all. You have to marry the job. Good news if you don't want to marry an actual person, I guess.' Aisha tore off the whole label from the bottle and rolled it up into a long cylinder.

'But you still want someone. You're human,' Faye finished the thought for her. 'Just because your work's going to take most of what you've got, doesn't mean you don't get to have love, Aish.'

'It feels that way sometimes.' Aisha sighed. 'Even now. Doctoral study is hard. And I haven't met anyone I like at uni. Or I'm too shy to meet men when I go out. Like tonight.'

'I know. I'm the same! I mean, when they look at me, I just want to hide away.' Faye laughed. 'Look at us. A pair of wallflowers. At least we've got each other.'

Aisha smiled.

'But you're beautiful. You don't know how many guys look at you. You don't even see it.'

It was Faye's turn to blush.

'I don't think they do, much,' she said, quietly. 'And you are a beautiful, intelligent, interesting young woman, don't forget. But anyway. Your time will come, Aish. Remember the spell.' She reached over the table and squeezed Aisha's hand. Yet as she did so, all she could think about was the door flying open and Aisha walking out of it as if she was in a trance; and the strange expression on her face when she returned.

'D'you really think it'll work?' Aisha asked again, like she had before in the shop, just after they'd done it. Like she needed the reassurance; like she didn't really believe, but she wanted to.

'Is this your scientist brain making you doubt magic?' Faye asked, with more of a smile in her voice than she felt. Doubt of the truth she had grown up with always made her sad; not being believed by the rest of the world was a burden her family had borne for generations, and it sat heavy on her shoulders.

'No. The more you study Genetics, the more you realise how magical humans really are. Anyway, the wisest of us know that we still have so much to learn.' Aisha stood up, chafing her hands together and looked back into the bar. 'God knows what's encoded into our DNA. No, it's just… I dunno. Human frailty. Not daring to believe, I guess.'

'You don't lose anything by having faith.' Faye smiled. The vision, whatever it had been, was still with her, but it was like waking up from a dream which receded quickly. It seemed real when you were in it but it soon became a memory.

'I guess. D'you want to go back in?'

'Sure,' Faye stamped her feet on the ground; it was cold, sitting outside on an April night in Edinburgh. Aisha nodded.

'And... thanks. Sometimes I feel really alone, y'know? It helps. Having you and Annie around.' She leaned forward and gave Faye an awkward hug.

'That's okay, Aish. Anytime.'

Faye took a deep breath and followed Aisha back into the bar.

The tune played around her again, and she could see it as a magic in itself, weaving its way in and out of the crowd. She watched the faces of the others around her; some were so entranced that their eyes were almost rolled all the way back; they swayed, totally unaware of where they were. She could sense that they *were* somewhere else, to all intents and purposes.

She wobbled, then reminded herself that she was a witch. She'd been caught off-guard the first time, but she had to remember that she could take control.

Standing at the bar, she took care to imagine herself cocooned in a black cloak with a hood; she imagined drawing it over herself, and closing the seven energy centres in her body, the rainbow-hued chakras that everyone had, head to groin. Starting with the white crown energy at the top of her head, she imagined the balls of light closing to a pinprick: to the indigo of her third eye, the blue of her throat, pink of the heart, yellow, orange and down to red at the base. Instantly she felt better, more grounded; for good measure she imagined tree roots growing out of her feet and down through the sticky wood floor of the bar and into the dark Edinburgh earth.

Grounded, she let herself look at him again: he was just as beautiful, otherworldly, even. His hair was a lighter blonde in the stage lights, and the horse tattoo on his side seemed to writhe with the music.

As she watched him, she had the impression that he was searching for her; his blue-green eyes scanned the crowd, not finding her. *But why would he be looking for you?* Her inner voice, the doubting voice she was so used to hearing, reasoned. *He doesn't know you're here. And even if he did, you're just some shop owner that he passed the time of day with. Why would he remember you?*

And yet, something in her knew it was true. That, perhaps, as mad as it sounded, he knew the vision she'd had. Perhaps he knew all the places of reverie that the audience were in right now...

The searching feeling grew so strong that Faye raised her hands to her long auburn fringe. Though she was only wearing an imaginary robe, her hands grasped the edge of where the hood would be, and she brought her loose fists to her shoulders. Removing the disguise that she had imposed on herself, she unveiled herself to him.

The music pooled around her in sharp, quick drifts, like snow; Finn had brought the flute to his lips again and the female singer with the dark hair in so many plaits keened a gentle melody over it. Faye's heart surged; the tune was haunting yet mournful, and she felt an overwhelming longing take her over, though she could not have explained exactly what she was yearning for. It was as if she was homesick; she felt it like a longing for a love she had never lost.

As her heart filled with the melody, Finn's eyes found her at last. She didn't disappear into the vision of the beach again, but it felt as though the room cleared, and it was just her and him there together. Finn took his flute away from his lips and started to sing with the black-haired woman and, this time, Faye understood every word.

He sang a lament for his lost love; for a part-human, part-faerie-woman. He sang for the woman he had searched for all his life, and never found. He sang to summon her from her remote castle in the sea, to join him in his bed.

A smile played on Faye's lips as she listened; and, as he sang, Finn Beatha's eyes never left hers.

Chapter 8

Faye usually made a good effort not to run into the minister, but the day after the show she was still half in another world, even after a night's sleep. All night she'd had strange dreams of Finn: kissing him, dancing together in a strange place, dark and lit with lamps. Sometimes they were alone, and sometimes in a loud, whooping, spinning crowd. Just before she woke up, he had put that same rose-gold necklace that she had seen in her daydream around her neck and whispered something in her ear: she forgot it immediately on waking.

In her dreaminess, it was too late to avoid the white-haired man, who was coming out of one of her neighbour's houses, holding a sheaf of papers, when their paths crossed on the pavement outside.

'Oh, sorry. Hello.' Faye stepped back instinctively to let him go past. She'd popped out of the shop in a quiet moment to get some milk and bread.

'Good morning, Miss Morgan,' he replied frostily, but didn't move. Faye assumed he was waiting for her to go first, so she nodded quickly and strode out in front of the house, only to bump into the minister who had clearly thought the same thing. He cleared his throat.

'No, after you.' He waited for her to pass. Ordinarily she would have left it at that but today, for some reason, she felt wicked.

'I wouldn't hear of it. How are you, minister, on this fine day?' She gave him a huge grin.

'Oh. Well. Very well, yes, thank you, Miss Morgan.' He frowned uncomfortably.

'I'm so glad. I'm very well also, in case you were wondering,' she replied brightly, standing in his way. She couldn't say why, apart from that she was filled with the question: *Why should she scuttle out of this man's way?* She had as much of a right to be in this village as he did. *And he's an ignorant little man*, said a voice in the back of her mind. *Cardigans, jumble sales and cheap biscuits do not a man of power make.* It sounded like something Moddie would say, and she smiled to herself.

'Good,' he replied, looking past her at the street. 'Anyway, I really must be on my way.'

'Of course.' She looked down at his hand; the knobbly knuckles held leaflets printed on a light green paper. 'May I have one of those? What are they?'

He held them to his leg, instinctively, in a protective gesture.

'Oh. Parish business,' he said, not meeting her eye.

'Well, I'm one of your parishioners. So I think I qualify, don't I?'

He squinted at her suspiciously, but Faye smiled all the more sweetly and held out her hand.

'Err… yes, I suppose so.' He handed a leaflet to her unwillingly. She scanned it, expecting another afternoon tea or charity event.

'Are you kidding me?' She looked up at him, waiting for him to, totally uncharacteristically, laugh and jab her in the ribs or something like it was a joke. But the minister coughed and looked away.

'The proposal has been put forward, yes. For a statue of James the Sixth of Scotland – James the First of Great Britain – to be erected in the village,'

'James the Sixth. Author of *Daemonologie*? *That* King James?'

'Yes. A great king. Bringer of peace and union to Britain.'

'A great king who wrote a book that was responsible for the murder of thousands of innocent people. My ancestor, in particular,' Faye spat back at him, furious. 'That book provided a reason for the witch trials to take place. He made up all that *nonsense*, fuelled by his lurid, sadistic fantasies about torturing and killing women, and with it he gave other sadists free rein to accuse anyone they didn't like the look of—'

'That's your view, Miss Morgan. Many would disagree,' the minister pursed his lips, and Faye wanted to hit him.

'It's not my view. It's historical fact!' Faye recognised the familiar sensation of fury edged with a raw hopelessness when faced with this kind of entrenched forgetting. The minister probably still thought that most people who had died in the witch trials had deserved it in some way.

'This is immoral. Who proposed it?' Faye scanned the leaflet, but all it gave was the time and date for a village meeting to vote on the statue. Anger flashed through her like a knife.

'The council has some money left in the local budget. We thought, in these difficult times, it would be good to have a symbol of unity in the village. Someone that represents a pivotal point in our proud history.'

Faye almost choked.

'Our proud history – the Statutes of Iona? That man broke up the clans. He forbade Gaelic to be spoken here. He ruined our culture as well as advocating the torture of women. I'm not proud of that. Neither should you be.'

'You can have your say along with everyone else, at the town hall.' The old man sighed. 'I simply serve the community.'

Faye glared at him.

'Fine. I'll be there. And, I might add, the Morgans were helping the community long before you got here. I still do.'

'I know many parishioners that hold you in high regard, Miss Morgan. I can't say I agree, but I'm wise enough to accept that old folk beliefs can be particularly intransigent in remote communities like these. Now, I really must be on my way.' He turned away from Faye and started walking up the path, back straight, as if that would shield him somehow.

'Perhaps that's because folk beliefs work, and people do well to hold to the old ways. Perhaps that's because people in *communities like this* know that I have power!' she shouted at him, making two nearby women frown at her as they walked past.

'I'm not here to take part in a conjuring contest with you, Miss Morgan. Unlike some, I have work to do, not sitting in my shop all day, reading tea leaves,' he called over his shoulder.

Faye wondered briefly if it would be unforgivable to curse at a minister; not that she needed his forgiveness. She let the moment pass, taking a deep breath. He was an old man, and she should keep her dignity.

'Fine,' she muttered. She stood and watched him go, until she remembered what she had set out for, and went into the bakery.

'Havin' a disagreement with the minister, are ye, sweetheart?' Muriel in the baker's loved a gossip, but Faye wasn't in the mood.

'No. I don't agree with this new statue being built, that's all.' Faye sighed. 'Granary please, and a pint of milk,'

Muriel shook her head as she turned away to get the bread.

'Ach, I know, lassie. We should ha' a woman at the very least. The world's full enough of stone men,' she chuckled. 'Still, at least that way, they don't talk back.'

'Hmmm.' Faye looked out of the window, feeling dejected.

'Like how there's women on the banknotes now. We had the scientist woman, what's her name? And the poet,' Muriel handed the soft brown loaf to Faye over the counter and put the cold container of milk next to it. 'It's the small things, aye. Slow and steady wins the race. That's two pounds for ye, sweetheart.'

Faye handed Muriel the money and took the bread. She was halfway out of the door when the idea came. If not a stone man, then a memorial of another kind.

'Muriel, you're an angel!' she called back to the bemused baker and strode back into the street.

Chapter 9

The bell jingled as the shop door opened and Faye looked up, hopefully; since she'd seen Dal Riada with Aisha last week there was a part of her that expected Finn Beatha to walk in at any moment. She caught herself in the hope and frowned – it was silly to expect to ever see him again, though she really wanted to go and see the band when they played at the festival in June.

Rav caught her confused expression and laughed.

'Good day, Mistress of Magic.' He tipped an imaginary cap to her and looked around at the shelves of incenses, tarot sets, books and a row of brightly polished brass cauldrons.

'Oh, hi.' Faye smiled and sat back down behind the counter; she realised that she'd sprung up when the door had opened and blushed, embarrassed at her keenness to see Finn again.

'Expecting someone else?'

'Ah, no… you surprised me, that's all.'

'You do know that this is a shop? Probably best if people do come in, I'm guessing?' He came up to the counter and picked up a novelty spell book next to the till. 'How's business?'

'Not too bad.' Faye felt herself relax into Rav's easy company like that day at the beach. She watched the minister walk past the shop;

Rav followed her gaze. 'Not that some people wouldn't like us to go under,' she added, narrowing her eyes.

'That guy? Tell me about it. He's not keen on Abercolme Rocks happening, let me tell you. Turned up at the house yesterday complaining about it. Thinks it's gonna bring undesirables into town.' Rav shook his head.

'*Undesirables.* I'd rather have a few music fans once a year than a bloody statue of King James.' Faye shook her head. 'Have you heard about that? It's outrageous,'

'Yeah. You not a fan of the monarchy, then?'

'Not so you'd notice. But, more to the point, that particular king was a key figure in the witch trials that happened in Scotland. I'm fuming, to put it mildly.'

'Was he? I didn't know that.'

'If anything, history views him as a reasonably good king because he avoided religious wars and unified the country. A bit of woman-torturing on the side's all right, apparently. My direct ancestor was tried as a witch because of the book he wrote. A kind of witch-hunter's how-to.'

Rav raised his eyebrows.

'Wow. I didn't know. Sorry.' He looked confused 'But… wasn't she, though? I mean, I thought you…'

'I am. She was. But being a herbalist or a midwife or someone that liked to talk to the faeries isn't quite reason enough to burn them at the stake, is it?' she snapped, annoyed at Rav's thoughtlessness. 'Anyway, I've decided to a make a counter-proposal. A memorial for my ancestor, Grainne Morgan, and the other women of Abercolme that were murdered at the North Berwick witch trials.'

'Wow.' Rav smiled. 'That's going to ruffle some feathers.'

'I hope it does,' Faye snapped. 'I'm sick of the people here not acknowledging what happened to Grainne and the others. Like we're all supposed to forget. I can't forget and neither could my mother and my grandmother and all the women in between. We carry that grief with us.'

'Sure, of course.' He nodded. 'I can relate to that. My great-grandparents, they lived in Rawalpindi, in Punjab, in the 1940s. Then Partition happened. You know what Partition was, right?'

'Overall, yes. But not in detail,' Faye leant forward, listening.

Rav sighed.

'They don't teach you it at school, why would you know? In Punjab, Muslims went to the west part that became Pakistan, Hindus and Sikhs went to the East. My great-grandfather was killed, protecting my great-grandmother from a gang. She had to move the whole family to the east side of the border after that, otherwise the whole family would have probably been murdered. She was a lone woman protecting three children; women were committing suicide rather than let the gangs get hold of them, if you know what I mean. It was the same on both sides of the border.'

Faye shivered, and squeezed Rav's hand. 'I'm so sorry.'

'People were terrified. Hundreds of thousands – even millions – died just in Punjab, never mind the other states that got ripped apart. Families split, displaced, murdered; the scars are still there. We carry that with us.'

'That must have been so terrible for your… was it your mum or dad's family?'

'Mum's. My grandparents moved here in 1960; she was born here. But my *Dadi* – my grandmother – she remembered. She was afraid to go outside the door in England for a long time, Mum said. She thought it could happen any time, someone could break down the door, attack you for being the wrong person in the wrong place.'

'That's terrible.' Faye imagined it and felt tears building behind her eyes.

'I know. To be honest, I still feel it in places like this… a bit. I mean, don't get me wrong. Nothing like as bad as *them*. And everyone's great, for the most part, you know? We were really happy to get the contract for the concert up here when it came up – me and my business partner Roni, we were looking to expand north and everything. But I have to say, moving away from London…' he trailed off and gave Faye a rueful smile. 'People who are different in these small communities… let's just say we stand out a lot.'

'I'm well aware of that,' Faye rolled her eyes, and Rav grinned.

'Look at me, pouring my heart out to the village witch.'

'That's what I'm here for,' she smiled back, liking their back-and-forth.

'It's nice to have someone to talk to, to be honest. It's kind of stressful being away from the office, up here on my own. I'm supposed to recruit some temporary help but I haven't got around to it yet. It's all been pretty last minute – we put in the application for the festival last year and then suddenly, about a month ago, got this call.'

Faye's eyes flickered to the fireplace, remembering how she, Annie and Aisha had sat on the sheepskin rugs on the stone flagged floor, passing their poppet dolls through the incense smoke. *Magic works in its own weird way*, she remembered Annie saying.

'I suppose that's how it goes, sometimes,' she said, guardedly.

'Yeah. So, anyway. Anything I can do to help with your memorial thing, let me know. It's important that people remember the difficult things, as well as the good.'

'Some moral support at the meeting would definitely be very welcome.' Faye's hand was still on his, and she lifted it away awkwardly; he smiled, his eyes on hers.

'More than happy to provide any support necessary,' he continued to gaze meaningfully at her until she blushed and looked away.

'If you think it'll make any difference me being there of course.' He yawned. 'Sorry. I haven't been sleeping properly.' Rav rubbed his eyes, then flicked through the little spell book he was still holding. 'Maybe I need one of these.'

'Why not? What's up?' She warmed her palms on her faerie face mug; today it was a calming herbal tea blend. 'Oh. D'you want a tea?'

'Love one, thanks.' Rav went to the hearth and sank into one of the easy chairs. 'Is it okay if I sit here? Sorry, I should have asked. It just looks so comfy.'

'It's fine. That's what they're there for.' Faye went into the little kitchen at the back of the shop and filled the kettle, flicking it on and looking in the cupboard for some biscuits.

When she came out with a mug of tea and a packet of her favourite chocolate biscuits, Rav was immersed in the Scottish faerie lore book she'd got in a few weeks ago. She was surprised it hadn't sold, but it would probably go when the tourists started drifting in for the summer. Most people who lived in Abercolme were well aware of the local myths.

'So what's wrong in *your* world?' Faye settled into the chair opposite Rav and took a biscuit. He put the book down.

'Oh, it's weird. Mind you, I guess I wandered up because I thought you might understand, of all people.' He looked down at his mug, embarrassed. 'Well, and… I wanted to see you again, too, if I'm honest,'

A flare of emotion caught in Faye's stomach like a hare's kick.

'Oh.' She didn't know what else to say, and looked away. She wasn't used to this kind of thing, though if Annie was here she'd roll her eyes and say, *Faye, sweetheart, you're a lovely looking lassie, and you're a witch to boot. Men love that*, or something to that effect.

'Well, anyway,' Rav continued, hurriedly. 'I don't know that many people here yet, so…'

Faye felt immediately that she hadn't responded in the way she should have. She should have flirted back – wasn't that what people did? That was normal. She liked Rav; liked his quickness, his sense of humour. She liked that he had a kindness about him. His eyes were beautiful: dark and long-lashed. He was slim and tall, appealingly boyish; today he wore black-rimmed glasses and a t-shirt from an 80s rap band she dimly remembered hearing about, under a black hoodie.

'Sorry, I…' She didn't know how to turn the conversation back so that she could respond differently – but even if she could, she didn't know what she'd say.

'It's fine. Look, the thing is, don't think I'm deranged or anything, but I think the house is haunted.' He took a sip of the tea.

'Haunted?'

'I know. It's mad. But ever since I moved in, there's been these weird noises in the night. Running footsteps in the hall. Sounds of laughing. And when I go downstairs, there's been a few times when the fridge door's been left open and stuff pulled out. Food all over the floor.'

'It's not mad.' Faye crunched her biscuit. 'You know there have always been stories about that house. No-one ever stayed there long, not since it was built.'

'Really?'

'Remember, I told you at the beach that day?'

'Did you? I don't remember.' He gazed into the hearth, frowning. 'It's scary, Faye. I mean, I'm embarrassed to say it, but I don't want to sleep there right now.'

'You don't have to be embarrassed. These things happen all the time. Spirits that haven't moved on – occasionally people with powers they don't know they have, affecting their environments. The minister would probably do you an exorcism.'

'*Should* I have an exorcism?' Rav took a biscuit and dunked it in his tea.

'You could do. But I'd be happy to come and have a look for you first. See if we can't give the place a good cleanse. That might be all it needs.'

'You think so?'

'Why not? I can come and see, anyway. Take it from there.'

'That would be great.' Rav looked relieved. He sat back in his chair. 'Honestly, Faye. I'm knackered as much as anything. I haven't had a good night's sleep since I moved in.'

She looked at the antique clock behind the counter; it was almost four.

'Come on. Drink up. You can show me now,' she said, taking another biscuit for the walk and going to get her coat.

'Now?'

'Sure, why not?' She came back into the shop and started turning the lights off. 'Real witches are better than novelty spell books, and you have a real witch at your disposal.'

'I do?' It was his turn to look wrong-footed; perhaps it wasn't too late to let him know she liked him; she was just really bad at flirting.

'Yeah.' She held the door open for him, keys in hand. 'What're you waiting for?'

'Nothing! I had no idea that witches had this kind of immediate response time. I mean, I'm going to have to rethink my next 999 call.'

'I don't come out for less than a level 3 haunting. Just so you know.'

They walked companionably down the high street, towards the beach. Rav's hand brushed hers as they walked, and Faye fought an impulse to take it. It felt natural to do so, but she cautioned herself to be careful. After all, though Moddie had never said it as such, the implication always seemed to Faye that if you loved a man, he would inevitably leave you at some point. If that was the case, it was smart to stay at a distance from them. Not that hand-holding was love, but it was confusing nonetheless.

So she walked next to him, and wondered how anyone ever managed to fall in love, and what the sense of it all was.

Chapter 10

The house was cold. That was the first thing she noticed, which was odd because the late afternoon light was streaming through the floor-to-ceiling windows. Faye hugged her coat around her; an old dusty-pink one of Moddie's with a rounded collar and big pink buttons down the front. Faye liked it because it hung loose like a cape, and it had deep pockets for collecting stones and shells and feathers from the beach.

'Sorry it's cold. As much as I turn the heating up I just can't get it warm in here.' Rav ran his hand over one of the white-painted vintage radiators that sat against a wall of exposed brick. Most of the internal walls were glass with long blinds rolled up at the top, but there were a couple in that designer-styled exposed brick that gave it the feeling of a trendy loft apartment. He pulled his hand away. 'It's boiling hot to touch. Just won't spread to the room. The perils of a house made of glass by the Scottish coast, I guess.'

Faye frowned.

'I'm not sure. I'd think that it was built to be energy efficient. Some kind of house of the future. It's more likely that the cold is connected to the haunting.' She walked into the steel and glass kitchen; it still looked unused. The cold was worse in there, and as soon as she walked in, she got a sense of being watched, and a prickling on her skin.

'Connected to the haunting? You're saying that like it *is* haunted.'

'Something along those lines, yes.'

'But you've only been here for three minutes. How can you be sure?'

'What you told me isn't normal. I didn't have to come to the house to know you're having some kind of supernatural disturbance.'

'So why did you, then?' Rav opened the fridge and got some milk out. 'Coffee? Think I still have enough.'

'Thanks. Because I don't know exactly what the problem is without coming here. It could be anything. Old spirits attached to the house that need to be moved on. A poltergeist. A curse. A malfunctioning witch bottle.'

'Witch bottle?' he frowned.

'An old folk custom. To protect your house, put rusty nails in a bottle, pee on them, close up the bottle and wedge it up the chimney,'

'Nice.' Rav raised an eyebrow as he spooned ground filter coffee from a packet into a silver cafetiere.

'Or it could be you, sleepwalking. Night terrors.'

'Well, I've never sleepwalked as far as I know.' He poured hot water into the jug and let it stand.

'Well, that probably rules normal reasons out, then, unless you've got foxes. Mind if I take a look around?' She felt drawn to the glass hallway that ran down one side of the house, connecting the kitchen with the lounge that looked out to sea and three large bedrooms.

'Go for it. I'll come and find you.'

Faye stepped into the glass corridor, and her world changed instantly.

Instead of standing in a modern floor-to-ceiling glass-walled corridor, she was ankle-deep in a sea of grass. Small, twinkling lights and orbs, like a child's blown bubbles, bounced in the air and rose and fell in anarchic fashion on the grass, which was long and green-blue, like the shifting colour of the sea.

There was no glass on either side of her, but a metre or so away from where the outer edge of the house had been was a row of tall white stones, painted in blue spirals and other strange markings. Faye saw that they marked a path towards a radiant green-gold light just over the brow of the headland. To the left, the sea was still there but the muddy, dark sand of Black Sands Beach glowed white, as if it was lit by bright photographers' lamps.

She was not alone on the pathway; as she stood there, adjusting to the strangeness of the vision, she became aware that the grass held legions of small faerie creatures. Some of the ones in the grass were a little like the faeries she'd seen in the books Moddie read her as a child; tiny, winged creatures with petals for clothes and twigs in their hair. Some were half-caterpillar, half-fae; butterflies with faerie faces flew past her, and there were large, iridescent beetles.

But there were also taller creatures that pushed past her; some were singing, dancing, laughing; many didn't progress in a straight line but circled around her, pulling at her clothes. One, a bearded half-man, half-goat, tweaked her nose, and then, unexpectedly, her nipple, as he passed her.

Some had a greenish skin; three faerie-women passed her on horseback with a procession of courtiers before and after them. They were beautiful, in draping, diaphanous garments, but their expressions were forbidding; one horse was black, one white, and one was blood red. Each of the horses had silver ribbons plaited into their long manes.

Rav's hand touched her on the shoulder, and she blinked. And as soon as she had, the grass disappeared under her feet and she was standing back in the long passageway.

Faye could only stare through him as she tried to process what had just happened.

'What?' he gave her a strange look.

'I… I just…' She couldn't find the words – any words – at that moment. She felt outside herself in a different way than she had before, even when doing magic.

'It feels weird out here, doesn't it? I knew you'd pick that up.' He handed her a mug. Faye took a sip, instinctively, and then again as she felt the drink reconnect her to her body again.

'I just… I wasn't here. This is a faerie pathway.' She pointed outside the house to the edge of the beach where scrubby grass gave way to the sand. 'To about there, where the sand starts. It leads over the hill, there. To the headland.'

'A what?' Rav gave her a look.

'A faerie road. I saw them. The fae, the spirits of nature. So many different kinds. This was all grass. It was… beautiful.' She felt a wave of exhaustion come over her, and she slumped against the wall.

'Wow. Okay, let's get you to a seat.' Rav took her coffee and guided her to the lounge where she fell back into a yellow leather sofa. He didn't seem to have done much moving in except for a tall, wide box-shelved unit that held what looked like thousands of vinyl LPs.

'So. I don't really understand what you're telling me. Faeries? I thought that was just made up for kids.'

'Of course not. Few things that are talked about that much aren't real. Even if they weren't real to start with, they become it because of being so imagined. Magic 101,' Faye snapped. 'Don't ask me to come here and solve your problems and then tell me you don't believe what I'm saying. I'm the expert, you wanted my opinion. That's my diagnosis.'

'Wow. Testy, dude.'

'You asked, I'm telling you.'

'Faeries?' he raised an eyebrow at her, questioningly.

'Yes.' Faye stared at him, unblinking.

'But, like… and I'm not disrespecting you, Faye. Really. But, as far as I know, faeries are these little tiny winged things. Like the ones in the flowers. My sister had those books. C is for the Cinquefoil Fairy, D is for the Dandelion Fairy… It doesn't feel like they'd be the ones trashing my kitchen and pounding the house so hard it sounds like an army passing through.' Rav sat forward, awkwardly, on the orange leather easy chair facing her – *classic single man décor*, Faye thought briefly to herself – and put his coffee glass down on a packing crate that was positioned as a table between them.

'You weren't reading that book of faerie lore, then? Earlier, in the shop?' She sighed and sat forward, wondering if she'd ever meet any man that she didn't have to explain herself – and the natural world – to. They were always so disconnected from the real, textured life of nature under their feet.

'I was flicking through it,' he said, defensively.

'Fine. So, basically, faerie is the realm of the spirits of nature. There are all kinds of faerie. Some tiny with wings. Some huge and terrible. There are spirits of the sea, of the rocks, of the plants, of ancient species that are from other periods of human development, and non-human time. When humans interact with them, as long as it's respectfully, they tend to take their shape from the frame of human perception. Hence you get regional variations on the same thing: selkies, mermaids, kelpies are different riffs on a similar energy. A water spirit that appeared at different times to different people.'

'So you've seen them before?' He sat back a little, taking in what she was saying.

'Only a couple of times, and nothing like that. They don't like to be seen, as a rule. They don't want to be disturbed by humans. Once,

I was sitting on my rock out there…' She pointed out to the beach. 'And I got a sense there was someone else there. I saw what looked like a little girl dart behind one of the other big stones, but then, when I went to go and look, there was no-one there. I was the only one on the beach that whole time. No children ran on or off the beach.'

'So… what you saw. It was like that?'

'No. That was way more vivid. It was a grass road, like I said, and it was absolutely heaving with them. All sizes. All kinds. I could see them all. They could see me, but most of them left me alone,'

'So…?'

'So, this house is sitting on a faerie road of some kind. All the disturbances you're getting are because of the sheer amount of traffic going up the hill to whatever that glowing thing is up there. Which would explain why no-one's ever settled here. The fae must have been livid when this house was built. They're very protective of what they consider to be their land. Faerie mounds, roads, passageways.'

'How do you know that?'

'There are documented cases of people having to placate faeries when they've built on their territory. In Iceland they build roads around their elf-hills. They wouldn't dream of knocking them over.'

'Really?' Rav chuckled. 'That's amazing.'

'Oh, it's a serious business. There are people that are brought in specially to negotiate with the elves when a new road is to be built.' Faye smiled.

'So what're you saying? That I need to pacify the faeries?'

'I would say so.'

'Well, what are we talking about? Saying a prayer or something?'

It was still cold in the room. Faye looked around her; it was beautiful, this house, but unless she could sort this problem out, Rav would move out in a month or so. And she realised that she didn't want him to go. She liked him, and she liked him being close by. And this was a special place; she'd always thought so. She felt suddenly sure that if the faerie road problem could be solved, it could be a place of power here.

'No. I think it's going to take more than that,' she mused. 'Do you own this house? Or are you renting it?'

'Renting. Had to move up here so fast it was the only option.'

'Ah. Well, I remember reading about a house that this happened to. They stopped the disturbances by rebuilding the corner of the house that was impinging on faerie land.'

'You've got to be kidding.' Rav let out a snort of disbelief. 'That's mad. Not that any landlord would let me do that anyway.'

'I'm not kidding at all.' Faye gave him a serious gaze, pushing her fringe out of her eyes. 'This kind of thing is serious. People spend a lot of effort appeasing the fae.'

'Well, I'm not doing that. I can't, even if I wanted to.. Forget it. I'll just get some earplugs.'

Faye sighed. What she couldn't say, or even explain to herself, was that in that moment when she stood on the faerie path, she had felt at home. What could she say to Rav that would help him understand that? She hardly understood herself.

'Look, I never said it was an easy option. Perhaps I'd better go.' She stood up, jamming her hands in her pockets. She felt uncomfortable being here now, and it wasn't just because of the faeries.

'Don't go. I didn't mean to be rude. Just… there must be something else we can do?' Rav stood up and reached out for her shoulder; his hand felt warm through the coat. 'I'm new to all this. And I… I really like you, and I trust you. But you've got to admit it's kind of crazy, too. Please, Faye.'

He sighed, and shook his head. 'Mum always said I should be more spiritual. I've just never really... connected with that kind of thing, you know? She had an altar to Lakshmi and Vishnu in our house when I was growing up, she went on pilgrimages now and again. It's just... not my thing. Or, it never has been. Maybe it's something I should explore? But... take it easy with me, I guess.'

'Okay.' She put her hand to his on her shoulder and they shared a long look. Faye felt the attraction again between them, like the heady mist of faerie, but she felt a disappointment too. She wasn't experienced with men, and maybe that meant she was too romantic about them. She didn't like it when the sparkle rubbed off, even a little.

She'd wanted to imagine that Rav was different, but he was like all the rest: his doubt was hurtful, like little thorns in her heart. But she'd spent her whole life among the doubt of others, and she couldn't blame him for it – Grandmother had always told her, *it's us that's different, not them. Have patience, wee one.*

'Well. Other things you can do – you can cleanse the place, first. With sage or rosemary. I bet no-one's done it the entire time it's been here.' She paced around, looking up at the walls and the ceilings.

'Right, I've heard of that. Does that work, though?' Rav frowned; Faye could see he was trying not to look too doubtful, and a warm flare of affection for him spread in her heart. He was trying to understand, and there were many people who wouldn't.

'Sure. You can get a bundle of either herb and burn it, smudging the smoke into the corners of all the rooms, around the doors, that kind of thing, or use the rosemary with water.' She cupped her left hand as if it contained water and mimed a flicking motion with her right hand. 'Like this.'

Rav copied her, his expression totally serious. 'Like this?'

'Right,' Faye wanted to hug him, suddenly, for trying, but she held herself back. 'And you should set up a faerie altar, and leave offerings for the fae. It might make them a little happier, at least.'

'An altar. Like, stuff on a table?'

'Specially selected stuff on a table, laid there with intention,' she corrected, smiling. 'Usually the offerings are bread and milk, or cream. Nothing too fancy and nothing too simple. Something just right.'

'Like the three bears.'

'Exactly,' she said. 'I can help you find things for the altar. It doesn't have to be elaborate; in fact, it's better that it isn't. This house is built next to the sea. The fae are of the sea and the land. The way that we show them we're honouring them isn't by loading up a table with plastic knick-knacks. Some stones, shells and feathers would be good. And those things bring the power of nature to your sacred space indoors.'

'Oh. And the bread and milk?'

'Yes. Can you do that? Change the food and drink every other day, maybe. You don't want to leave anything that's gone off.'

'I can do that.' Rav frowned, then smiled at Faye watching him. 'I'm grateful, really I am, Faye. I hope it'll work.'

'I'm sure it will. It can't hurt, anyway,' she smiled again.

'Can you help me? Find the stones and shells and things?' Rav leaned forward and reached for her hand.

'Of course. Let's go out there while there's still light.' She squeezed his hand; it felt good in hers.

Chapter 11

The sunset hung over the sea like a spell, temporarily changing Black Sands Beach into another place entirely: an in-between place where a faint smell of roses laced the salt of the rippling tide. Faye wondered where the smell of roses came from; perhaps an early blooming garden somewhere in the village.

'That's some beautiful sky,' Rav whistled as they stood there, suffused in the deep pink of the heavens. The red sun lit the sea dramatically; an unusual hush was on the beach. Faye felt the heartbeat of the land pounding through her toes; she took off her shoes and sank her bare feet into the sand. It was Beltane tomorrow, the first of May: the fire festival of the Old Ways. Sex and revelry, drinking, dancing. The energy was thick in the ground under her; Nature was bursting, full to the brim with bounty. Faye blushed as the fullness – no, it was something else – the *ripeness* of the feeling took her breath away.

'Yes… it's… um. It's bonny,' she replied, without knowing how to say how she felt. She had felt the surge of life in the earth before, but never when standing on a beach at sunset next to an attractive man. She had always imagined that attractive men were cads, acted like assholes, full of the ego of their own beauty. But Rav was shy, respectful; he made her laugh. There was an essential niceness about him that was relaxing to be around. And he was beautiful, perhaps without knowing it.

'Let's look, then,' she broke the moment, unsure of herself around him still. 'Shells, feathers, hagstones – that's stones with holes in them – anything like that. Whatever you like the look of.'

'All right.'

They walked along the beach together, picking up things when they saw them.

'It's hard, isn't it? Family expectations.' Faye broke the companionable silence, and bent down to pick up three iridesvent blue mussel shells; there were so many on the beach that the small, broken bits of blue shell gave the sand a jewelled sheen in the twilight. 'Your mum expecting you to be more into religion, I mean. I sometimes wonder what I'd have been if I hadn't been a Morgan.'

'Would you have been a witch, you mean? he asked, holding out his hand for her as she stood up.

'I guess so, aye. I wonder that sometimes.' Faye picked up a flat, round stone and skipped it into the sea. 'Did you always want to work in music? Was it always your thing?'

'Pretty much. Practically came out of the womb with headphones on. I remember being like three, four maybe, and listening to all of my brother's hip-hop CDs. And Mum and Dad's Indian music. Like, everything I could get my hands on; I still like a massive range of stuff. I studied sound technology at university but I wasn't quite good enough to make it in a studio, so I ended up on the business side. Roni and I started our company straight out of uni. We used to make flyers for indie bands in London, then we booked a tour for a friend's band, then a few years later we were doing all sorts. Management, tours, marketing, the lot. It grew pretty quickly.'

'Sounds like you were meant to do it.' Faye grinned and pushed the hair out of her eyes.

'Yeah, but it was mostly hard work, you know? Some people believe in fate. I don't. I think it's what you make it.'

'Maybe it was fate you came here,' Faye teased as she picked up some slick crow feathers from the sand.

Rav laughed softly.

'Maybe it was,' he conceded. He held his hand out for hers again, and this time he didn't let go after she took it. Immediately she felt a heat rise between them, even though the evening was cool and the wet sand was cold on the soles of her feet. It was the heartbeat in the sand; the rhythm of the land that, in that moment, at this point in the year, was focused on bodies, sex and making babies. In the old agricultural year, it was a time of giving thanks for the ripeness of the crops. *Ye can sugar coat it all ye like,* Annie had said in the shop yesterday, now that she was back from the acting job she refused to talk about, *but there's nae doubt that Beltane's comin'. I need that spell to work soon, if ye know wha' I'm sayin'...*

Rav's gaze was soft, and he leaned in to kiss her.

Faye pulled back, unsure.

'What is it?' Rav asked, stepping back quickly. 'I'm sorry, I—'

She felt silly, but it was hard to explain the caution she felt. Love was a subject haloed in doubt and mystery in her mind; Moddie and Grandmother had taught her to be wary of it. And yet, she possessed a rebellious dislike of their constant carefulness. Even Moddie, with her flower power *joie de vivre*, was cautious. About boys for Faye when Faye was a teen, about men for herself, and about magic itself. They were witches, that was accepted. That was their heritage. But the fear of persecution persisted. Grainne Morgan, apparently a beautiful black-haired woman, had 'enchanted' several local men so badly that she 'possessed their minds, turning them aside from their wives'. That she was a witch was true, but her power – her magic – was intrinsically connected to her sexuality, and the people of Abercolme had resented it.

'No, I'm sorry, Rav… I…' She didn't know how to explain. *It's not the sixteenth century any more*, she thought angrily, hating herself for pulling away. Hating herself for the confusion on his face. There was a legend that Grainne Morgan had not in fact been drowned as punishment, but that when it came time for her execution, an army of faeries had swept in with the sea, flooding the harbour at North Berwick.

It was a legend, Grandmother said. How could it be true? But in that moment, in her mind's eye, Faye saw the faeries riding on the waves towards her, to Black Sands Beach, and she was suddenly filled with a kind of velvety, warm wickedness which dispelled the doubt and anxiety like a shot of morphine. A pleasurable lull relaxed her taut muscles; a sweetness filled her blood and she reached for Rav, wrapping both arms around his neck and pulling him to her. Without saying anything more, she kissed him fiercely.

As she closed her eyes, Faye was overcome with sensation. Rav's lips were soft, and for a moment she could feel his surprise in the kiss; then, he kissed her back, harder. His fingers stroked her cheek, and then came to her bottom lip as they kissed. It felt *right*, delicious: the kiss became hot, slippery, wet. At the same time, she had the sense they were not alone; for a moment it was as though they stood on a beach thronged with people. She had the feeling of being knocked into, walked past. She heard laughter, snatches of speech she didn't understand, giggling. But when she drew back briefly from Rav and opened her eyes, they were alone.

'What is it?' he asked huskily, his face close to hers still.

'Nothing, I just… thought I heard something.' The sun was setting fast and the moon was rising already; it would be full tomorrow.

He kissed her again, and now Faye felt a sense of urgency in herself she wasn't used to. She'd had so few lovers. For a moment she smiled as his lips brushed hers; the spell had worked, anyway.

'Come back to the house,' Rav murmured against her ear. Faye looked up at the rising moon and shook her head; she wanted to stay outside. Here was where she felt most alive. Rav kissed her again, his lips tracing the line of her neck now; she felt his hot mouth on her collarbone. He pushed her clothes away from her skin and started to unbutton her blouse underneath the pink coat. Pleasure made networks on her skin, like a trail of small fireworks following his kisses. She sighed and let her head hang back, accepting Rav's worship of her body. She was hungry – starved of affection, even; she had forced herself into drought; denied herself this. 'Please,' he begged her between kisses. 'Come back inside.'

'We're fine here.' She pulled him down to the ground and he knelt next to her.

'Won't we get covered in sand?' he said, smiling.

'A little, maybe. It comes off. Don't worry about it.' She reached into her pocket and took out a large, creased cotton scarf and spread it over the sand under them. 'There. No sand.'

'You've done this before.' He raised his eyebrow, pretending to be arch. 'Seducing me under the moon, is that your plan?'

'Aye, you're just this week's conquest,' she reached for him, lying back on the sand and he came to her, laying his head next to hers. He gazed into her eyes.

'You've captured me, then. What now?'

She didn't know, but let instinct take her over. He rolled onto his back, reaching for her, and she kissed him deeply, touching his chest, feeling it firm and muscled under her light fingertips. She wanted his skin on hers, so she pushed up his black sweater and the soft tartan shirt underneath it; she placed her ripe mouth on his stomach, feeling the electric buzz of connection between them as she did so.

He moaned as her kisses covered his chest; both had forgotten any kind of chill in temperature, and the aura of roses still hung in the air, at the edge of perception.

He reached for her greedily, pulling her up towards his face for a deep kiss; as he drew away slowly he bit her top lip gently.

'Take this off,' he asked softly, and she took off her coat. He slid his hand under her half-opened blouse and bra and stroked her breast, pushing its lace to one side.

'Rav... Oh, oh god,' she murmured as he ran his tongue over her soft skin. She straddled his hips and leaned forwards so that her full breasts, skimmed with the white lace bra, were in his face. He licked her nipples through the soft lace and silky material of the bra, and moaned as he kissed both of them. She reached behind her, unhooked the bra and pushed it up so that her rounded, soft breasts were his to adore. She could feel him harden and push instinctively against her; she ran her fingers in his black hair as he moaned and sucked on her nipples. She felt wildly alive; she knew she was so wet already from his mouth on her that she could climax with just a few strokes of him inside her, or with his hand stroking her clit.

As if he could sense her thoughts, Rav reached under her and stroked the crotch of her jeans. She unbuttoned and unzipped them, taking them off and throwing them to one side, and rolled beside him so that he could touch her more easily; his gentle sucking was intoxicating and her body had now entirely taken over with its urgent need for pleasure. If Rav was surprised at how far their teenager-ish making out was going, then he adjusted quickly: he pulled her pink cotton knickers to one side and stroked his finger over her clit, maddening her with his deliberate slowness.

'Oh god, oh god…' Faye began moaning, having no control over her voice now. She closed her eyes and, just for a moment, had the sense again they were not alone on the beach; it was as though she could feel eyes on her dishevelled clothes, on her naked breasts under the moonlight. As Rav moved his mouth towards her stomach and continued stroking her softly, she closed her eyes and spread her arms out on the scarf, her palms on the sand. Shapes and shadows formed and dissolved on her eyelids as if figures stood by, watching her pleasure build, but she felt no shame or embarrassment. Indeed, as Rav quickened his stroking and pleasure filled her even more, she spread her legs wide. Just the act of doing that aroused her further: she wanted to be seen. She wanted to be completely open, receptive to all, to everything to fill her with pleasure. She felt the gazes of the shadows feeding her. Their desires building hers.

Come and watch me, come and feel this, witness my pleasure. Worship me, adore me, she thought, the words coming from nowhere. She felt his finger enter her, moving slowly in and out of her, and then, as she was so wet, he pushed two fingers into her. She gasped at the sensation of them stretching her in just the right way: he twisted his two fingers into her slowly, and then pulled them out again in a gentle corkscrew motion. She felt her climax coming hard, then, just as his hot tongue met her clit; as her muscles started to contract, the heat of his mouth was on her and she grabbed his head and pushed it into her as the wave of ecstasy came, and came like a hardness and a softness at once.

Her whole body was lit with intense pleasure, from the soles of her feet to her heart and her head. White-hot pleasure filled her lungs, her throat, her blood. She had had good orgasms before, but this, with the strangely rose-scented air on the beach, the salt of the sand and the moonlight on her skin, was different. She cried out in deep pleasure, a wordless, animal cry halfway between a moan and a scream.

The shadows disappeared, and Faye and Rav lay back on the sand. Faye laid her head on his shoulder and shivered.

'Thank you,' she smiled, feeling herself come back to earth. He half-sat and reached for her coat and jeans next to them, and draped her coat over her.

'You're welcome,' he grinned. 'So formal. Here, don't get cold.'

'Sorry, I…' She started to try and apologise for herself, then stopped.

'You've got nothing to apologise for, except being unbearably sexy, Miss Morgan.' Rav kissed her forehead, nose and lips and hugged her in closer.

'But you didn't get to…' Faye had been so lost in her own pleasure that she hadn't considered Rav as anything other than pleasure-giver until now. She felt guilty immediately, but he laughed.

'Um, I don't know if you noticed, but I was actually enjoying myself quite a lot just then.'

'But don't you need to…?' She looked shyly at him.

'It's not compulsory. I will next time.'

She smiled, realising he was telling the truth, and a weight lifted from her heart, knowing that Rav was this thoughtful. She liked him anyway, but she felt herself relax around him even more now.

'There might not be a next time,' she said playfully, pulling her bare legs up under the pink coat and wrapping them in his.

'Oh. Well, then, thanks for the memory. I'll take it to my grave.'

'*You're* welcome,' she grinned, and shivered again. 'Argh, I'm really starting to get cold now.'

'Right, come on. I'll make you a hot chocolate. Or a brandy. Or both.' He hugged her tight. 'We can collect feathers and shells for the faeries another day.'

She pulled on her jeans and put her coat back on, shaking the worst of the sand out of the old scarf and stuffing it back in her pocket.

'Okay.' Faye watched the strip of moonlight across the sea as Rav took her hand. She felt odd, suddenly, as if they had wandered into another time and place here, with the way that she had reacted to him; with the smell of roses in the air.

Rav's mention of the faeries had unsettled her, somehow; while the sense of being watched had aroused her earlier, as part of a fantasy, but now she felt vulnerable. What if, when Rav had been touching her, they really had been watching? She had seen the faerie folk in his house, and felt the cold they had cast about the place; she knew from the old stories that they were not always pleasant or kind.

She looked around, peering into the dark, but she couldn't sense any other presences now. Yet she felt a sudden disinclination to go back into Rav's house and be among those showy energies again. In her ecstasy, she had invited them to feed on her pleasure. In a more sober state, she really didn't want that at all.

'Actually, thanks but I'm going to go home.' She turned abruptly, pulling her hand away from his. 'I've got some things I need to do at the shop. Just remembered.'

'What?' He turned in surprise. 'But... we just... I mean...' He looked dumbfounded.

'I have to go. I'll see you,' she said, feeling stupid but not knowing how to explain. The beach was different now, but she couldn't describe how; this had been her place of worship for so long, and she was sensitive to its energies. She had often drawn on the elemental power of the beach in working magic, but whatever she had felt just now was different. Sex had brought a different energy, maybe that was all it was. But that feeling of being watched – and of her own wicked, sexual response – had unsettled her.

'I need to go home,' she repeated.

'Okay.' He cleared his throat, as if there was a lot he wanted to say, but was choosing not to. 'Will I see you again soon?'

'Oh. Yes, of course!' She felt awful then, but it was too late. 'Come back with me? To the shop? I'll make *you* a hot chocolate!' She was annoyed at herself for not suggesting it before, but the energy had changed between them now and her slow thinking – she was still befuddled by the strangeness of what had happened – was to blame.

'No, it's all right. Really. I should probably get an early night.' He smiled carefully at her, and gave her a little wave. 'See you around.'

No, no! Not see you around! she berated herself, and watched him take the path up the beach to his house. She sighed. Why did she always get it wrong?

She turned her back on the moonlit water and started off for home, pulling her coat tight against a wind that had started up suddenly. And as she stepped carefully around the rocks where the grass met the sand – where, she often thought, the real world met this in-between place of power – she heard strange voices calling her name. *Faye, Faye*, the wind seemed to carry an echo of someone calling her. *Faye Morgan*. But when she looked over at Rav's house, he couldn't be seen, and there was no-one else there.

Chapter 12

Annie knew instantly when Faye opened the shop door the next day; it took her all of three seconds to look Faye over and make up her mind that something had happened.

'Morning.' Faye stood aside and let her friend in; today, Annie was wearing a belted red trench coat over a baggy Breton stripe shirt with flappy pockets, a denim miniskirt and thick orange tights with biker boots. Faye felt dowdy in comparison in her jeans and sweater, though the cornflower-blue colour of her top sat nicely against her hair.

'Don' give me yer *morning*, Faye Morgan, like nothing's going on. Somethin's happened. I can tell,' Annie threw her coat on one of the easy chairs and stalked around her friend like a cat. She peered at Faye's neck and grabbed hold of the frayed collar of the old sweatshirt, pulling it away from Faye's skin and scanning her skin.

'What are you doing, you madwoman?' Faye pulled away, laughing at Annie's manic expression.

'Looking for love bites, my sweet dahhhling,' Annie trilled in her actress voice. 'Remainders of the love act. The shadow of a kiss.' She stood back and narrowed her eyes. 'You've had sex. Haven't you? I can tell.'

Faye laughed out loud. 'My god. What are you, like, some kind of sex detective? Yes, I did. Happy now?' she folded the neck of her sweatshirt back to normal and tried to look normal, though she didn't feel it.

'Ye *didn't*. Tell me yer not makin' this up!' Annie screeched, lapsing back into her normal accent.

'I'm not making it up.' Faye fiddled with a basket of crystals, sliding her fingers between the cool smoothness of the clear quartz.

'Who? When? *Where?*' Annie demanded, letting out a whoop of delight. 'I cannae *believe* it! This is big.' She sat down behind the counter and leaned forward, drumming her fingers on the glass. 'C'mon. Tell me. I want it all.'

The door opened and Aisha strode in, smiling. The bells tinkled, and Grandmother's hagstone charm twisted gently with the movement. It looked a lot better now that Faye had given it the once-over.

'Aisha. Yer just in time, sweetheart. Seems that the spell's worked. Faye got laid last night.' Annie nodded to Faye, who was feeling increasingly uncomfortable.

'Annie, I don't think…' she began, but Annie glared at her.

'I hope yer not tryin' to weasel out of telling us, Faye Morgan. When we're the ones that did the spell with ye. Grandmother Morgan would frown on that, ye know. She didnae have anyone to share her magic with except your maw and ye. We're a coven now, aye. Ye share yer magic. In fact…' Annie opened the store cupboard and drew out Grandmother's book. 'Here. We should be writin' this all down. Keepin' a record.'

She took a pen from the counter and sat down again, leaning forward.

'Annie! You are NOT going to write about my sex life in Grandmother's book!' Faye snatched the pen from her hand and closed the covers of the thick volume, full of Grandmother's spidery handwriting.

'We should put in the details of the ritual, though. An' the results,' Annie replied sulkily. 'It's only common witchcraft practice.'

'Fine. But only the ritual, and the fact that it seems to have worked.' Faye sighed.

'Tell us, then.' Aisha perched on the closest easy chair. 'This is so exciting!' She grinned, but there was a catch in her voice. Faye remembered their heart-to-heart outside the bar. Perhaps Aisha was sad that something had happened for Faye, as a fellow wallflower, and not her. Annie uncapped the pen and waited, expectantly.

'Well, there's not that much to tell,' Faye lied. After all, there was a lot she could say; about the strangeness of the feeling of being watched on the beach and about the fact that Rav's house was sitting on a faerie road, but she wouldn't. Those things were private. And her wild pleasure was also hers; not for gossip. 'I told you I met someone at the beach, the other week. Remember?'

She had mentioned it to Annie the day after meeting Rav, but had played it down at the time.

'Ye told me ye had a chat tae some guy. Not that he was some kinda new sex puppet for ye.'

'Annie! He's not a sex puppet.'

Annie waved her hand dismissively.

'Aye, he's a mega-brainy yogic philanthropist, I'm sure. Get on with it.'

'He's new to the village. He moved into that 60s house on the beach? You know the one?' Annie and Aisha nodded; they both knew Black Sands Beach well. 'His name's Rav Malik. He's from London originally, he's just moved up because he's organsing this new music festival in the village. He's… thoughtful. We had a really good talk about our families, about… it's hard to describe. About both having experience of families that have undergone trauma of different kinds. He's not into anything like this –' she gestured around her, at the shop – 'but he said his mum was a really religious, spiritual woman. He thought his house was haunted, and when I told him it was the fae that were

displeased… that house sits on a faery road, d'you know that?' Her
friends shook their heads; Annie raised an eyebrow.

'Explains a lot, though,' she said. 'Continue.'

'Yeah. Well. When I said that, his first reaction was, like, *this is
mad.* But then he took it seriously. He tried, anyway. I mean, I don't
think we have that much in common. His whole life is music; I'm not
really that into it. And I don't know what he thinks of me being from
a family of witches. But I really like him.' Faye was aware that she had
been gabbling a little; usually she didn't say as much.

'He's probably fascinated with the witch thing,' Aisha replied. 'And
you don't need to have that much in common. You just need to have…
I dunno. *The feelings.'*

'D'you have tha feelins?' Annie demanded. 'What happened,
anyway? Ye went over there tae look at his haunted hoose? An' then
what? Which, by the way, is a new one on me, aye. Goin' to have to
keep that one in the bank for when I'm tryin' to seduce a witchy type
in the future.'

'We kissed. And…' Faye felt uncomfortable saying much else. 'One
thing led to another, I guess.'

Annie screamed and punched the air.

'Yesss! Is he like what ye asked for, sweetheart? What does he
look like? Faye, you have to introduce us. I take it yer going to see
him again?'

Faye shrugged. 'Maybe. I don't know.'

Annie looked concerned and wrote something in the book.

'Oh, sweetheart. It wasn't any good?'

Faye smiled, thinking of the way that Rav had concentrated on
giving her pleasure; of the way that his mouth caressed her, brought
her to the intense ecstasy of the night before.

'No, no… it was very good.' She felt her cheeks colour. 'He's… I don't know if he's like what I asked for. He's tall. And he's really sweet.' Faye remembered her doll. The wool hair with golden flecks that she'd braided; the way she'd tattooed its skin with her words. It wasn't Rav… but it *did* look awfully like someone else she'd just met. Her eyes widened at the realisation. If the spell had worked, and Finn Beatha was its result, why was it that she had made love with Rav last night? Where was Finn?

'I feel like there's a "but" moving in the general direction of this conversation,' Aisha said.

'There might be a but,' Faye conceded.

'Why? He's nice?'

'Yes,' Faye smiled.

'He made you come, aye?' Annie looked concerned. 'Tell me he made ye come, sweetheart,'

'Annie, that's none of your business!' Faye glared at her friend.

'Just say yes or no,' Annie prompted. 'I'm not going to write it down. Look.' She put the pen down. 'I just wanna know. Yer my pal. I want to know ye had a good time.'

'Fine. *Yes*,' Faye hissed, grateful they didn't have any customers in the shop while this excruciating conversation was taking place.

'Good! So what's wrong with him? Ugly, is he?' Annie made a sympathetic face. 'Ye might get used to it. If he knows what he's doing, like.'

'He is very good-looking! Stop asking questions.'

'So what is it then?' Annie and Aisha were frowning at her, and Faye couldn't explain it to them. She was still unsettled by what had happened – she had acted so out of character in going so far with Rav at the beach, and she didn't know why. Stranger still had been the sensation of something watching them as they made love. If

Rav's house did sit on a faery road, as she believed, had it been faery creatures that had watched them, lost in their passion? Had the faeries influenced their abandon in some way? Either way, Faye felt exposed and shameful. In that moment, she had obeyed her desire, but now, she felt uncomfortable. She wondered how Rav felt about it. Was his desire real, or influenced in some way too?

She liked Rav, and she believed that he liked her too. Yet, as she talked to Annie and Aisha, her thoughts strayed briefly back to Finn Beatha. She had asked for someone kind who wanted her, and Rav had arrived....

But was he the one that she wanted?

Chapter 13

'Blue-rinse brigade out in force, I see,' Aisha murmured to Faye as they walked in, taking her arm. Folding chairs had been set out in lines facing the front of the room where the minister stood, talking to the local butcher. The front half of the hall was already full, mostly with the older members of the community.

'Hmph. Hope some of them are sympathetic to a witch memorial,' Faye sighed. The meeting was at six, so they'd come straight from the shop after closing up.

'Though they weren't witches, were they? Just normal people that got accused by, I dunno… jealous neighbours.' They stood at the refreshment table where Muriel from the bakery was handing out scones and pouring tea.

'Hi, Muriel. Two please,' Faye handed a china cup and saucer to Aisha and balanced her own cup on a plate with two scones. 'No, they weren't witches, but Grainne was. She helped most of these people's ancestors; childbirth, herbs for ailments, that kind of thing. She kept them connected to the old ways. They owe her a debt.'

'D'you think they see it that way?' Aisha whispered as they found seats at the end of one row.

'Probably not. But I'm happy to remind them,' she muttered. Aisha smiled and sipped her tea.

'I have no doubt of that,' she grinned. 'Don't know if I'm helping or hindering you, being here, you know,'

'What do you mean?' Faye smiled at the people filling the rows; these were people she'd lived alongside all her life. Some of whom, she knew, had an uneasy relationship with her and her family. Some, like Muriel and Annie, were enthusiastic about witchcraft. Muriel had been a close friend of Moddie's when she was alive, and when Moddie held a circle in the shop on a Friday night, there had been quite a few familiar faces that Faye had watched honour the old gods in the flickering candlelight.

'You know what I mean. Villages like this one don't like outsiders. Especially not ones like me.' Aisha touched her brown cheek. Faye sighed.

'I wish it wasn't like that for you. It's not fair.'

'Tell me about it. I was born in Scotland. Not good enough for some of them, though,' Aisha smiled too brightly. 'Most people are lovely. Just, occasionally, I get that *where are you from* question. Baffles them when I say Glasgow.'

'They're very suspicious of new people to the village. Or people that have been here for generations.' Faye sighed. There were many villagers that still avoided the shop altogether. And there was whispering, had always been sideways glances when Faye had been at the shops with Moddie or Grandmother; there had been a need to keep their chin up, as Morgans, and ignore the things that might have been said by some. Faye had learned this from a young age, when she had started school. On her first day, after she had bid a tearful goodbye to Moddie, who had mussed her hair affectionately and told her that she'd have a wonderful day, she'd gone inside and hung her coat on the peg with her name on it. Bel McDougall, her mud-brown hair in two scratchy plaits, had peered curiously at the bulge in the cream lining of Faye's coat.

'Wha's that?' She'd touched the rounded shape of the black tourmaline Moddie had sewn into Faye's coat for protection. Faye, accustomed to Moddie's ways – crystals and lavender bags under her pillow for good dreams, herbal tinctures for coughs and colds, searching for faerie toadstool rings for making wishes – had shrugged.

'Black crystal to keep the bad spirits away,' she'd explained quite naturally, smiling at this new friend. But Bel's eyes had widened, and she'd run into the classroom calling out, *She's a witch, she's a witch*, laughing but casting baleful glances back at her at the same time until Faye felt she was being made fun of, though she didn't know why. Tears had welled up in her eyes until she felt a small hand in hers, and turned to see five-year-old Annie's earnest face topped with a mop of unruly dark blonde hair staring into hers.

'Ye can sit with me,' Annie had led her to a green hexagonal table with two boys who were reasonably sensible, and they'd begun a discussion about what their favourite colours were. After that day, Faye learned that there were plenty more Bel McDougalls, but there was also Annie, who, rather than run away, always seemed to be propelled towards Faye with a combination of fierce curiosity and even fiercer love.

But Annie wasn't here to fight for Faye today; she was away at another audition. *I hope she gets something soon,* Faye thought, as the minister banged the table for attention. Still, it was heartening to have Aisha with her: not for the first time, Faye thanked whatever fair wind had blown Aisha to Mistress of Magic's door.

The minister outlined the proposal; it was more or less as he'd described to Faye. There was some budget spare in the village's coffers, despite the fact that the roads hadn't been repaired for some years and the street lights needed updating. There wasn't enough for that, but there was enough for a statue in the village. Faye rolled her eyes at Aisha. *Obviously*, she mouthed. Aisha grinned, but her expression altered as she looked over Faye's shoulder.

'What?' Faye mouthed, and Aisha signalled with a nod of her head to the back of the hall.

'Who's that?'

Faye blushed and looked back to the front of the hall.

'That's Rav. The one I told you about,' she whispered.

'He's fit.' Aisha turned back round to look, and Faye elbowed her.

'Aish! Shhh,' she hissed; Mrs Robison in the seat in front of her glared at them both.

'What?' Aisha whispered, but Faye shook her head. She wasn't about to explain her and Rav's erotic encounter on the beach in a town hall full of pensioners. She knew that she'd asked him to come to the meeting in passing the night before, before things got physical. But she hadn't expected to see him: it was kind of him to turn up, considering her behaviour.

'So, the proposal to put in front of you as residents is for a life-sized sculpture of King James the First,' Minister Smith said, his voice well used to addressing a large and yet usually sparsely attended stone church. 'We haven't yet sourced an artist. We can take suggestions if anyone has any. But we thought – the church committee, that is – that if we were going to have a statue, what better person should we have than the unifier of Great Britain? A King of Scotland that became a King of all Britain.' There was a general murmur of assent from the hall.

Faye took a deep breath and stood up. This was her moment.

'Minister Smith. With respect, I'd like to propose an alternative statue, if this money really can't be spent on anything more useful.' Her legs felt wobbly and her voice shook, but she was determined to speak out. She felt everyone's eyes turn on her; her shyness threatened to take over, and she wanted to sit down and say *never mind* and give up on the whole thing altogether. But Aisha smiled up at her. *Go on*, she mouthed, and she was reminded of Annie's hand in hers that first day in school.

'Miss Morgan,' Minister Smith sighed, and beckoned her to the front. 'By all means, come and tell us your idea.'

Faye stepped over Aisha's legs and walked slowly to the front of the hall, feeling the kindly and not-so-kindly stares on her back. *She's a witch, she's a witch*, she heard Bel McDougall's voice in her head over and over, and felt the snide comments and the sudden silences that still arose sometimes when she walked into the library, the supermarket or the garage.

Faye turned to face the room and smiled as confidently as she could. She cleared her throat.

'Hi. I'm Faye Morgan, I run Mistress of Magic on the high street. I think I know most people here. Anyway, I'd like to propose, as an alternative to James the First, that we have a memorial in Abercolme for the people that were wrongly executed for witchcraft during the Scottish witch trials.' She tried to avoid Rav's eyes, like she wasn't looking for him, like she didn't know he was there, but he was right in her line of sight and gave her a little wave. She smiled shyly at him and looked away, feeling herself blush again. It was awkward, and she didn't know how to make it easy again – but for the moment, she had to concentrate on her speech.

There was a dead silence for a moment, followed by a largely indignant rustle of voices. Faye cleared her voice again, but it wasn't enough. Minister Smith banged his hand on the table for silence; Faye looked at him in surprise.

'Whatever ye might think of me, Miss Morgan, I respect democracy,' he murmured, unsmiling, and nodded to her to continue.

'Right. So, as I was saying. Several members of our community died at the infamous North Berwick witch trials in 1590, including my own direct ancestor, Grainne Morgan. Other innocent members of our community suffered in local ad hoc trials and were similarly put to death,' Faye shivered, but took a deep breath and continued. 'None of these people – men and women, but predominantly women – deserved their fate. Accused witches were tortured until they confessed to the lurid accounts of completely fictional devil worship that the inquisitors told them to repeat. Someone could be accused as a witch for the most basic of reasons – having looked at a cow that became ill, for enchanting a man to fall in love with them—'

'You sell love spells at yer shop, lassie, don't ye, though?' someone shouted out. Some of the villagers laughed.

'Yes, and I don't expect to be murdered for it,' Faye snapped back. *Keep your cool,* she told herself. *You're not going to get people on side by being angry.* 'Anyway. I would like to put forward the option of a memorial to the men and women who suffered so horrifically. Whoever the village chooses as the sculptor is fine, I don't have anyone particular in mind. Actually – just a plaque with their names on would be fine. But this village has a dark past, and I think we have to do something to make amends.'

She breathed in, her heart hammering. There was a sullen silence.

'Is that all?' Minister Smith enquired.

'Yes,' Faye muttered and returned to her seat. She caught a few kindly stares, and many not as kind. Aisha gave her a smile of solidarity as she sat down.

'Well done,' she whispered.

Faye gave Aisha's arm a squeeze, but she felt disappointed. 'Fat lot of good that did. I tried, anyway,' she muttered. She didn't know why she'd bothered. In what world would conservative, rural Abercolme choose to remember innocent scapegoats over a king? She sighed.

'All right then.' Minister Smith clapped his hands together. 'You'll all be receiving a ballot pack in the letterbox, with the written proposals from both parties, and we will vote on the matter by casting ballots here in the village hall at a time to be agreed. Miss Morgan, if you could see me after the meeting, I can give you the details of what's required. Are there any other matters anyone would like to propose before we leave?'

Someone at the back of the hall put their hand up.

'I see that music festival's still going on. Ma customers aren't happy with it. More and more unsuitable bands going on the list, aye. Village is going to be full of layabouts an' hippies, mark my words!'

Minister Smith had noticed Rav and beckoned at him to come to the front of the hall. *Ah. That's why he's here. Not for me*, Faye thought, and felt ridiculous for thinking he was there to support her in the first place.

'I asked Mr Malik to be here with us, as I thought many of you would have questions about the festival,' the minister explained. 'Perhaps he can provide more information?'

'Uh, hi.' Rav made his way to the front of the hall; Faye noticed he was nervous. 'I'm Rav, I'm the promotor organising Abercolme Rocks. So, we've got some amazing bands on the schedule; Science Fiction Pulp Novel, Dal Riada, Green Apple: Red Apple, Kollectiv and Aspirational Terrace so far. Tickets are selling really well but we have limited them to 5,000 because of the space in the castle grounds.'

'Why did we have to have a music festival here at all? We were perfectly happy without one.' Mrs Kennedy, in her seventies, with a flowered scarf knotted around her head and dressed in a fleece of indeterminate colour, stood up and flicked her hand dismissively at Rav. 'Ah don't know who ye spoke to, to get permission in the first place, aye. Nobody wants ye here.'

'Well, you can take it up with the council. They put out a tender for a festival and my company won it; it's part of their regeneration project. I've produced a lot of festivals and music tours all over the world. I can promise you that this will be a good opportunity for Abercolme. Your businesses will benefit – accommodation, taxi services getting people to and from the venue, catering, retail; and I'm going to be creating some temporary jobs in terms of site services.' He opened his arms in a welcoming gesture. 'Honestly. I know it's new, but you're going to find that this helps Abercolme rather than hinders it. I promise.'

'It's going to ruin the castle! That's ancient, ye know. That's our heritage. We don't want hippies runnin' around it with no clothes on, spray-painting the stone, breaking things. It isn't respectful.' Mrs Kennedy wasn't going to let it go, clearly. Rav smiled nicely and nodded, waiting for her to finish.

'Of course I understand your concerns. I will say that a festival audience for the type of event Abercolme Rocks will be are much more middle-class: responsible people who love good music; I imagine there will be quite a few parents bringing children; it's a pleasant outdoor festival event that starts in the afternoon and finishes around eleven, so won't keep anyone up too late into the night.' Rav ran his hand through his hair; Faye liked the way that his fringe got in his eyes; he pushed it away impatiently. Today he was wearing skinny jeans, another hip-hop t-shirt and a dark blue blazer.

'We will have the proper security attached to the event. We'll be holding the festival in the castle grounds, away from the main building; people will not be allowed access to the castle for the duration of the day.'

Rav's tone never wavered from a practised, steady pleasantness, but Faye sensed his frustration under the professional veneer. It couldn't have been the first time he'd had to deal with a difficult crowd: Faye supposed that diplomacy was part of an event manager's skill set. Yet, she noticed that his left hand was clenched into a fist: as Rav caught her eye, he smiled subtly, knowing that she'd noticed his tell, and stretched out his fingers, returning his hand to his side.

'All necessary risk assessments have been done. I think, if you came along, you'd enjoy it.' Rav twinkled his sweet smile at Mrs Kennedy, and Faye was amazed to see her look slightly mollified.

'Well, I still don't like it, but I see I've not got much of a choice, aye,' the woman muttered and sat down.

'Tell you what, you can have two free tickets so you can come and see for yourself. How would that be?' Despite her awkwardness at being in the same room as Rav, Faye snorted with laughter and coughed to disguise it.

'Get on with ye! I wouldn't want to come.' Mrs Kennedy sounded scandalised; Faye wished she could see her face from where she was sitting.

'All right. Well, if you change your mind, let me know,' Rav said. 'In fact, if anyone's not sure about the festival, come and talk to me about it. And I'm happy to provide free tickets to anyone here that would like to come.'

Everyone started filing out of the village hall.

'Miss Morgan, if I may?' the minister beckoned Faye to the front of the hall as everyone else left.

'So.' Minister Smith handed her some papers. 'You need to write something to make your case. If you can get that to me in a week or two, then I'll make up the letter with all the information to be sent out with the ballots. All right?' he smiled thinly at Faye.

'Fine.' She took the paperwork without looking at it. 'What do I have to do, exactly?'

'Make your case. Write something persuasive for the villagers to think about. No more than five hundred words. They'll most likely go for the King James statue, but you're welcome to try.'

'They might not.' She felt the minister was probably right.

At that moment, the village door banged open, blown by a sudden wind. Faye, Rav and the minister looked around in surprise at the rain which had suddenly come out of nowhere, outside.

'Scottish weather.' The minister shivered as the rain drummed on the windows. It was suddenly dark outside where before it had been a normal spring afternoon. 'So. Any questions?'

Faye looked up at the rain on the high windows. For just a second, she thought she saw faces in the water, looking in at them; otherworldly faces with large, watery eyes and open mouths. As if they were laughing. Or something more savage. As if they were hungry.

'No,' she said, turning away. She walked cautiously out of the hall, through its thick, old double doors.

'Weird weather.' Rav was standing by the doors, adjusting the collar on his blazer.

'Oh. Yeah.' She looked away, embarrassed. Though he was being sweet, Faye was painfully aware that they had been shockingly intimate so recently; the feeling of having been exposed returned to her, and she swallowed awkwardly. What must he think of her? *I don't normally do that kind of thing*, she wanted to say. *I wouldn't usually be so... abandoned. We had just met.* But these were modern times; she didn't feel she should apologise. She wasn't puritanical, either. It was more that it had just been strange. The whole time – on the beach, at his house – in retrospect, she had felt odd throughout. As if she was under some sort of spell.

'Good speech.' He reached for her hand, and held it. 'Hope you win the vote,' he added.

'Oh, err, thanks. So do I,' she replied. It wasn't getting any less awkward: in fact, holding his hand just made it worse, because it made her want to hug him. 'Buying your way into their good books, are you?' Faye blundered on. 'The free tickets, I mean.' *Oh God, what am I saying?* she berated herself. *Sorry. Just say sorry for running out on him.* But though she wanted to, she couldn't make herself say the words, because that would mean acknowledging what had happened, and she was too ashamed.

'Oh... right.' Rav shrugged and let go of her hand. 'Worth a try. That woman with the headscarf, what's her name?'

'Mrs Kennedy. She does the flowers in the church.' Faye's heart sank. The moment had gone; if she was going to say anything, she should have said it by now. They had been hand in hand: that was the moment where she should have looked up into his kind brown eyes and tried to explain. Rav was trying to talk to her, trying to connect to her, but she was doing it all wrong.

'Mrs Kennedy. Okay. Thing I've learned about places like this is, go for the ringleaders and the rest fall in line. I'll make friends with Mrs Kennedy and we'll see how many complaints there are about the festival after that.' He smiled warmly at her, and she felt awkward again.

'Oh. Well, good luck.' She opened the doors; getting drenched was better than making a fool of herself with Rav. 'And... I'm sorry. For... you know,' she blurted, confused, and ran into the rain, berating herself. *Get back in there and talk to the man, idiot!* Annie would have said. But Faye couldn't.

'Faye!' Rav called after her. He sounded confused and a little annoyed. She tried to wave over her shoulder, but it came out wrong, like a flailing madwoman. She was running away.

It was nice that Rav still wanted to know her but, after that performance, Faye doubted she'd be seeing him again anytime soon. Letting herself into the shop, she berated herself. *Stupid, stupid.* She'd had a chance at something. A real romance with a real man. But she'd blown it.

Summoning love with a magic spell might have worked. But magic wasn't responsible for what happened afterwards, Faye was learning.

Chapter 14

A week later, Faye woke in the middle of the night, thinking about the faerie road.

She lay on the oak double bed that had once been Moddie's and stared at the ceiling for a moment. When she closed her eyes, she was back there instantly, walking the grass road that existed somehow inside Rav's house. But this time, instead of Rav making love to her on the beach, Finn Beatha stood at the top of the hill, and he was beckoning her to come to him.

She opened her eyes again. She knew she was still in her bed, safe in the grey stone house of the Morgans. But, at the same time, she was somewhere else.

She felt a sudden need to be at Black Sands Beach. She hadn't heard from Finn; *it wasn't specifically about him,* she told herself. But her heart yearned towards the beach, her special place of magic.

Well, I'm not getting back to sleep anytime soon, she thought as she swung her legs out of bed. *So I might as well go.* Experience had taught her to obey her instincts when they were this insistent. It was times like these when she imagined the spirits of her ancestors pulling at her hand, compelling her to act. It would be rude to deny them.

She got dressed quickly: leggings, a heavy long woollen dress over the top, socks. Downstairs, she wrapped a thick blue and green tartan scarf around her neck and put the long pink coat on again; she pulled on her high, practical walking boots. They had a thick sole and she knew she could walk through water in them, and climb wet rock if required. She grabbed a pair of thick fleece gloves from under the counter and let herself out of the side door.

The street was deserted: she looked at her watch. 1:30 a.m. – no time for anyone to be awake in Abercolme. Even the pub shut just before eleven. Or, if people were up, they were sensibly indoors.

It wasn't that cold, being May. It was a full moon too, and when she got to the beach, the clouds parted so that the intensity of the light beat down on the flat water. She looked up at Rav's house, but it was in darkness. She felt embarrassed and hoped he wouldn't see her out here. She didn't know what she would say to him.

Instead of going to her rock to sit and look out to sea, she went to where she imagined the beginning of the faerie road might be and closed her eyes.

It was there, immediately, as if it had been waiting for her. The long grass where she knew there should only be sand; the twinkling lights that floated around her like stars in a tide of light mist. She had walked this place so many times and never known.

Or perhaps she *had* known: Black Sands was a magical place. It had always been that way; Moddie had brought her here as a child to make simple shell shapes on the dark sand. She had squatted down on her bare heels next to her daughter. *Make a wish, Faye. When the tide takes your spell, it goes to the faeries.*

Moddie made shapes Faye recognised: circles, spirals, stars. She often wrote things within the shapes with her finger; symbols and letters. And, occasionally, she would dispatch Faye to collect as many shells as she could from around the beach to make one large heart shape which she would always trace the same name into: Lyr. *What is Lyr, mummy?* Little Faye would watch Moddie draw the looping script into the sand. *Nobody, darling. Just a memory,* she would reply.

Not many others came here. But she and Annie had spent hours here as teens, asking all manner of boons from the sea and the wind and the air: To pass their exams. To get people to like them. To get the new boots they'd had their eye on in the one village shoe shop.

She closed her eyes and followed the sparkling path. She was no longer cold, and she took off her gloves and coat, letting them fall to the ground.

The fae were around her again, in varying size and colour and type. The butterfly fae fluttered past, moonlight glimmering on their wings. When she looked up, the moon was still there and the sea rippled calmly to her left. There was a distant sound of hoofbeats on grass, and a pleasurable thrumming rhythm that vibrated up from the faerie earth into her body.

This time, she followed the path to the top of the hill where the golden light shone as it had before. And when she reached the top, she took a breath of wonder.

Before her, far out at sea, was a huge golden castle, ringed by a vast green maze. In reality, if you stood on Black Sands Beach and looked out, it was onto the Firth of Forth that ran into the North Sea; there was a small island off the coast that monks had once lived on; before that, druids.

But now there was no island: instead, tall towers plunged upward through the dark Fife sea, looking as if they were formed of golden seawater. The maze that led to it was impossible. There was no way that such a strangely manicured puzzle could just be there, dotted with flower gardens, fountains and strange golden statues. And yet it was there, made of a kind of hedge which ran at head height. Faye could see many small faeries scurrying about in it, the hedge towering above them. It seemed that the maze was the only way to the castle, and it seemed to reach on forever.

The air was scented. Faye could pick out rose, jasmine and lavender, but she knew there were more fragrances that made up the smell of this place; lingering, heavy, like an incense or when she walked past the perfume counters in the fancy department stores in Edinburgh. She remembered the smell of roses when she had made love with Rav on the beach. It was the same smell; the same perfumed air.

Well, I might as well follow, she thought, and approached the entrance to the maze. *This is what everyone else seems to be doing.* Though 'everyone' wasn't really the correct term; the faeries were so varied. In front of her, floating into the maze opening, was a beautiful fae woman about Faye's height. She was wearing a green skirt. She was naked from the waist up, and her golden hair floated down her shoulders like a cloak. Yet when her skirt swished to one side, Faye saw she had black goat legs underneath.

'Through the maze, this and there, the faerie castle is here. Beware! Beware, humans, ere time is lost! Beware the years that the faerie realm cost!
Through the maze, this and there, the faerie castle is here. Beware!'

Two gnome-type little men with beards – rather like the gnomes Faye had in the garden behind the shop where she grew herbs for her homemade incenses – sang the song as she trod past. One looked up and nodded at her as she grew closer to the opening of the maze.

'Blessings, miss. Ready to try your luck in the Faerie Maze?' he chuckled rather unpleasantly. 'Most humans don't come back if they go in. But there's fine food and dancing to be had. Don't be shy, little miss, in you go!' and he reached out a little hand and tickled the back of her shin so that she leaped forward.

'Hey!' she cried, not sure what to do. She didn't want to get lost, wherever she was. Moddie had read enough faerie stories to the young Faye for her to know that getting lost in Faerieland was no laughing matter. The realm of the fae was dangerous; faeries were capricious, changeable; they might grant your wishes or help you around the house, or they might try and drown you, steal from you or hurt you in a thousand little ways.

And of course there were the tales told of unlucky villagers who, on moonlit evenings, had come across a faerie ring of toadstools or a faerie mound – the ones that the farmers preserved in the middle of their fields so as not to upset the Fair Folk. They were transported into the land of the fae where they might have been treated well or badly, but when they returned, it was many years later and their family had all died of old age and no-one knew them.

She stepped back, but the other little gnome-man followed her and looked up into her face.

'No, no! She's not one of them. She's *sidhe-leth*. Let her pass,' he said, and bowed deeply from the waist. 'Many apologies, madam. We have not seen your like for many years.'

Faye was confused.

'But I don't want to be lost here. It was a mistake. I'm going.' She turned away and followed her footsteps back to the beach, though she really didn't want to at all. Everything in her being sang out for the faerie castle; she wanted so much to go, to be in it. It was more than wanting, in fact; it was a need, a sense that it was part of her.

'You will not be lost, madam. You can pass.' The gnome bowed again. 'You will know the way.'

Faye turned again and looked at the castle before her; it seemed to loom even more golden and bright against the strange sky. Though it had the same full moon as above the beach, it was neither day or night but a strange pink-orange in between, like sunset or sunrise.

She wanted to, but she was afraid.

Then, as she looked into the maze, at the end of the first turn, she saw Moddie.

Chapter 15

Without thinking, Faye ran forward.

'Moddie!' she cried; she hadn't called her *Mum* since she was small. Moddie had preferred her own name; she'd been a young mother, only twenty-one when she'd had Faye. When Faye was in her teens, their relationship had been more like sisters.

Moddie's hair was loose and curled and reached her waist in long ringlets. She wore a white dress with a full skirt and long, bell-shaped sleeves. Her feet were bare, and she wore a golden circlet on her head. She beckoned to Faye, smiling, then turned a corner.

Faye ran through the maze pathway to the end and turned left as Moddie had. The hedge of the maze wall was fragrant and brushed against her legs as she ran.

'Moddie! Wait!' she cried again, but her mother moved fast through the turns and twists, not looking back. Faye followed as best she could, being careful not to crush the small faeries as she passed them; ladybirds the size of cats, leather-apron-wearing, bearded goblins that carried metal tools, more diaphanous, beautiful fae that seemed to float by without touching the earth. They were all heading for the castle, and there was an excitement among them that Faye picked up on. As she grew nearer, her heart beat faster; she felt a pleasant sense of anticipation, though she didn't know why.

Will I be lost? she wondered, but she felt that Moddie wouldn't lead her astray. There was that strange sense of familiarity, again; though she didn't understand how that could be. And the more she breathed in the strange faerie air, the more a kind of lassitude entered her veins. It was like having drunk two glasses of wine: the same light-headedness and pleasure at everything.

Faye followed the turns of the maze as best she could, trying to stay focused, fighting the lulling influence of the air and a growing disinclination to hurry at all. Moddie led her through long, dark tunnel-like passages where the hedge seemed to have almost completely grown over at the top, making a leaf-hatched ceiling; on other stretches the hedge was replaced by long walls of sandy brick or red stone; one section was made completely of a thick blue-tinted glass through which Faye could see the black ocean under her feet.

Further on, when the hedge had returned, small winged faeries fluttered around her head, singing, and she found herself laughing, holding her hands out for them to land on. She was fascinated with them all, shivering delightedly as four white faerie horses ran past her, their flanks covered in sweat, their hooves pounding on the flattened dirt. Faye stopped walking and let the rose-scented air overpower her. There were other voices that joined in the singing; she wanted to sing too. She felt her eyes closing, and pleasure washing over her. Moddie had died and left her long ago. It probably wasn't her mother that was leading her through the maze; most likely, it was another type of faerie that looked like her. That wanted to trick her.

Come to us, Faye, come to us, sidhe-leth, the voices sang to her, and, as her eyes closed, the edges of the maze seemed to melt away, leaving Faye in a slow, soft kind of dance with all the creatures undulating around in a circle, this way and that. *Come to us, be with us, Faye Morgan, kindred soul.*

Faye felt a pinch on her arm and opened her eyes; the dream, whatever it had been, of the faerie dance disappeared; she was alone again. She rubbed the sore spot on her forearm, frowning; it was like a sudden hangover come way too early after the pleasant tipsiness of a moment ago.

Faye. Wake up. It was Moddie's voice; even though she hadn't heard it for eight years, she knew her mother's voice as well as she knew her own skin.

As she looked up, Moddie's foot and the hem of her dress flickered around the far corner. Faye's head cleared; she knew it was Moddie, and that if she should put her trust in anyone or anything, here in the realm of faerie, it should be her mother. *The fae realm is treacherous*, Grandmother and Moddie had told her so many times. *They are beautiful, but you cannot trust them.*

Faye ran after her mother around the next turn, but Moddie had disappeared, and Faye didn't know which of the three possible openings she might have gone down.

Panic replaced the giddy pleasure of the faerie maze. Faye peered into each opening, but each one was empty and shadowed. She stopped and rested her hand on the thick hedge. She was lost again, and this time, it didn't feel so good.

Moddie, please help me. I don't want to be lost here, she thought, but there was no answer; no flickering of a dress in the distance, and no further pinches on her arm. She had to choose one of the ways forward, and she had nothing but instinct to go on.

Taking a deep breath, Faye chose the middle path. And as soon as she stepped into it, the open doors of the golden faerie castle towered, vast, above her.

Chapter 16

The walls of the faerie castle seemed to reach to the moon, which sat pregnant and full above Faye in the coral-pink sky. Its golden towers, when she gazed up at them, seemed to lean towards each other to join under the moon, the golden petals to its glowing centre.

The moon was far larger here than Faye had ever seen it in the ordinary world. Dimly she remembered reading once that the moon would have looked much bigger than it did now to people in the Stone Age, because it was closer to the earth then. Was it the same moon here as the one she was so used to? Or was this another, different, faerie moon that pulsed with a different kind of fierce and sweet power?

Intricate Celtic decoration covered the castle doors and, she saw as she walked through them, the walls inside. Spirals and Celtic knotwork scrolled over the gold and stone; similar designs to the ones on the jewellery she sold at the shop. There were words too, but Faye recognised they were in Scots Gaelic, and her grasp of it was shaky at best. Yet as she passed through the doors, she lost the thread of comparison to the real world altogether; it was like passing deeper into a dream, and whatever grasp she still had of her shop, of Abercolme and Annie and all the things she knew disappeared.

Faye found herself in a square, open-air courtyard. Faeries of all kinds milled around market stalls, which sold all manner of beautiful fruits. Faye remembered the old poem about the dangers of eating the faerie food – *Morning and evening, Maids heard the goblins cry: Come buy our orchard fruits, Come buy, come buy!* But she felt thirsty, and goblets of some rich red liquid were being poured by a bearded centaur from what looked like a crystal jug on the stall closest to her, with its bright red-and-white striped awning.

The centaur held out the drink to Faye with a wink.

'Drink for my lady, *sidhe-leth*? Thy beauty surpasses all, but this drink will make thee beautiful for ever,' it said in a seductive tone that thrilled Faye and made her shiver with pleasure.

She reached out before she knew what she was doing, then pulled her hand back sharply and shook her head.

'No, thank you,' she said, politely, and looked around for Moddie. The throng was getting bigger and busier, and she was being pulled into the crowd. She started to feel threatened instead of delighted.

The centaur – at least, Faye thought that was what it was, as she was a little hazy – had called her *sidhe-leth*, like the gnomes at the edge of the maze. What was that? She knew *sidhe* was a Gaelic word for faerie, but she didn't know what *leth* was. And she wasn't a faerie, so what did they mean? It must be some other term they gave to humans – perhaps as she had been a witch her whole life that made her different somehow.

The singing, catcalling and shouting was starting to ring in her ears; it was increasingly loud, so Faye pushed through the crowd as best she could, aiming for one of the entranceways leading off the courtyard. She couldn't see what lay beyond, but a soft gold light shone in each one – one to the north, one to the east and one to the west.

The closest doorway to Faye was on the left-hand wall, which was what she was used to thinking of as west at home, though here she was unsure which way was which. She managed to elbow and *excuse me* her way through the crowd until she had passed through it and emerged on the other side, where the noise of the courtyard faded away quickly.

The room was lit by candles, and their warmth licked the carved stone walls from which hung ultramarine and emerald-coloured tapestries. She couldn't see anyone else in the room, so she approached the nearest one and stroked it with the tip of her finger. It was soft, made of something velvety. The pattern wasn't one she recognised, but as she gazed at it, she thought for a moment she could see horses in the waves; then she decided they were seals on rocks. It was impossible to say exactly what was on it, but the colours and the sense of movement gave her a deep sense of wonder and beauty.

A hand on her elbow made her jump.

'I see you like the wall-hangings. They were made by our most talented weavers,' a deep, musical voice said, and Faye turned to face Finn Beatha. 'Welcome, Faye Morgan, *sidhe-leth*.'

Chapter 17

'Oh!' She couldn't think of anything else to say and felt stupid straightaway.

Finn let go of her elbow and bowed to her, though his eyes never left hers, and he smiled mischievously as he did it. 'The faerie realm is pleased to have you here.'

'You? How did you get here?!' Faye spluttered, shocked. Part of the surprise was seeing him, of course, but seeing him also made her remember where she had seen him last, and the memory took her back to earth, which, in the strange dream she was in, she had temporarily forgotten. For a brief moment, a clear vision of Mistress of Magic replaced her opulent surroundings: the hearthfire lit with the flame flickering cosily. It was a dark day, rain battering at the windows, and she had been arranging the stone mantelpiece which displayed her biggest crystals. A row of large amethyst crystal clusters sat next to a number of extra large yellow-gold citrine and smoky quartz crystals that had been polished into pyramids and pillars. On days like that, the shop was a snug, safe haven: she clutched at the memory as if it could steady her.

'I am of this place,' he replied, as if that would explain everything. 'I hoped you would come.'

'You're... faerie folk? But I saw you. At the bar, onstage! That's not what the fae do. My mother told me stories.' *Moddie.* She remembered that she had been following her mother through the crowd. 'I have to go. I need to find her. She's here…'

Faye would have recognised him anywhere, but Finn was dressed differently to the last time she had seen him, onstage in the packed Edinburgh bar. There, he had been bare-chested and barefoot, wearing only a blue and green kilt that sat on his hips, showing off his flat stomach and strong, rangy torso. Now, he wore a dark blue jacket with gold piping on the shoulders which looked somehow military; fitted trousers of the same material highlighted his strong thighs and calves. His dark blonde hair had the same golden flecks in it as she had noticed before – exactly the same colour as the wool she had used on her poppet doll in the spell, she remembered blearily, though the thought already felt distant – but this time, he wore a golden crown, studded with pearls and opals.

'She resides with us now. You will see her again in due course.' Finn took her hand this time and she felt the light-headedness that had overcome her before return, but this time, at a much greater intensity. Instinctively, Faye fought his power, though it was intensely strong. She tried to do what she had in the Edinburgh bar – to shut down her energy centres and cloak herself in darkness to regain some kind of control, but it was impossible to retain enough focus to do it properly. She kept finding her mind wandering, and the focused power she was used to raising and directing in spells and ritual eluded her, like snow blown into drifts and eddies by a strong wind.

'What do you mean? How can she…' But Faye's words trailed away as Finn drew her to him. Being this close to him was like a drug; something raw and wild swept through her. She felt, suddenly, as though nowhere else in the world existed, and as if she herself was changed: her old self was sloughed away, and some new yet original, as yet unknown self, remained.

'I will answer all of your questions, Faye Morgan,' he said, quietly. 'But first, follow me. I will show you this great land of mine.'

He released her from the embrace and took her hand. There was a part of her that knew she was being entranced; that this was a strange place where she very well might get lost. Faye fought it as hard as she could, and, just for a moment, as she focused hard on Mistress of Magic and on the rain on the windows and the leaping firelight, she felt her own power return a little. She pulled her hand away from his, concentrating on the vision of the shop to steady herself, but he took her palm in his again, chuckling in amusement, and Faye lost what brief advantage she had gained.

His hand was warm in hers; though she was walking, she hardly heard what he said. All she could focus on was the energy coming through his palm and into hers. It was a tingling wave of headiness she'd never felt before, and it surrounded her, circled her, so that she felt she was walking in a cloud. They walked through room upon room filled with tapestries and treasures; each one flickered with that strange candlelight, and hummed with a distant music – sometimes like a lullaby, sometimes a fast reel that made Faye's feet want to dance and tap.

He told her of the faerie realm. Old stories about this castle, where he and his royal family resided.

'Your court?' she asked, noticing that the noise – clapping, laughing, and the wild music – was growing louder.

'Yes.' He smiled at her; his eyes were like warm sapphires.

'You are a… king?'

'A faerie king. My sister is the queen of this place. Murias, the Castle of the Cup. The Palace of Water.'

'How long have you been here?' she asked wonderingly. Grand-mother had told her that the fae were as old as the world itself.

'As long as the moon, perhaps longer.' He smiled, raising her hand to his mouth and kissing her palm. 'I was a child once, but long ago, in your eyes. We do not age as you do in the human realm. I played here, with my pets and the other faeries of the court until I grew to be King. When we could not sleep, my sister and I, the faery pipers played us lullabies. When our hearts were broken, in the days when we were foolish in our love with mortals, they played to cheer us and mend our sorrows.' He smiled at her expression. 'You do not think our hearts can be broken? The fae creatures have suffered much at the hands of humans.'

'I... I don't... I mean, I didn't...' Faye shook her head. 'I don't know. I've only ever heard about faeries enchanting humans, not the other way around.'

'Well, *sidhe-leth*, believe me: it can happen.' He gazed meaningfully at her, and Faye had the same sense of disquiet as before.

She pulled her hand away from his. Immediately her head started to feel a little clearer; she looked around her at the room they were in. It was as grand as the others, but when she looked harder, she could see that the walls and the floor had shadows of tree roots within them.

Faye peered at the scene on the tapestry that hung closest to her. Like the others, it had figures that appeared to be dancing, in the midst of great revelry. Yet when she really looked at it, she realised that several figures hung upside down, hung by ropes attached to their ankles, their faces obscured. And, under the feet of the revellers, there were skulls and bones.

'Am I dreaming?' she asked him.

'You are not dreaming,' Finn's voice pulled her gaze from the tapestry, back to him. He reached for her hand again, but she refused him and held it to her side, suddenly unsure.

'What is this place?' she demanded, fighting the sleepy desire that had come over her. A part of her remembered that being in the faerie realm was dangerous and that she should be on her guard; she looked back at the tapestry, as if looking at it was an act of self-preservation. It was a reminder of danger; a reminder that she shouldn't forget she might be in peril. 'I… I shouldn't be here. I want to… I think I should go.'

There was a knock on one of the doors to the room and, frowning, Finn stalked across the room and flung it open. Some of the rooms Finn had led her though had had many doors in and out, and some just one. It made her think of the castle like a maze itself. She had found her way through the labyrinth outside, but could she leave this one, now that she was inside? She realised that Finn had led her through many rooms and she didn't know the way back out.

'What?' he demanded as he opened it; his demeanour had changed, suddenly, in a fraction of a moment; there were edges now, where there had been none before, and Faye felt wrong-footed.

There was a murmured conversation which she couldn't really hear; Faye stepped quietly towards where Finn stood, curious to see who he was talking to. In the shadow beyond the tall, carved wooden door, she could see there was a tall figure standing in a corridor. Dim candlelight flickered in the hallway; there was just enough light to ascertain that whoever it was, they were dressed in some kind of reflective material, a little like armour.

'I don't care. Just do it!' Finn barked at the intruder, making her jump. He slammed the door and stood with his back to her for a moment, tense; Faye didn't know whether to ask what was wrong. She felt confused again; it was so changeable here. *I should go home, I don't belong here*, she panicked. *What am I doing?*

Finn turned to her, scowling, and, without warning, reached up and tore the tapestry she had been staring at off the wall, letting out a shout of frustration as he did so. Faye, startled, shied away from him. He glared at her fiercely for a moment and, in that brief second, all his former warmth was gone. His deep blue eyes narrowed.

Faye ran to the other side of the room and tried the door.

'This was a mistake, I shouldn't have come here,' she muttered. 'I... this isn't right, I...'

But before she could open it, his hand was on her shoulder, and sweetness began to suffuse her whole being again.

'Forgive me, Faye,' Finn's voice was honey again. 'It was bad news. I apologise if I made you feel uncomfortable.'

She was still tense; despite his soothing presence, her body had kicked into fight or flight response. Finn stroked her arm.

'You... startled me,' she protested, pulling away from him.

'Please accept my deepest apologies, dear Faye. I would never intend to alarm you,' Finn's tone became urgent, his eyes full of anxiety. 'My kingdom is in conflict with Falias, the realm of Earth. The faerie realms are often at war with each other. Boundary disputes, that kind of thing. But I should not have let it affect my time with you.' He clasped her to his chest in a hug that felt tinged with desperation. 'I'm sorry. Dearest Faye, I should never have lost my temper. I know I am... difficult, at times. Please forgive me.' He sounded as if he was on the edge of sudden tears, and Faye wondered at his changeable mood.

'It's all right. You frightened me, though.' She felt as though her apology was required by him, and that it would be politic to give it whether she meant it or not.

Finn released her from his arm and, reaching past her, gently opened the door she had been struggling with. Immediately, a blare of music pierced the room.

Faye looked down from a balcony onto a large, ornate hall below where a party seemed to be in full swing. Faeries of all kinds sat at long tables which were piled with food and drink, and a band played on a raised circular stage in the middle of the room, which Faye recognised as the music she had heard distantly all the way through the castle.

It was a little similar to the music Dal Riada had played that night in the bar: a kind of fast, folky music with fiddlers and flutes, but this was performed on unusual instruments: Faye leaned over the balcony and peered hard at the players, trying to make it out, but she couldn't tell what they were exactly, only that they were made of wood and branches and other woodland elements.

The music, also, was faster and louder than Dal Riada's, and the dancers that circled around and around the stage were frantic and crazed. There were no dance moves that she could discern in particular, just fierce running, jumping, skipping and howling along with the music. As she watched, one slight-looking female faerie fell down as she skipped wildly to the music and was trampled by at least ten others before she got raggedly to her feet again. Faye's eyes widened in amazement.

'Come,' Finn, watching her face, took her hand and guided her to the top of some golden stairs which led from the balcony to the hall below. He was not barefoot, as he had been onstage at the gig, but wore some kind of gold slippers on which he walked soundlessly.

'Oh, no. No, I couldn't,' she murmured, and stepped back into the room, but Finn held onto her hand.

'Will you not take a dance with me in my own royal hall?' he asked and, as he touched her again, that golden lightness entranced her, and the music outside filled her with a wild delight. 'And I will answer all your questions. I promise.'

At that moment, the musicians stopped playing one song, and, after a brief pause, launched into something slightly slower. Faye certainly had questions, but her body had caught the rhythm of the new tune and she felt herself nodding.

Hand in hand, they descended the golden stairs and reached the ballroom. Finn bowed and clasped her around the waist and swung her into the outer throng of dancers that had formed around the wildest ones, closest to the stage. Rather than join the running, trampling faeries that seemed possessed with a kind of fury, Faye followed Finn's lead in a much more stately fashion, though it still made her dizzy.

The other dancers made way for them as they circled and dipped around the room, and Faye saw that many of the fae nodded and bowed as they spun past.

'What were you doing in that bar, in… in the real world? Your band. If you are… what you say you are?' Faye asked him, trying to follow his lead.

'You can hardly doubt that I am anything else,' Finn replied seriously as they danced. 'But you are correct. The fae sometimes go forth into your world. Not very often, now. Once, human and fae intermingled happily. It was a golden age; I remember it with such fondness.' He sighed. 'Now, everything is different. Everything is wrong, out of balance. We all mourn the passing of that time in the human world, where your kind knew us and honoured us. Even though we dance and laugh, sadness is in us all.'

The pipers and drummers paused again and commenced a much slower song. Finn smiled, and put one hand on Faye's waist.

'My grandmother told me old tales of the faeries. She said we had a house faerie called Gussie, who kept the hearth swept for us and the milk fresh, but he was very particular about how we honoured him.

As a child I left a bowl of the creamiest milk and a slice of bread out for Gussie every night, but one night I wanted to put out a scone. Grandmother said no, Gussie would take that as an insult in the same way as if no offering was left at all,' she said, feeling a blush come on her cheeks as she looked up into Finn's strange eyes. He was disquietingly beautiful. His hair was a dark gold in the light of the ballroom; when she had seen him onstage with Dal Riada, and in her shop that day, it had looked darker, more of a dirty blonde.

'Your grandmother was a wise woman,' Finn smiled. 'The fae have their ways that humans used to respect. Now they have all but forgotten us and built upon many of our dwelling-places.'

Faye blinked hard. Finn's comment had made her come out of her faerie dream a little again and remember Rav's house which had been built on the faerie road, the path that led here. It was very easy to forget the real world completely and she reminded herself she was not a faerie; that she had to keep her wits about her here. She also had no idea if she was, perhaps, dreaming especially vividly, and might wake up in her own bed any minute.

'She was a witch. She taught my mother the old ways, and they taught me,' she said. They danced slowly now, and the rhythm of the tune patterned her heartbeat in a delicious, sensual repetition. Finn's face was close to hers, and their breath met between them. She was aware of breathing in when he breathed out, he following suit as she exhaled in an intimate synchronicity of air between them.

'Yes, I know.' He smiled around them at the many dancers that called out a blessing or a greeting to him.

'You didn't answer my question.'

'I didn't?'

'About why you play music to humans. In the band.'

He gave a little laugh.

'You are persistent.'

I'm not nearly as persistent as I should be just now, Faye thought. Her head was spinning.

'Hmmm. Well, perhaps I like the audience.'

'You have all the audience you need here, surely?' The hall was full of hundreds of faeries feasting and dancing.

He raised his eyebrow and smiled. 'Quite so. Well, then. Perhaps it is that we need humans. We need your attention to survive. We need your love,' He smiled, looking at her deeply, and she felt her breath catch. 'We were banished from your world, or near enough, when you stopped paying us our due. As the spirits of the land. As the ones that should receive offerings so we would give you good luck, help you, keep your babies healthy. We didn't ask much, but it was too much for humans in the end, and it broke our hearts. Now, we are mostly confined to our own places. But as I am king, I can choose whether to go forth into your world or not. And I choose to be loved again, and give love. It is no more than an act of a broken heart looking to be healed, my time with Dal Riada.'

Faye didn't know what to say in reply; Moddie and Grandmother had told her as much in their stories – that the old spirits of the land had been forgotten by most; made fun of, ignored and maligned. That was the explanation they gave to the young Faye for why she couldn't see faeries in the garden and under the stones on the beach she so assiduously turned over, from one end of the dark sand to the other.

Finn nodded to another couple that danced next to them. The woman – or, as Faye corrected herself, the faerie-woman – was dressed very grandly in a violet and silver dress with a bodice and full skirt very reminiscent of fashion from many hundreds of years ago. She wore red roses in her dark golden-blonde hair, which was plaited intricately around them. Her partner was, as far as Faye could tell, human – a dark-skinned young man with a dazed expression who couldn't take his eyes from the faerie queen in his arms. The faerie queen was high-cheekboned and full-lipped, and her eyes had the same oddness as Finn's; as if they were made of jewels that held great depth but still remained somehow impassive and cold.

'Greetings to you, *sidhe-leth*.' The woman nodded imperiously to Faye, and her human partner smiled briefly before he swung the golden-haired beauty away.

'Who was that?' Faye murmured to Finn, though she was having trouble focusing on anything apart from Finn and the music which had entered her blood; it felt as though it was powering her actions from inside a formerly hidden part of herself. A part of herself that was as wild as the trees and the rivers, and wanted to sing and dance and – most of all, as Finn pressed her against his firm, well-muscled chest – kiss this beautiful faerie king.

Their faces were so close together now that their lips almost touched; Faye's awareness of the dancers around them dimmed so that it was only she and Finn moving as one inside the music. If she inclined her head less than an inch, her lips would meet his; the idea thrilled her more than she had ever thought possible.

'My sister, the Faerie Queen Glitonea, Queen of the Powers of Water,' he breathed.

'And the… the person with her?'

'Her lover.'

'Is he human?' she murmured. 'Like me?'

'Yes.' Finn smiled, and traced the line of Faye's cheek with his fingertip. He did it lightly, but the trail of his fingertip felt like a pleasurable fire that lit her whole body up in desire for him. She sucked in her breath. 'But not like you.'

'Are you... close to your sister?' Faye was curious about the faerie queen, and Finn's relationship with her. His eyes had glowed when they met hers, and Faye had felt something pass between them: an unspoken understanding, a deep connection.

'Of course. She is Queen, I am King,' he replied, dismissively, but on seeing Faye's expression, he softened a little. 'She is made of the same stuff as me; the same as all faeries, just as other humans share much in common with you. But she and I are of an old, old family: our forebears are the spirits of the first oceans. What is between us cannot be between anyone else – it is impossible for you to understand, as you are not like us. We are Murias, and Murias is us. This is one of the mysteries of my kingdom, *Sidhe-leth*: it would take you many more lifetimes than the one you have to understand.'

'What is that name? *Sidhe-leth*? I have been called that by many of the... fae here.' Faye resisted the impulse to say *people*, where they were most certainly not.

But instead of a reply, Finn brushed her lips with her fingertip and, gently, kissed her.

Chapter 18

It was like being underwater, but being immune to drowning.

Faye's eyes fluttered closed, and she was subsumed by the kiss; pulled under into tumultuous waves.

Behind her eyes, she saw nothing but the ocean, lit by the full moon that shone its reflected light down onto black-and-green waves; she looked back at an unfamiliar horizon that ended on a distant silver beach.

But she was not alone. Finn was with her, among and within the waves, and they were of the water, together; made of it, somehow, rather than their heavy bodies which were uncomfortable by comparison. Faye experienced a sense of dissolving into him, and he into her, as they kissed deeper, and the sky rolled back into indigo nothingness above them.

Dimly she was aware of them walking away from the dancefloor, but they were both already somewhere else. They were something else other than they had been separately: combined, even in a kiss, they had half-merged, and both felt the fierce pull of the elemental power that demanded they return to it immediately.

The music quietened; Faye's eyes cleared a little as she climbed the golden stairs up again to the room with the balcony where they had started. She had no sense of time, or how much time had passed since she had been in the faerie world. But she didn't care. The flashes of her real, human life that she'd had since she had been there seemed like trivial memories. Compared to Finn, compared to the strange music that inhabited her blood, it was that life that seemed a dream now.

He led her down a corridor and into a bedroom. Faye followed, her hand in his.

In the centre, a golden four-poster bed was covered in green and blue silk and velvet coverings; the walls of the room were covered in the spirals and carvings that were everywhere in the castle. One whole wall was glass, and looked out over a waterfall outside the castle that she hadn't seen on her way in, but the castle itself was large, and she wasn't exactly in an analytical headspace at that moment. The glass wall reminded her briefly of something, somewhere familiar she'd been recently, but she was so deep inside faerie now that the pull of the human world was very weak. Faye was now heedless of the danger she was in; the link to her old life was weak now, and it would take very little to sever altogether.

He pulled her to the bed and she fell into his arms.

Finn kissed her again, deeply, and Faye felt the full power of the faerie realm close over her like a cloak of soft seawater. She pulled back from the kiss and gasped as she felt the strangeness come over her, but when Finn kissed her again, she dived gratefully into it.

His lips found her neck, and she moaned in pleasure. His hand caressed her breast through her clothes, and the sensation of his touch on her was like lightning on a black sea. She shivered in rapturous delight as his lips found hers again and they went under, merging with water. She closed her eyes and watched a storm roll over the same unfamiliar sea. Her hands were in his hair, on his chest. He unbuttoned the jacket he had worn which was a little like an old-fashioned doublet; a dark indigo, piped with gold on the shoulders and cuffs which fitted his slim yet muscled chest and shoulders. Underneath the jacket he was bare-chested, but his golden skin held the tattoo she had seen when he stood shirtless on the stage, a horse that reared up his body in a blue the same dark indigo as his jacket. Spirals followed his shoulders and continued down his arms, which Faye saw as he took the jacket off altogether.

She sat up and pulled off the woollen dress she only dimly remembered putting over her vest and leggings when leaving the house. Finn kissed her collarbone and followed the line of lace along the edge of the vest's neckline, then moved his mouth lower and she felt his warm breath through the flimsy jersey as he kissed her breasts through it.

Faye moaned louder, then, and felt herself grow slick and wet with desire. Finn peeled away the vest and leggings, leaving her completely naked on the bed. The material below her, like silk but something different, seemed to kiss her skin. He knelt and caressed her body, kissing and touching her with a sweetness and ardour she had never experienced before. He was gentle but in control and, as he touched her, she felt her pleasure building like the momentum of a song; like the increasing rhythm of the faerie pipers whose music had inspired such delicious anarchy in her soul.

She wanted more, and couldn't get enough of his skin; warm, as if he had been in the sun, and which tasted of the sea. Her lips were swollen from kissing him, but she couldn't stop, and as her lips trailed down to his waist, he pushed down his matching indigo trousers. She went to take him in her mouth, craving all of him, but he smiled and shook his head.

'Not yet,' he said, and pulled her back to him. He took one nipple in his mouth and licked and caressed it with his tongue, while stroking her clit gently. Faye felt herself close to orgasm almost immediately, and he seemed to know, because he stroked her more slowly and returned to kissing her mouth and neck.

'Please. I don't want to… come… yet,' she gasped, and reached for him. He was hard with desire for her, and he moaned deeply as she moved her hand gently up and down.

'Faye. Faye, *bruadarach, neach-gaoil*,' he murmured, opening his eyes to meet hers.

'I want you,' she breathed, unable to look away from the sapphire depths of his eyes. 'I want… I…' She was deep in enchantment, and even telling him she loved him seemed inadequate in that moment, though she knew nothing about him other than this dreamlike ecstasy.

His hands were warm on her thighs as he pushed them apart, and bent his head to her openness. And when she was moaning loudly, lost on the waves of desire and pleasure, and had no control of her body, he pushed deep into her.

He filled her totally, and their bodies fit together as if they were one. Faye had no consciousness apart from pleasure; the hot, sweet orgasm rose from her like an unstoppable wave, reaching and reaching higher and higher as Finn stroked in and out of her slowly, deeply. She was with him under the waves again, in the rolling of the salt water that was their sweat and saliva; they were the power of the ocean, and they were life and death and pleasure combined.

Finally, she shouted for him to come into her as hard as he could, and felt herself clutching and biting his shoulder as her climax came, bigger than she had ever had before.

Her whole body was aflame; pleasure screamed and sang in her stomach, in her elbows and toes. She was screaming his name and other words she had no awareness of. She came again and again against him, feeling him deep and hard within her, returning his urgent, hot kisses as he called out her name, mixed with the Gaelic words she had no idea of. And, yet, at the same time, woven amongst her cries of ecstasy, Faye felt an undercurrent of danger. Perhaps it was because they were in the faerie realm, where time operated differently, but there was an uncountable moment when Faye saw a darkness open up around her. It was like being at the bottom of the ocean, and she felt the terror of drowning. And in the second before she opened her eyes to return to her body, Faye remembered the expression of Glitonea's human lover, lost in a desire he could never control.

She came back to her body with a sense of foreboding that nestled alongside the pleasure of being next to him, feeling his skin against hers, and dismissed the visions – of drowning, of the ocean, and of Glitonea's human lover – as a moment of mindlessness.

They lay entangled in each other; he kissed her forehead, the end of her nose; taking her hand in his, he kissed her fingertips. Her heart felt as it never had: open, raw, like a rose that had bloomed before time; it hurt a little from the intensity of their connection. She felt tears start in her eyes, and wiped them away. But the ache wasn't pain or regret; rather, it was a sadness that she had waited all this time to know this kind of pleasure, given so freely.

He kissed away her tears.

'What troubles you, *neach-gaoil*?' he said, concernedly. 'You are safe with me. Do not be frightened. You are my lover now; remember, mine is a broken heart that needs to heal. Be happy that you are doing that.' He put his hand on his heart, then on hers. 'Here. To here.' he kissed her again, tenderly. 'There is a bond now, not easily broken.'

'No, it's not that. I'm… I'm fine,' she murmured, and snuggled against his chest. 'I just… I haven't known that before.'

'You are a virgin?' he looked at her, surprised.

'No. Just... I haven't... not like that,' she finished. He smiled, and gathered her to him closer again.

'You have a special magic in you, Faye, that I doubt you know exists,' he murmured. 'And we can make each other whole, if we let ourselves trust each other: human and faery, in balance, as we should always have been.' Faye felt sleep come over her like the calm after a storm. 'I will adore you, Faye Morgan, if you do me the same kindness,' he whispered. 'Give me the whole of yourself and I will give you the world. I will give you everything that my whole heart can command.'

But in her dream, Faye was drowning again, and Finn's voice was the sound of waves on savage black rock.

Chapter 19

Faye woke up in her own bed to the sound of birdsong. She rolled over groggily, patting the quilt for her phone. Locating it by her feet, she pressed the display and looked at the time. 6 a.m.

She swung her feet out of bed and rested them on the wooden floor, then frowned and pulled up her right foot, resting it on her knee. The skin between her toes was sore. She rubbed her foot gently, waking up, then took her hand away and felt the sand on her palm.

She stared at the tiny granules of dark sand for a minute or more, feeling unease unfurl in her like a stray ribbon.

Faye stood up and caught her reflection in the mirror. She was naked, and a pile of clothes – jumper, dress, thermals – lay on the floor by the end of the bed as if she had stepped out of them there, but she had no memory of doing so. She knew she had got dressed last night and gone to the beach, but then… then, it had felt like a dream. And, listening to the birds at dawn, it seemed highly unlikely that she had in fact been in the realm of Faerie all night.

She went to the bathroom and leaned over to run a bath. As she reached out her hand, she saw the ring on her hand.

It was a large round opal set in rose gold on her thumb. Faye gasped and stood up in shock, looking at her hand, which suddenly seemed completely alien. This wasn't any ring of hers; usually she wore a silver pentagram ring that had been Moddie's on her right index finger and a vintage tiger's eye on her left for protection. It wasn't a ring from the shop that she'd slipped on by mistake either, as she definitely hadn't seen it before.

She took it off and held it up to the light. The opal sparkled with unusual gold, pink and orange accents that reflected unexpected hints of magic. She stared at it as the water for the bath filled up slowly.

'What on earth?' she muttered, and placed it down on the windowsill as she opened a jar of her own handmade Full Moon bath salts and shook them into the water. The smell of lavender filled the bathroom; Faye sat on the edge of the bath and picked up the ring, replacing it on her thumb. It felt wrong to have put it down, somehow.

She got in the bath, breathing in the fragranced steam, and let it cover her. She closed her eyes and held the ring to her forehead. It was an instinctive gesture, but as soon as she did so, she saw Finn Beatha in her mind's eye, as if he was with her, in the bathroom. She opened her eyes with a start but there was no-one there.

Cautiously, she held the ring to her third eye chakra in the middle of her forehead again and closed her eyes. As soon as she did, she remembered.

They had just made love – and it was love, fierce and hot and out of any normal frame of reference – that was something she knew, deep within herself, although she didn't understand it. And, sometime in the night, she had half-awoken, twined in his silk bedsheets. He had kissed her awake and, when she roused, half-sat up in his huge bed, he had placed this ring on her thumb.

'A gift,' he had whispered. 'Wear it and think of me.'

Sleepily, she had held it up to the moonlight, slanting through the window and watched the magic in the stone flicker like fire. She had thanked him, said, what? She couldn't remember – she was growing drowsy and must have fallen asleep next to him.

Wear it and think of me. She stared at the ring. How was it possible? Any of it? Grandmother and Moddie had told her plenty of tales about the faeries, but she hadn't ever really believed any of them, if only because she knew that the fae had left Scotland a long time ago, driven out by modernity: industrialisation, pollution, lack of belief. And *Moddie.* She had seen Moddie there. What did that mean?

If it wasn't a dream, Finn Beatha was really a faerie king. And Finn Beatha wanted her. At the thought of him, she felt a rush of desire, and instinctively stroked her own body, thinking of him: his tall, rangy, well-muscled body; his arms, covered in the tribal tattoos, and his lips. His pouty, ever-so-slightly scornful mouth that begged to be kissed, and even bitten. She closed her eyes and turned the hot tap back on with her toe. The warm water covered her fully, and the pleasant heat of the water felt like a kiss on her skin.

Faye wondered about Finn: who he really was. He was a king, and he had proved himself a remarkable lover, but she knew very little else about him. He seemed deeply emotional, yet he was guarded. He was powerful and yet tender when he chose to be. Now she was back in ordinary reality, she pondered what he had said about his realm being heartbroken about the lack of – how had he put it? – a *balance* with humans. That he sought lovers as a way to balance their relationship as two races upon whose harmonious existence the world depended? Grandmother had told her as much with her old tales, but Faye wondered whether Finn was telling the whole truth. Was that really why a faerie king appeared as the frontman of a band in the human world? Or were his reasons much more plainly carnal?

She found she was already wet from arousal, thinking of Finn and their lovemaking. She started stroking herself with one finger and then two, feeling the water on her like Finn's tongue. She yearned to be with him again. She moaned and spread her legs as far as she could within the bath, and put two fingers inside herself, stroking now with the other hand too. Feeling the orgasm coming, quickly, wildly, uncontrolled, she heard herself speaking his name, calling it, as her pleasure heightened and spread over her like a net, like a spell of desire. *Finn, Finn, Finn, come to me, love me, Finn, oh, oh, oh.*

When she came it was as though his lips were on hers and his tongue was on her at the same time; the water held her, and he was somehow part of it. She closed her eyes as the pleasure ebbed through her, and saw him again, clearly. She felt another orgasm coming, and she pushed against her fingers hard this time, feeling her insides contract hard, over and over again. She screamed out in pleasure, disconnected from the mundane world. It was like being truly awake for the first time in a life that had only been a dream until now.

When it was over, she got out of the cooling water and dressed. She padded down to the kitchen behind the shop and made breakfast: she was suddenly powerfully hungry. *Probably a good idea to ground*, she thought; the easiest way to ground yourself, to come back to earth after doing magic of any kind – never mind visiting an alternate dimension, or whatever the realm of faerie was – was to eat and drink. She gulped down a mug of strong tea and made some toast under the grill.

As she ate her breakfast, some of Faye's spirit returned to her. If she saw Finn again – and she hoped that she did – she resolved that she would keep her head a little better. It was understandable that she had been so thoroughly taken over by being in Murias, and by Finn's attentions, but she had been raised a witch. She could do better.

Slowly, she started to feel more human, and looked at the clock with the mottled brass rim that hung on the wall behind the counter. Every now and again Faye had to cull the postcards and letters around it that she received from visitors from all over the world, otherwise the clock would be lost under reams of paper and card. Moddie would be proud that Mistress of Magic had, in its own quiet way, quite a following.

With a practised hand, she lit two charcoal discs and placed them inside a large abalone shell, then dropped resinous lumps of dammar gum and frankincense on top of them and rested the incense in its shell on the edge of the shop counter.

The fragranced smoke made the shop smell and feel like a temple and Faye was grateful for its familiar sweet and sharp tang, which gave her a sense of power as surely as the stone flagstones under her feet.

Remembering how the vision of the shop had grounded her, even just for a little while when she was in Murias with Finn, Faye spent a few moments picking up and holding some of her favourite curiosities: possessions belonging to other Morgans, from Grandmother and back into the past. Opening its sealed display cabinet, Faye reached in and carefully took out the Morgans' crystal ball: not like the acrylic ones she sold in the shop, this was an ancient sphere made of pure quartz. It had one very fine fissure through its middle, like a dim lightning bolt, but otherwise the crystal was without any flaw, which made it incredibly rare.

It had been a long time since Faye had scried with the crystal ball: you had to have the patience or the gift, Grandmother said, and Faye had always found she had neither, though she found it beautiful. Today, she wanted the weight of it in her hands: to be reassured she really was back in the ordinary world. Yet as she turned it over carefully, she thought of all the Morgans that had used it. *Wasn't that her power as*

*much as anything? Her heritage, the blood of all the other witches that
flowed in her veins?*

It was almost opening time, so she replaced the crystal ball in its case
and locked it. When she opened the shop door and looked out onto
the street, she saw Annie a few doors away, coming in to start her shift.
Faye waved, and the opal ring on her thumb caught the morning sun.

'Hey! Morning, ma sweet darlin',' Annie grinned as she walked in
past Faye, and instinctively, Faye put her left hand down by her side
in the fold of the long dress she'd pulled on today. It was a deep cerise
with a low neck and romantic bell sleeves; not at all the kind of thing
she would usually wear. 'Ye look gorgeous today! New dress?'

'Er… yes. New stock. Thought we could take a few,' Faye panicked.
In truth, she had no idea where the dress had come from; it was hanging
in her wardrobe earlier and she'd put it on without even noticing.

'Suits ye,' Annie called out, hanging up her coat in the back room.
'Dunno what you've been doing last night, but ye look beautiful.' She
returned, sipping a glass of water. 'Ye saw Rav, eh? Out of the bad
books, is he?'

Faye twisted the opal on her thumb; she wanted to tell Annie
everything. The words lined up on her tongue, but instead of being
able to say them, a tightness seized her throat and she coughed.

'Ye all right, pet?' Annie banged her on the back. Faye nodded, and
tried again, but the same dry, airless sensation assailed her, and Finn's
voice spoke in her mind.

*The gift is for you, Faye Morgan. But I am your secret. Tell no-one what
has passed here tonight, or you may not be permitted back into my realm.*

She knew she wasn't supposed to talk about being with Finn, but
she hadn't expected his prohibition to be so literal. Annie offered her
the glass of water, and Faye took a gulp.

'Alright?' Annie looked concerned.

'I'm okay,' Faye nodded, a shiver of unease rippling through her body. She didn't like lying to Annie, but Finn had made it very clear. She felt a momentary guilt that she hadn't thought of Rav at all when being away; Finn had taken her over completely. *How was that possible?* Was it something to do with being in the faerie realm itself? Being there exerted a power over her that made her... different. That made her forget the real world and everyone in it. And it seemed that the enchantment was not completely gone; Finn's power reached out to her here, still.

'Phew,' Annie smiled, then looked at her phone and frowned. 'Ah. Slight change o' plan, lassie. All right if I hop off early later? Got an audition. Nice ring, by the way.'

'Sure. Fine. Thanks, it's... new.' The less Faye had to be around Annie today, the better. She didn't want to lie to her any more than she had to. 'Take the day off, if you want? It's going to be quiet, I'm sure.' She dropped her hand by her side to avoid any further comment on the ring.

'Thanks, sweetheart,' Annie grinned. 'I'll stay and have a gossip for a bit though, aye? I tell ye what, Aisha's been acting odd recently. Have ye noticed?'

Annie was running on about something – about Aisha not turning up for work, about seeing her walking on the beach alone, but Faye wasn't listening. She was twisting the ring on her thumb.

Chapter 20

When the bells by the door jangled the next day, Faye looked up for Finn's graceful shadow blocking out the sun; she didn't know how she felt about seeing Rav's boyish frame instead.

'Hey. I've been messaging you but I didn't get a reply.' He smiled his shy, sweet smile and Faye looked guiltily at her phone. She realised that she'd spent the last hour staring off into space, reliving her night with Finn; Aisha, who was working that day, had given up talking to her and had turned on the radio. Faye heard the Dal Riada song be introduced by the DJ with little surprise; she was so obsessed with Finn now that it seemed perfectly natural for his voice to caress her, as if reminding her that he was with her always, now. And that, somehow, there was a subtle, fine network of faerie that she was now tuned into.

'Oh. Sorry,' she blushed, knowing that he knew it was a lie, but unable to explain. Rav looked around at the shop, which was empty apart from Aisha, unpacking a box in the corner, back again at Faye, and at her phone, next to her on the counter.

'Oh.' His smile faltered, and he took a step back.

Dal Riada, there, Scotland's hottest new band, burbled the local radio as the track had finished. *Set to be headlining Abercolme Rocks this year; the first Midsummer celebration for many a year up this way. It's gonna be a banger, get your tickets soon cos they're selling out!*

'Are they? Selling out?' Faye gave Rav a big smile, picking up her pack of dog-eared tarot cards she kept at the counter and shuffling them to have something to do with her hands; it made her feel less awkward. She pulled three cards without any particular questions and laid them on the counter, facing up. The King of Cups on one side, the Knight of Wands on the other, and The Empress in the middle. *Two men that desire you.* Two men – well that was easy enough. The King of Cups was Finn, and the Knight was Rav. The Empress was herself – sexy, desired, fertile; the ultimate woman. Faye remembered that sometimes the Empress card could mean a Mistress, too; she raised an eyebrow. *Whose mistress?* she wondered.

'Doing all right, yeah.' Rav watched her cautiously. 'Word's getting out there. People love that band. Not my thing, but whatever.'

'Aisha really loves them. Aish, come and say hi.' Faye beckoned her over.

She pulled two more cards, more consciously now. On the King of Cups she placed The Lovers; on the Knight of Wands, 7 of Swords. The Lovers was obvious. The Swords card meant deviousness, guile; betrayal, sometimes. She frowned and picked up the cards, slotting them back into the deck. *Betrayal,* she thought, avoiding Rav's eyes. *But who betrays who?*

'Hey, Rav,' Aisha finished arranging some new salt crystal lamps on one of the shelves and came over, wiping her hands on her jeans; it was fairly obvious she'd been giving Faye and Rav some space until now. She stuck her hand out and he shook it, hardly taking his eyes from Faye. 'I heard you're organising the festival. Faye's right. I'm a huge fan of Dal Riada.'

'Oh. Cool! Nice to meet you.'

Rav shifted his smile to Aisha. For a moment Faye saw Aisha through Rav's eyes: young, bright, enthusiastic; Aisha loved music as much as

Rav. She had been wearing her hair down more and wore makeup most days now which made her dark brown, long-lashed eyes look like those of a cartoon doe. Faye had always thought that Aisha was a hidden beauty and had encouraged her to feel more confident about the way she looked, but for the first time, she suddenly felt envious and hated herself immediately for the feeling. *What was wrong with her?* Aisha and Rav were allowed to talk to each other: she didn't own either of them. Faye could feel something encircling her, constricting her throat and casting a kind of haze in front of her eyes. It was a similar feeling to when she had seen Annie earlier, and had been unable to tell her what had happened with Finn. She shook her head to try and clear the feeling, but it persisted.

Aisha and Rav were chatting amiably about music, and Faye made herself go and rearrange something on a shelf that didn't need it. *Let them talk,* she told herself, resisting the jealousy that had risen in her.

'If you need any help with the festival, I've got some free time. I'm at university but I've got a few weeks free at the moment and I love music. I'm really into a lot of the bands on the line-up. I used to run a music blog, so... I mean... it'd be a pleasure to help.'

'Oh. Really? That'd be great. I can't pay you, I don't think, though.' Rav sounded apologetic. Faye's heart started beating harder, and she was alarmed at herself.

'Ah well. Festival tickets'd be enough?' Aisha smiled innocently.

'Oh, sure! That I can do.' He nodded enthusiastically. 'You're serious? You can help out? I need admin help, like, emails, social media, local advertising, that kind of thing.'

'No worries.' Aisha scribbled her number on a scrap of paper and gave it to him. 'Give me a call. I'm free Mondays and weekends... or evenings, if you need a hand then.'

'Okay, cool. Thanks, Aisha. That'd be a huge help.'

Rav isn't yours, Faye berated herself. *You gave him up when you took Finn Beatha as a lover.*

Yet, when she looked up from the spell bags she had organised into neat lines, Rav was staring at her. She felt his gaze flicker to her breasts in the pink dress. She looked back at him, letting the pleasurable fugue she had felt in Murias overcome her again. As she did so, the strange sensation of constriction relaxed, and she let the delicious power of faerie suffuse her limbs and her blood. It was suddenly as though all her insecurity had been washed away, replaced by a new seductive power.

Interesting, Faye thought. *It's like Rav's under a spell when he looks at me. My spell.*

She smiled over at him, touching her top lip with her fingertip, tracing it along, watching him watch her as she did it. She felt so different, so *good*, suddenly, and she was enjoying it. *Perhaps she didn't have to make any decisions just yet...*

Rav followed her across the shop, leaving Aisha to return to her tasks.

'You seem... different,' he blinked. 'Did you... I don't know. Do your hair differently?' he asked Faye, frowning.

Faye ran her hand through her hair, not breaking eye contact with him.

'No. Just the same as always.'

'Oh.' Rav stared at her again, hungrily, his desire open on his face, then looked away, obviously trying to control himself.

'Actually, I wanted to ask you about the—' he lowered his voice, '*faerie problem.* It doesn't seem to have worked, leaving out the offerings.'

'Oh, hasn't it?' she asked. 'I'm sorry to hear that. I'll come and take a look.'

'Cool… Could you come tonight? It's just that… the noise. I can't sleep. Knocking noises. And it still sounds like they're running through the house. Obviously whenever I go to investigate I can't see anything.' Rav shrugged and rubbed his eyes; Faye could see he looked exhausted.

'Of course I'll come,' she said, feeling sorry for him; the desirous, wanton Faye receded and she felt her normal self return somewhat. 'I close up around five. I'll come over after. Okay?'

'Thanks so much. It's just, with the festival coming up, I've got so much to do. I could do with some sleep.' He grinned sheepishly and yawned. 'I though the faeries liked music? Surely they should be blessing me or something?'

'Who can say what the faeries want?' Faye responded, honestly. The whole day had been full of extremes, of dramatic emotions and oddness. She felt both wrung out and soaring out of control, hallucinatory, out of sync with her own self.

What was this new, strange power she had over Rav? Was it connected to her visit to Murias? Perhaps enchanting Rav made her more like Finn. And she had no idea whether that was a good thing or not: only that it confused her even more.

She smiled reassuringly and gave Rav a chaste kiss on the cheek.

'I'll see you later,' she said: a friendly tone, nothing more. He looked confused again, and she didn't blame him at all. There was a brief second when she knew he considered kissing her again; she saw it in his eyes, but she stepped back. *Not until I can control this,* she thought. *Whatever it is.*

Rav met her gaze for a moment, and looked like he was going to say something, but he just nodded. 'Okay. Later.' He let himself out the door, gving a friendly wave to Aisha. Fresh air cut through the shop from the street outside, but right at the edge of her perception, Faye could smell roses.

Chapter 21

'Can't you feel it? It's got colder. And there's this loud knocking, like, pretty much going on all day and all night now,' Rav hugged his arms around his chest and shivered. 'If this goes on I'm going to have to move. I can't live here with it like this.'

Faye walked slowly around the circumference of the living room, which was still sparsely furnished. In her mind's eye she had a sudden vision of what it could be like – golden shafts of sun slanting through the floor-to-ceiling windows, through diaphanous gauzy curtains that floated on the breeze coming in from the sea outside; soft chairs in neutral pink and silver velvet; elegant, simple furniture, with tall, rose-gold-coloured lamps in the corners, ready to be lit in the evening when the windows would be thrown open to watch the moon rise over the waves. Above the modern fireplace, in which artificial logs were burning behind a glass screen, she imagined a seven-pointed star, made of opals.

She ran her hand over the back of the leather sofa and caught sight of the opal ring on her thumb. The rose-gold lamps were like the precious gold that sang on her skin; an opalescent glow that shot unexpected trajectories of rainbow light from inside itself. Her vision for this room was a kind of homage to faerie, she realised: or, perhaps, a move to bring the house in sympathy with the energy it rested upon and within.

Faye could not feel the cold of which Rav spoke; in fact, as she closed her eyes and saw the room as it should be, she was filled with a warm joy.

'It feels fine to me.' She made her way to the fireplace and stood in front of it, gauging the temperature. 'In fact, I'm actually a bit hot over here.' She took her coat off and unwrapped her scarf. She listened for a moment, too, but heard nothing. 'I can't hear any funny sounds. Are you sure you're not imagining it? Or maybe you're a bit under the weather? That would explain feeling cold. Maybe you'd better go to bed?'

Rav looked at her with an odd expression. 'Faye. It's freezing in here. Put your coat back on.'

'No! Really. I'll be too warm.' She shook her hair over her shoulders.

'There! That sound! You couldn't hear that?' He pointed to the long glass hallway and stared at her expectantly.

Beautiful singing was drifting through the house now; Faye's whole body responded to it with joy. It was different to the fast reel the faeries danced to in the great hall: this was a lilting song that wove itself like water. It flowed through the room, a song made of delicate stairs of crystal and faint, tinkling bells. Faye followed the lone female voice out to the hallway with a pull of longing in her heart. She walked as if she was in a dream, her arms held in front of her, eyes half-closed. She was being called by this beautiful song, back to where she belonged now. Back across the sea, to the castle of Murias and Finn Beatha's arms.

'Banging. Like someone dropping a pile of saucepans or something.' Rav followed her out to the hall; immediately, the music stopped and Faye felt her connection to faerie severed, savage and sudden. 'Didn't you hear it?'

'Oh, it's gone. It was so beautiful.' She sighed, momentarily exasperated with Rav.

'Beautiful? It's a fucking racket!' Rav shouted. 'I don't get it. What's changed? You got it before, but now you're acting like there's no problem, Faye. I thought you wanted to help me?' He went to the faerie altar and pointed at it. 'I did everything you said. Milk in the bowl every other day. Flowers, feathers, shells. I've even said a fucking prayer to the faeries every day to leave the house alone but, if anything, it's got worse. And then you come back here, floating around like some kind of princess, and act like everything's okay! It's not fucking okay, Faye! I feel like I'm going mad!'

Tears filled Rav's brown eyes, and Faye felt a wave of sympathy for him.

'I thought you… I thought we had a connection, something… I thought you liked me.' He wiped his eyes in frustration. 'But you're being really weird with me and I don't know why.'

'I'm sorry. But I really didn't hear the noises. Just… a really lovely singing.' Faye was frustrated. Rav was sweet, and he tried to understand, but whatever was happening to her now – whatever this enchantment was, that meant she felt half in the ordinary world and half in the glorious magic of faerie – it was too much, too alien for him.

'Singing?'

'I can only tell you what I heard,' she said, still a little stiffly because he'd shouted, and called her a princess. And there was a voice inside her that said, *If anything, you call me your queen.*

'It must have been in your head. But I don't know how you didn't hear that banging sound. And the knocking is absolutely doing my fucking head in. I'm… I'm so tired, Faye. I'm not sleeping. And I'm trying to get this festival sorted and all the bands are being completely pathetic, and…' He trailed off and took a deep breath. 'Sorry. You don't want to know about all that. But I am sorry for shouting.'

She approached him cautiously. 'That's okay.' She stepped forward and he opened his arms, accepting a hug. He sighed and laid his head on her shoulder, then pulled back slightly and gazed at her.

'I missed you, too. Can't say that hasn't been part of what's keeping me up.'

Faye felt the energy between them change. The pull of faerie was strong in this house, standing as she now knew it did on sacred faerie ground, and being here reminded her how much she wanted to return to it. And that part of her, whose hair was pulled by the moon and who longed for the sea-castle of Murias and its strange enchantments, was impatient with Rav's earthbound ignorance.

'Oh.' She didn't know what else to say. How to explain that since she and Rav had been intimate on the beach, she had been whisked off to faerie and found a faerie lover that was so entrancing she could barely remember to eat, never mind be interested in mortal men with their imperfect bodies and bad morning breath and dull little routines? That one night with Finn Beatha had moved her, pleasured her, *satisfied* her more than all the other nights with human men put together? That faerie kings did not complain about having too much work to do, or confess they didn't know how to solve the problem of their house being haunted. Finn Beatha just *was*, like a force of nature.

'Why did you run off that night? After we… you know? Were together? You've been so distant. If I did anything wrong, please tell me. I don't want to have offended you without knowing.' Rav stroked her cheek, and Faye looked into his eyes properly for the first time since they had kissed on the beach.

There was a great deal that kept her standing there with him, even with the memory of Finn still on her lips and under her skin. Rav was gentle and kind. He had never shown any hint of the sudden rage

Finn had, even though he had contained it quickly enough; he was here, in the real world, and Faye didn't need to find her way through a treacherous labyrinth to find him.

The heady pull of faerie was at odds with with Faye as a practical, powerful earth witch. She was a flesh and blood woman, a woman of power; she was a Morgan, she ran her own business. And this Faye, the one whose magic wove the power of crystal and smoke and rain-soaked earth wanted Rav – this Faye wanted a good man she could trust to love her, to honour her as she should be honoured. That Faye fought the power of faerie that wanted to overpower her altogether, and suck her in its undertow.

'I just... it's hard to explain.' She brushed his lips with hers. 'But I'm here now.'

'Is this happening? Is this for real, now? Because I don't think I can cope if I have you and lose you again. I like you, Faye. Please don't... I don't know. I just want to know where I am with you,' Rav appealed to her. Faye realised with alarm that he was holding back, protecting himself from her.

Is this really who you are now? Faye wondered, stepping outside of herself for a moment. *How have you, Faye Morgan, become someone that inspires such uncertainty? And such desire?* She didn't recognise Rav's vision of her, and it was troubling to have that double sense of herself.

'I like you too,' she murmured, touching his cheek and meeting his gaze as honestly as she could. She would give him all of herself that she could; he deserved more, but Finn was a secret she was unable to disclose, even if she wanted to.

He returned her kiss like she knew he would. But, warring with her heartfelt connection to Rav was a smoky shard of the faerie world that remained within her. And that wild part of faerie that was inside her now, knitted into her lungs and liver and heart, closed its eyes and let its soft darkness unfurl.

She was torn, because part of her could grow to love Rav. Now that she was with him again she remembered how he made her laugh, something not many people except Annie ever could; she was serious, as a rule, quiet and watchful, knowing what had happened to outspoken witches all those years ago.

And she couldn't deny that there was also a chemistry between them. It was as if he was lit from within with some kind of candlelight or the soft glow of an orange-peach sunset; she realised that she wanted to be near him because of that light, for the way it made her feel happy and safe but also as if she had found a long-forgotten friend. Finn made her feel powerful, sexy and invincible. On the other hand, being with Rav included insecurity and awkwardness; she had felt awkward on the beach after they made love; normal life was edgier and bumpier than the strange, effortless lull of faerie.

But being Finn's lover, and feeling herself changing so rapidly was a roller coaster ride. She didn't know Rav at all, really, but she wanted to; and, when she was thinking straight, she knew she wanted some stability in her life. Usually, the only person in her life that gave her any support was Annie; it would be nice, she admitted to herself, if there could be someone else who was in her corner.

This wasn't an ordinary dating situation. Faye examined her motives for being here. If it was hard for Rav to compete with a faerie king, it was also true that having been in faerie had given her the confidence to pursue Rav – to respond to him – in a way she wouldn't before.

For long, velvety moments, Faye revelled in the softness of the kiss; she felt made of honey under Rav's touch.

Suddenly she was pulled away – through the air at great speed by rough hands that pinched where they held her; she knew without being told that the faeries had her, though she didn't know how or why. The sound of cruel laughter cut the air, slashing at it with knives, cutting away the air she needed to breathe; Faye saw the blue air like icy diamonds cut by steel fall from around her towards a blurring of brown and green below. *Stay away from the human man, sidhe-leth*; Finn's voice sounded like he stood next to her, but as she whirled around, looking for him, there was no-one there. *This is a warning.*

Before she had time to take breath, she found herself standing over a chasm that fell away to nothing under her, and she reeled from sudden vertigo, slipping from her tenuous footing. She flailed, reaching for the mossed rock on both sides of her, not knowing where she had been taken to, and marshalled her instincts as quickly as she could. *What was it that had grounded her before?* She reached for the vision of the shop, her place of power. Closing her eyes, she remembered the security of its stone-flagged floor under her feet; of Grandmother, sitting by the fire with a blanket over her knees. *I am a Morgan, you cannot take me. Return me immediately!* She commanded whatever force had taken her, and concentrated on the symbol for earth: a downwards-facing triangle with a line through the middle. *Earth. The ordinary world. I am human, I am of earth, I am a witch, you cannot take me like this.*

Faye's eyes snapped open as she heaved in a ragged breath, doubled over by the – what? A kind of slippage into faerie, an out-of-body experience? – that had just happened without her even trying. Yet Rav again wore the enchanted look he had had in the shop earlier.

'Rav. *Rav!*' She shook him, and he came back to her.

'Sorry, I… I don't know what happened there. I was kind of… transported. I don't know… I,' he stammered, confusion muddying his expression. 'Were we…? I thought I was kissing you, and then you… disappeared,'

'It felt strange to me too.' She didn't elaborate further, but she didn't want to repeat the strange and rather unpleasant sensation she'd had of being stolen away. Rav stepped back, away from her.

'I don't know what's going on, Faye,' he murmured, rubbing his eyes. 'This is getting weird,'

'I know,' she said, smoothing down the cerise dress. Something in the faerie realm objected to her being here with Rav; either that, or the line of power that ran through the house was growing stronger as he had described.

'Perhaps I should go.' She frowned. The faeries didn't want her here, that was obvious. But Rav looked so disappointed that she felt terrible.

'Please don't go.' He took both of her hands in his. 'I need you. Please, keep me company at least for tonight? I don't want to be here on my own again. And… I know it's weird, but at least you understand what's going on. Please? Stay?'

'Okay. But I'll have to do some research. About what I can do to… rid the house of the fae,' she offered, though she knew she couldn't; this was faerie territory. They were here first and wouldn't leave even if she tried to force them to.

His face brightened.

'Thank you.' He kissed her again, and she felt herself respond. He took her hand shyly. 'Maybe I can persuade you to come upstairs? I think we've got some unfinished business,' he murmured.

He held her hand as they walked down the long hall upstairs – the one that sat directly above the one that was so troublesome below. Vintage music posters lined the walls; Rav told her about Woodstock, Janis Joplin at the Filmore, Bowie at the Montreal Forum in 1974.

'You wish you'd been there,' she smiled at his eager expression as he described buying the Janis Joplin poster from a specialist dealer.

'Yeah. Too young, though.'

'You love your job, though, don't you?' she asked.

'Yeah. Too much, in a way.'

'What does that mean?' She looked along the hallway; the posters hung next to each other uniformly in frames all of the same size. Even though the poster sizes were different, Rav had clearly gone to some expense to make them all fit neatly into the space.

'Why too much?'

'Ah, well. Workaholic. Built my own company up from the ground with my best friend – I mentioned it before, didn't I? We're doing really well now, that's why we opened the Edinburgh office. Expansion is good, and all that.'

'Sure,' she agreed. 'Sometimes I think I'd like to open another shop. Or more than one. A little witch shop empire. We could branch out: homewares, more clothes. Not just practical supplies. The whole lifestyle.'

He smiled and squeezed her palm. 'Sounds great. You should do that.'

'I don't think I want it enough yet,' she shrugged. 'Maybe one day.'

'Fair enough. You've got to give everything to running your own business. It takes over. Cost me my relationship. With my ex.' He sighed. 'Don't get me wrong, I love what I do. But it means I've spent long months – years – working late, only seeing Roni, eating takeaway… and, you know, I love the guy, but I don't want to wake up and I'm forty years old and still single with no family. Mum's practically at boiling point that I don't already have kids. She wants to be a grandma, and I want her to be one. I'd love to be a dad, I just… it just hasn't

happened, mostly because I didn't have time for a relationship.' Rav
looked embarrassed. 'Sorry. This is supposed to be like, *come up and
see my etchings*, all sexy-like. Not good form to start talking about
wanting kids.'

'Don't be silly. I'm sorry to hear that, about your ex. And I'm sure
you'll be a lovely father one day.'

'It's fine. It wasn't working with her anyway.' He sighed and pointed
to a poster with a yellow background which featured a Hindu goddess
at the centre, holding a sleeping child.

'Anyway. Let's change the subject, okay? This is my favourite.'

'Altamont. Didn't people die at that festival?' she asked, trying to
remember – she'd seen a documentary about it once. The poster listed
the bands that had appeared at the show:

GRATEFUL DEAD, CROSBY, STILLS, NASH AND YOUNG, JEFFERSON
AIRPLANE, FLYING BURRITO BROTHERS, SANTANA. PLEASE BRING
YOUR OWN WEED.

'Yeah. Textbook example of how not to run a festival. Rule number
one: don't let the Hells Angels do security.'

Faye returned her gaze to the poster's garish retro-print style and
smiled. 'That seems like good advice. What happened, exactly?' Thinking
about it, Faye suddenly felt uneasy.

'It was a free concert, 1969. Four months after Woodstock; the
Summer of Love.' Rav made the peace sign with both hands. 'Three
hundred thousand people, mostly on drugs, descended on this place
that wasn't at all prepared. Bike gangs were on security. One woman
was stabbed to death, someone drowned in a canal because they were
so out of it, two people died in a car accident.'

'Oh, God.' Faye imagined the scene.

'Yeah. It was violent. Chaotic. It was so bad that the Grateful Dead didn't even go on. Why are you asking?'

'I don't know. I just wondered.'

'It's not going to be like that at Abercolme Rocks, you know.' He kissed her and Faye felt him harden against her. 'It's a nice, gentle Midsummer music festival. It'll be fine, I promise,' he murmured, and kissed her again, more deeply.

Midsummer, Midsummer, Midsummer delight; go to the faeries on Midsummer night; Take thee a maiden, take thee a wife... the song played on her mind again at the mention of the June solstice. Was there a significance about Finn playing Abercolme Rocks that she hadn't dared consider? Was it about more than satisfying his vanity, about more than feeding off the adulation of the audience?

The image of a rioting crowd, of the out-of-control chaos of the free festival at Altamont filled her mind, and she felt a shiver run through her that she didn't fully understand. She dismissed the thought with some effort; she had always had a vivid imagination. Finn Beatha was a faerie king, and music was part of his being. She had danced with him at the faerie ball and felt the raw electricity of the music in him then, and afterwards, when he had brought her to heights of ecstasy she still couldn't fully encapsulate into anything as imperfect as language.

'Ah, I don't know,' she whispered, taking in a jagged breath as Rav kissed her neck softly, and as his lips found her collarbone. So close to the faerie road, she felt divided; she could feel its electric energy running through the house, and she could feel the call of faerie which wanted to pull her away from Rav, and away from the material realm. She took a breath and grounded herself; imagined roots growing from her feet deep into the earth, closed her eyes and saw herself as part of

the planet, like hills and mountains and rocks and soil. The energy of
fae subsided a little, and she was relieved that she was starting to be
able to control it when it came, even if just a little.

'I don't expect anything from you. I don't expect to be your
boyfriend or anything, if you don't want that. We can take it slow. I
just want to be with you. Here and now,' Rav breathed. 'I've tried to
be in control of my feelings before, with women. But I can't control
how I am with you.'

But there was something about the danger, the prohibition of being
with Rav that made Faye's heart sing all the more as she surrendered
to his touch.

'I can't stop thinking about you; it's like you've possessed my mind,'
Rav murmured. 'I've never known anyone like you before. You're like…
I dunno… some kind of enchantress.'

He knelt in front of her.

'Perhaps I am,' she replied, seriously; her eyes were black in the
lamplight.

'Will you take this off for me?' He touched her dress, and she pulled
it over her head.

When she was naked, he knelt in front of her on the bed, kissing
the inside of her thighs, and when she was begging him for more,
pressed his head into her.

'I want to make love to you.' He sat back on his heels, stripped off
and kissed her again; behind her knees, the inside of her thighs. She
reached for him and lay back on the bed, drawing him to her. She
loved his soft brown eyes, the taste of him; like liquorice and whisky.
He kissed her neck, his hands on her breasts, on her waist and then
gripping her bottom.

Slowly, he entered her at just the right angle.

'Please. More,' she whispered, her lips full and eyes heavy-lidded with pleasure. 'Please?' He held her, gently but firmly, and drew in and out of her slowly. She started to moan and writhe as she felt the orgasm coming.

'I want to hear you. I love hearing you come,' he said, gazing at her full lips and then kissing them. 'You're so beautiful. Like a goddess.'

She didn't answer, but pressed his head to her breast and gasped as she felt his tongue on her again. She breathed in deeply as she felt the sweetness build inside her, deep, rising up her body.

'Oh. Oh, Rav, yes, yes, please, yes, yes...' She buried her face in his neck as she came, long and loud, with nonsense words, a guttural cry. She heard his cries follow hers; felt him tense as his own climax shook him.

'Rule number two: don't allow yourself to become intoxicated,' he murmured as he laid beside her. Gently, he tilted her head up to meet his lips, and kissed her, slowly and passionately.

'Rules can be broken every now and again,' she whispered back, as sleep came for her.

Chapter 22

Faye woke in the night and rolled over, unsure of where she was. It was dark, but the moonlight was enough for her to see the unfamiliar sheets she lay half under. She sat up and jumped as the movement was reflected back at her from the mirrored wardrobe on the opposite wall. It was Rav's bedroom, she remembered now. But the space next to her was empty.

Despite having woken up in the night, she felt more clear-headed than she had for a while. She sipped some water from a glass by the bed and took in a few deep breaths, feeling them ground her. Whatever happened last night before she had come upstairs with Rav – the faeries, clutching at her, Finn's voice forbidding her to be with Rav – seemed like a dream or a strange vision.

There was music coming from downstairs. Faye picked up Rav's bathrobe from the end of the bed and belted it around herself. At some point she had taken off the rose gold and opal thumb ring that Finn had given her, and laid it on the bedside table; she reached for it, but instead of putting it on her thumb, she slipped it in the pocket of the robe. The ring was a gift from Finn, and she needed to keep him and Rav separate in her mind.

Rav sat on the yellow sofa with his laptop, frowning at the screen. Faye recognised the David Bowie album that was playing; the vinyl sleeve for *Diamond Dogs* was propped up on the floor against a cabinet. Rav had put his jeans back on again and wore a sweatshirt and a blanket around his shoulders.

'Hi,' she said, shyly.

He looked up and smiled. 'Sorry. Did I wake you up?'

'Don't think so. Maybe it was the moon.' She ran her fingers through her hair to make it less wild.

'Ah, the moon, of course.' He grinned, put the laptop to one side and came to her, wrapping her in his arms. 'Aren't you cold?'

'No. You couldn't sleep?' She wriggled a little out of his embrace and kissed him softly.

'Mmm. That's nice. No. I'm kind of prone to insomnia anyway – always have been, and stress just makes it worse. I'm always on edge in this house. If it's not the weird noises it's the cold, and this general feeling of unease. Like I'm not welcome here.' He kissed her forehead and held her to him again.

'How long have you had the insomnia? I might be able to help with that – a herbal mixture or something,' Faye listed the herbs on her fingers. 'Valerian, hops, lavender. There are lots of things that can help.'

'I've tried some things, yeah. But sure, anything you can suggest. When I was a teenager the doctor said it was anxiety and I'd grow out of it, but I didn't. I suffered panic attacks pretty regularly when I was at university. Being away from home, I didn't have the ability a lot of my friends did to just get on with their lives. I really missed home.' He sighed, avoiding her gaze. 'What a catch I am, eh?'

'Don't be silly. Lots of people have depression, anxiety, all kinds of things. I know what it's like,' she reached for his hand. 'It's really common. I suppose I'm just sad that you haven't found any help yet. What kind of thing causes it? Are there, like, triggers? Things that make you anxious?' Faye asked. In a way it was good to know something about him, even if it was something he saw as a weakness. Actually, it made Faye like him more for opening up to her.

He sat back down on the sofa, looking dejected.

'No, well. Doctor offered me pills, but I didn't want them. Did some counselling and stuff, but nothing really helped that much,'

'Ah. Not unusual. I could suggest some other solutions,' Faye sat next to him but he refused to meet her eye, tracing a pattern on his knee with his index finger.

'No offence, but that's not really how I wanted this to go – me the patient, you the wise woman. I really… I really *want* you, Faye, okay? Like I've never experienced with anyone else. I have this completely obsessive, unwholesome passion for you. I mean, it's embarrassing, saying that. But that's how I feel. And I hate it, because I'm not in control of myself around you. That's the one thing I can depend on. I control things, because that's how I feel safe.' He gave her a sideways glance, half angry, half sad. 'I don't want you to cure me. I want you to want me as much as I want you. And I don't think you do.'

He stood up and walked to the window to look out over the beach.

'It's okay if you want to leave.' Rav's voice was jagged; he was trying to keep control, but it wasn't quite working.

'I don't want to leave,' Faye followed him and, shyly, wrapped her arms around his waist. 'I want to be here. With you,' she murmured.

They stood as they were, with Faye hugging Rav, for long moments. Eventually, he turned around, taking her hands in his.

'Sorry,' he kissed her gently. 'I don't know why I told you all that. I mean, I would have eventually… I just didn't mean to, right now.'

'I'm glad you did.' She kissed him back. Something had gone from between them; the tension that Faye had felt, the lustful power that had tried to make him her servant. She was herself again, and she was seeing him as he was, perhaps for the first time.

Rav bent down to pick something up from the floor; it was the opal ring Finn had given her, and as soon as she saw it, she felt a rush of revulsion and desire. *No, no*, she wanted to say, to refuse it, but she found herself offering her hand to him. She didn't want it; they had created a moment between them, a realness; Rav and she had connected, heart to heart. She didn't want to be reminded of Murias and Finn now.

'Oh. It must have fallen off,' she heard Rav say innocently, but, like before, Faye was unable to say what she wanted to; her body betrayed her, and she watched in dismay as Rav slipped the ring on her thumb.

There was a sudden rush, as if she was being thrust through the air at uncomfortable speed. She had the sense of breathlessness, and the blue diamond air surrounded her. Again, like before, she was panicking, falling, but now she couldn't wake up.

Chapter 23

'You kissed the human man.'

Faye opened her eyes to find herself inside Finn Beatha's bedroom and was immediately on her guard.

'You kissed him. Made love with him. On my land. That is not the behaviour I expect from my *sidhe-leth*,' he stared at her harshly, his voice ringing out even among the walls hung with their ornate tapestries. Today he wore something akin to a suit of armour, though it was still finely detailed with the Celtic spirals and intricate knotwork that was everywhere else in the castle, chased into the edges of the golden breastplate which accurately followed the contours of his muscled chest.

'I… I…' Faye's voice wavered; she felt choked by Finn's sudden change of temper. His intoxicating charm seemed like it belonged to another person; now, he was cold and inaccessible. 'How did I get here? I don't remember walking the faerie road or coming through the labyrinth.'

'Now that you are mine, I can summon you as and when I wish,' he said dismissively, looking her over and not answering her question. 'Though I appreciate you arriving so flushed with pleasure.' Finn grimaced, and his tone was sarcastic. 'Perhaps I shall keep you naked here, at my bidding.'

'You can't...' Faye wanted to argue, knew that he was wrong, but she was unable to bring the words to her lips. She recognised the delicious haze of fae descending on her, like too many glasses of wine with Annie after-hours in the shop, under the full moon, or luxuriating in an erotic dream, not wanting to wake up but knowing that the real world tugged at the edges of it, waiting for her to return.

'I can and, if it pleases me, I will,' Finn snapped. 'How dare you take another lover? Am I not enough for you? Am I not everything you desire?' he turned his back on her and paced the room sulkily, prowling like a cat. 'You are not the only lover I could have, *sidhe-leth*. Many others would willingly take your place.'

Faye couldn't respond: the same tightness restricted her throat, and she knew now for sure that it was Finn's enchantment that bound her words. In her right mind, she would have argued back, told him that it was over. That he had no right to treat her like this. But her thoughts were disconnected and vague. She felt tears of frustration springing to her eyes.

He turned and met her eyes, a speculative expression in his that were the colour of a tumultuous sea: his gaze had the power to drown or rescue her.

'I have not stopped thinking about you since the last time you were here. You know I want you; you are unlike a mortal woman, Faye. You and I are destined to be together.' He paused. 'You liked the jewel I gave you, I trust?' He approached her slowly, still prowling, still guarded.

Befuddled, she nodded, looking at the ring. Had it brought her here, somehow? As she looked down at her hand, a long, many-stranded rose gold and opal necklace appeared around her neck, spreading out to her shoulders and down, framing her breasts, the lowest opal resting just above her navel. Bracelets of the same rose gold, made of many interlocking spirals, made elegant cuffs on her wrists and ankles, and a brief triangle made of tiny rose-gold chains and silky pearlescent fabric, embroidered with opals appeared between her legs. She held out her arm and marvelled at the beauty of the design and, as the jewels nestled against her skin, the familiar lassitude of enchantment slipped over her like a robe. She fought it, though it was like trying to hold back a tide. She made herself remember her discomfiture at being transported here without warning; worse, being vulnerable like this, at the mercy of a man dressed for battle. She dimly remembered him mentioning a conflict of some kind, last time she was here; Finn hadn't told her anything more than it was with another of the kingdoms – she couldn't remember which one – and that faerie battles for territory were commonplace. She wondered if he had come straight from a battle, or was intending to go to it when she had arrived.

'See how generous I am, even to my faithless lover?' His voice was cool and steady, but anger still blazed in his eyes. 'And yet you betrayed me.' His tone was sharp and pointed; icy where once it had been honey. 'When I gave you everything.'

'I'm sorry, I…' She hardly knew what she was saying. *Was she really sorry?* She wondered at herself for a moment. She had felt right with Rav. But Abercolme already felt a million miles and a lifetime away from this moment. *No! You're not sorry!* She screamed at herself, but the words were coming out and she couldn't stop them: she was under Finn's spell, and said what he wanted her to say.

'Sorry is not enough!' Finn screamed suddenly, picking up one of the small golden bedside tables and flinging it across the room. 'Sorry is a human word! There are no apologies in faerie. There is love, and there is not. There is desire, and there is no desire. We do not have a single word that makes things right with no effort at all! Sorry is a lie. I do not want your sorrow. I want your love.'

Faye recoiled from his sudden anger. She knew that faeries were no strangers to lies, but she said nothing. She waited for his anger to pass, her gaze flitting from his face to his clenched fists until they relaxed.

'Promise that you will never see him again.' He stood facing her, and traced his fingertip on her cheek. His voice was calm again, and he kissed her cheek softly, as if she had imagined his outburst. Like it had never happened.

Faye looked up into his ocean-tossed eyes. She knew what had happened, and a part of her felt alarm; there was a warning here, and she knew she should take it. Finn was dangerous; his temper was explosive. But the power of Murias was too strong, and Finn, so close to her, was bright as the sun. And if the sun cast shadows, she knew that he called hers out: teased her darkness out from where her human-ness gripped it tight, refusing to let it see the light.

'I promise,' she whispered, knowing that he was compelling her, but also that there was something deep inside her that wanted to say yes, too. 'I am yours.'

'So be it. I will allow one mistake, Faye. But only one,' he was gentle now, and Faye wondered how she could ever have been startled by his anger. He had been hurt. He was emotional. He loved her.

'The lovers of faerie kings are richly rewarded for their adoration.' Finn Beatha smiled widely and turned her around so that she could look at herself in the mirror.

'They're beautiful,' she murmured, touching the opals. Finn's hand closed over hers, and he traced her own hand over her breasts, her waist and her bottom. She leaned back into him, and felt his arousal against her.

'You are beautiful,' he breathed into her ear, and Faye was willingly lost.

'Come.' He held out his hand to her and, at his touch, she felt the seductive, sleepy wave of faerie break over her, wrapping her in its seawater bliss. 'The faerie ball awaits.'

'So you weren't... aren't...?' She indicated his armour. 'You look like you're ready for battle.'

'The battle is over, for now,' he replied curtly.

'But... what's it about? Why are you at war with... the other realm?' She wanted to know, but Finn looked away, smiling.

'No talk of war now, *sidhe-leth*. It is not a matter for you. Listen to the music. Don't you care to dance?'

'Like this?' Faye was almost naked, and she hugged her arms around herself, vulnerable. It was one thing to be here with Finn, but quite another for the whole of Murias to see her dressed only in the intricate rose-gold chains. 'I... can't I get dressed? For a ball?' She remembered the lavish clothes that had appeared for her here, last time.

He smiled, and kissed her. 'You are the king's lover. In the faerie kingdom of Murias, *sidhe-leth*, I am all-powerful. And you...' He kissed her neck, watching her in the mirror, 'You are the object of my desire. And I desire them to see you as I do. More beautiful than the stars on the night sea. You may wear whatever you please. What do you want?' He caressed her naked breasts softly.

'Something magical,' she replied, and a sudden delight in her own body bloomed like a dark blood-red rose. She remembered the sensation of being watched as she had made love with Rav on the beach; the intoxication of eyes being on her as she claimed her pleasure. 'I want them to see me. Want me as you do.'

He clicked his fingers softly, and Faye felt the softest kiss of silk caress her skin.

'Then you shall have it,' he murmured.

Chapter 24

When they descended the golden spiral staircase, the music stopped and the faerie court stared silently at its king and his lover.

Faye looked down at herself, suddenly self-conscious. A coral-pink gown made of a slightly iridescent, translucent silky material was open to the waist to show off her elaborate necklace and naked breasts. Jewelled straps looped loosely over her shoulders, glittering with opals, pearls and diamonds, and a plain rose gold circlet sat on her forehead, covering her third eye. Her auburn-red hair had been braided around the circlet, and the rest of her hair was a mass of wild curls that spilled over her shoulders. The skirt of the dress swept the ground at the back but was open to the waist at the front, showing her thighs and the triangle of jewelled thong that sat comfortably against her flesh. A light breeze blew the gauzy material against Faye's skin, and she was aroused by the sensation of the silk – and Finn's hand – on her back. She wore flat slippers that seemed to be woven from a soft gold material that was nonetheless spongy and strong when she walked, and protected her feet from the cold marble and sometimes sharp shell floors of the castle.

Finn took her hand and bowed before the upturned faces of the court; Faye took his lead and bowed too.

'May I present the king's consort, Miss Faye Morgan,' Finn announced to the hall, his voice loud and commanding, then turned to Faye and, kneeling before her, took her hand and kissed it. 'This ball is in her honour,' he said, smiling up at her, and Faye's heart thrummed with ecstatic joy.

The crowd cheered, and Faye bowed to them. As they descended the stairs, the music started again and Faye felt her toes twitch. It was enchanted music; it made her want to dance and scream and laugh wildly; to pinch and bite and kiss.

As soon as they reached the floor, Finn's arm grasped her around the waist and he swung her into the throng. He still wore the uniform he had worn in his room; the light from a thousand or more candles glowed gold on his epaulettes and buttons. His eyes were wild, like hers must be too, she thought; joining the dancers was like going under a magical wave, and not needing air.

Large golden bowls of water alight with floating candles sat on top of numerous golden pillars around the edge of the wide hall; as they danced, Faye felt the fragranced air on her skin like kisses. Hanging from the ceiling above were strange decorations; some she recognised, like seashells and starfish, and brightly coloured coral that seemed to grow out of the ceiling. But there were other things, too; things made from knotted string and hair and bones that hung here and there, and that she didn't like to look too closely at.

The dancers were much as they had been before; varied as the faeries she had seen on the faerie road and in the labyrinth. Some were tall, willowy women, dressed in leaves, that bowed regally as Faye and Finn passed them. Some were short, fat faeries with ragged wings and dusty, moth wing-like garments. Faye glimpsed the beautiful woman with the legs of a goat under her long green dress; she remembered seeing her, or a faerie very like her, in the labyrinth.

'What are the names of all these creatures?' she whispered to Finn.

'The Faerie Court of Water is legion,' he replied, spinning her around until she was dizzy. 'There are dream-weavers, sprites, nixies, river maidens, topsy-turveys. There are frog queens and kings, undines. Many more that have not been given names by humans.'

Out of breath from exertion, Faye stopped dancing; the crowd continued to revolve around them. She spotted the frog queen, a naked, otherworldly beauty dressed only in an elaborate crown of pearls, with webbed feet and glistening green and brown spotted legs. The queen danced delicately yet unrelentingly fast with a slim young man who wore a baroque face mask that was as jewelled as her necklace, and a jewelled band around his neck that suggested a collar. He was human, Faye was almost sure; other than the mask and collar, his chest was bare, and he wore loose trousers in a dark green material. His chest puffed in and out rapidly with the effort of keeping up with the faerie.

Faye recognised Finn's sister, the Faerie Queen of Murias, Glitonea, approaching; she and Finn gave the same nod to each other that Faye remembered from before, and that same something passed between them: *like calls to like, deep calls to deep,* Grandmother used to say, and it was just that: of all the fae, they were something of their own. She danced again with the same young man – barely more than twenty, Faye guessed – who seemed frailer than before, but who still gazed at the faerie queen as if she was the gleaming spark at the centre of all things, and he couldn't believe his luck that he was the one holding onto her brightness. He too wore a mask this time, as did many of the faeries; Faye supposed that this was a masked ball.

Unlike last time, when she had been new to Murias and Finn had danced her past his sister without stopping to do more than nod, now Faye could focus on Glitonea in greater detail. Compelling in the same way that Finn was, the faerie queen was fair, tall, well-muscled and strong. She had the same high cheekbones and ravishing, penetrating gaze as her brother.

Finn smiled and bowed to the frog queen and her partner as they passed. Just before the frog queen grasped him by the shoulders and leaped into the centre of the crowd, laughing, the young man's outstretched hand glanced onto Faye's palm, and his eyes, in the slits in the mask, met hers.

As soon as they touched, Faye felt a jolt of pain all the way through her body, like being cut in two. She pulled her hand away. Panic filled her; the eyes that had held hers, she could swear, were full of pain. Was there an entreaty there, a cry for help? But before she could say anything, or hold onto him, the frog queen had dragged him deeper into the crowd.

'Who... who was that? With the frog queen?' He smiled, stroked her face and took her hand. His touch calmed her immediately.

'Her consort, just as you are mine,' he replied, simply. 'Do not worry. They come here willingly, like you,'

'But... I think he was asking for help. I felt... pain when he touched me.'

'I doubt that. The frog queen is a generous lover. He will not go unsated or underfed, *sidhe-leth*. Remember that the realm of faerie is not like the human world. Pleasure and pain are both sensation, and in faerie, we do not discriminate.' He smiled down at her. 'You know yourself that the desire you deny in the human realm can be free here. Humans come here to embrace their shadows as much as the desires that live in more plain sight. We do not judge; neither should you.'

Faye frowned. Under and among her intoxication at being in Murias she sensed a black thread of doubt weaving itself silently; she felt the tug of its shadowy teeth, and felt uneasy.

As if he read her mind, Finn measured her eyes with his.

'You know so little of us. Stay. Absorb our ways, our culture. Until you know us, you cannot understand,' he cautioned, and she nodded. He was right, and the call of faerie tugged at her hair and sang in her blood.

'Now. Will we have some wine?' Finn smiled, and Faye realised that she was thirsty.

Chapter 25

She woke up on what she thought was the third day after the masked ball, which had turned into a continual party fuelled by faerie wine and the sweet and deliciously sour faerie foods for which she had no name. Whatever the faerie fruits were, they had kept her and Finn awake – dancing, feasting and making love – for what felt like a long time. Flashes of memory, of contorted faces, twining limbs, of bodies and lips, slid in and out of her mind; she had a sudden, searing headache and her mouth was completely dry. She closed her eyes and felt her stomach heave. She was going to be sick.

Faye made it to the bathroom in time, and knelt by the toilet, retching until there was nothing left to come up. She slumped against the wall, the luxurious rugs under her legs, and tried to steady her breathing. Slowly, she got up, went to the sink and poured some water from a crystal jug into her hand and gulped repeatedly until she felt a little clearer.

She was a mess. Her face was pale, smudged with food and stained with wine. She was bruised from dancing in the faerie reel, which went on and on and on, never stopping – she and Finn had dipped in and out of the dancing, but many of the dancers never stopped, and she wondered at how they managed it.

Suddenly, Faye missed home. How long had she really been gone, in the time of the human world? Weeks? Months? It was hard to know, but she hadn't cared, until now. What would Annie think? What about the shop? And Rav. *Rav*. She covered her face with her hands as she felt her humanity, her body, fight back against the drunkenness Murias had seduced her with. She was sick again.

It was a purge of everything she had swallowed without question; of all the desire she had spent here. A sudden, vivid memory of making love to Finn in his bed while a host of faeries watched, laughed and pleasured themselves, came back to her, and she stared at her reflection in the mirror in shock. What had she done? Finn hadn't made her do it, she was fairly sure of that. She had done as she desired; deep down, she knew that exhibitionist desire. Finn had warned her that the realm of faerie was where humans came to explore their shadowy urges. And yet she had not expected it of herself.

Angrily, she grasped the gold and jewels that thrilled against her skin, and ripped them away, scattering the opals over the bathroom floor. She stood, one hand on the wall for support, as she was weak, trying not to regret doing it. It was beautiful, and she had loved being beautiful wearing it. She tore off the wrist cuffs which suddenly felt restrictive, like the collar she remembered one of the young men wearing; the consort of the frog queen. Had he really come willingly? Had she, lulled with whatever it was in the air here – the smell of roses, the taint of magic – that made her head swim and her desire take over?

She threw the cuffs at the wall and started to cry. She felt the shame for what she was cover her like mud. For what she had done. This wasn't who she was. Faye Morgan, daughter of Modron Morgan, granddaughter to generations of strong, practical, magical Morgan women. Had they come to Murias like this? Had they lost themselves in lust and excess? And yet, even though she was miserable, she also started to feel more awake than she had since she had first entered

Murias.. Anger gave her clarity; perhaps anger was a tool that could be used against faerie enchantment.

Faye remembered Annie talking about how she made herself cry onstage: *all ye got to do is think aboot somethin' really sad before ye go on, Like, really get yourself goin'.* She could do the same thing. In memory, Faye reached back to the few times she had been really furious and tried to place herself back in the moment.

'What are you doing, *sidhe-leth*?'

Finn Beatha stood in the doorway to the bathroom, rubbing his eyes. He was naked, his hair tousled, but otherwise as golden and beautiful as he had ever been; not dirty and bruised as she was. 'Come back to bed.'

'No. I'm leaving. Going home.' She stood defiantly, trying to look stronger than she felt. 'I've had enough. It... the party... it went too far. I wasn't myself.'

'On the contrary, Faye. You were more yourself than you have ever been. You have started to reclaim your fae nature,' he smiled lazily, watching her. 'And, may I say, it suits you. You were entrancing. Every fae wanted you for their own consort.'

She pushed past him, back into the bedroom.

'How dare you treat me like some kind of... sex slave! You can't buy me off with jewels. I'm not your whore, Finn. I'm not... not anyone's whore—'

He followed her; Faye felt his bare chest press lightly against her back and shoulders.

'Never my whore, Faye Morgan. Only ever my willing lover,' he murmured.

She was horribly confused. Finn's touch aroused her; it was unfailing, electric. Yet the fleeting memories of the last few days' revelries fuelled her anger and shame. She had believed this was a place of magic, of beauty. She had come here willingly. But she felt sick, exhausted, and now that the permissive haze of faerie had started to slip, she could see cracks in its beautiful veneer.

Finn touched her shoulder lightly then walked around the bed to the table where a breakfast had been left. He poured a green liquid into the two goblets and offered her one. Too late, Faye remembered that humans were never supposed to eat and drink in fairyland, or they would be lost there for ever.

'I didn't think humans could eat or drink in the faerie world. Perhaps I shouldn't have.' Her head echoed with their talking; everything was too bright. She wanted to close her eyes. Her anger sat at the bottom of her stomach, not gone, but waiting.

'Ah.' He smiled and sat beside her on the bed, biting into an apple. 'But that rule doesn't apply to you, *sidhe-leth*.'

'Why not?' she asked, tiredly, watching him.

'I thought you knew. You are half-fae. *Sidhe-leth*. That is what that means.'

Faye gaped at him, open mouthed. 'What?'

'You are half one of us, half-human. Your father was of the faerie realm.'

'My... my father? But I never knew him. He left us,' she stammered. 'He was just some guy. Mum said... he didn't want to be tied down. He was violent towards her, I think. He wasn't... a...' She broke off and stared at Finn, who took another bite of the apple and shrugged.

'This is how you came so easily into the faerie world, Faye. You would have found your way here much sooner was it not for the fear your forebears instilled in you. Your ancestors were burnt for consorting with us, for learning our gifts.'

'But why didn't they tell me? Moddie and Grandmother?' She felt sick again, but this time Faye didn't know if it was the shock or her hangover from faerie.

'I suppose they wanted to protect you. But connection to us is how you gain real power. Your great-grandmothers had real power; they lived alongside us. Learned our ways, honoured our lands. They made the appropriate sacrifices: a baby at Midwinter, a woman at Midsummer.'

'I always thought that was symbolic, the sacrifices.'

Midsummer, Midsummer, Midsummer delight; go to the faeries on Midsummer night
Take thee a maiden, take thee a wife –
Take thee a bairn for the rest of its life –
Midsummer, Midsummer, Midsummer delight; go to the faeries on Midsummer night.

The old song echoed in her mind, and Faye shivered. She'd never even considered, as a child on the beach with Grandmother, that the old song might have some truth in it.

Finn shrugged again and wiped the apple juice from his chin.

'Different times take different meanings. The babies, sometimes people would leave us an ailing one in the woods. It would die if it stayed in your world. We could take it and raise it in the faerie kingdom, then use it to strengthen our stock when it was old enough.'

'Stock?' Faye wrapped herself in a silky throw from the end of the bed; an unconscious gesture to somehow protect herself from the truth. Because it *was* the truth; she knew it, instinctively. She was half-faerie, and Moddie and Grandmother had never told her. To protect her, most likely, which was understandable. But at the same time, Faye was angry. She had always felt different, unusual, slightly out of things, but she never knew why. And they had denied her that part of herself all this time.

'Sometimes the faerie realm sickens without good stock from the outside to make us strong. And we need to be strong, especially when we are at war.'

'And the women? Taken to be lovers, like me?' Her heart sank at the thought that Finn might have brought other women just like her to his bed; it was easy for him to enchant a human woman. They were weak and pliable, unresisting. Like she had been. Like she was.

Her hand went to the intricate necklace of opals before remembering she had destroyed it. *Who else wore it? What other lips has he kissed, what other women has he pleasured like me? Am I no different to them?* She refused to meet his eyes and hugged in her knees to her chest. She wanted to cry. She was not a queen, just the latest in a long line of women plucked from her world to please a bored king. No: not just a woman. Something else; a new identity that she would have to explore. She was half-fae – different to Finn, different to Rav. *What was she? Who was she?*

'Sometimes.' He lifted her chin and kissed her softly; he tasted of apple. 'Sometimes they wet-nursed our children. That is the way of it, Faye. Time is different here. I have known many human women, but I am not old; though in your time I have ruled Murias for many years. Sometimes those women have borne children, half-fae, like you.'

She sat up, her heart beating wildly.

'Does that mean… am I… are you… my…?' She felt sick at the thought, but stupid not to have realised immediately what he could have meant.

'No, I am not your blood.' Finn made her look at him, serious now. 'That would not be the way of a king. Your mother loved another.'

'Who?' Faye stood up, holding the wrap around her like a cloak. 'I demand to know who my father is. It's my right.'

'I will not hold that information from you if you seek it. His name is Lyr. He is the King of Falias, the Faerie Realm of Earth. He rules that kingdom with his sister, the Faerie Queen Moronoe.'

'Lyr.' Faye was still incredulous. 'Moddie didn't love him. He threatened to kill her.'

'That is as may be. Still, he is your father.'

'Falias. The realm you are at war with now?' Faye remembered the name now, and Finn nodded.

'Yes.'

'Why are you at war with them?'

He sighed.

'Territory. The boundaries of faerie realms have shifted.'

Faye thought for a moment.

'Why is Moddie here? Her spirit, I mean. I saw her here.' Faye was trying not to feel as though her whole being was being unpicked and re-woven, like how grandmother used to roll up an old jumper of her own and re-knit it for Faye. The elements were the same, but the shape was totally different.

'I allowed your mother to come here in spirit,' he answered smoothly.

'Do you allow many humans to come here after they die?'

He looked away, avoiding her gaze.

'No,' he answered, after a pause.

'Then why Moddie?' Faye sought his eyes, understanding all at once. 'Oh. That's why. Her connection to him. She gave you something in return. Something she knew about him, perhaps.'

He smiled thinly.

'A bargain was struck. The details are between my sister, Glitonea, and Modron Morgan. No-one else.'

Faye got up and paced around. Her head was pounding but now that the veil of illusion had slipped from her a little, she wanted to use her lucidity while she could.

'Why did she want to come here?' she demanded. 'She's my mother. I have a right to know.'

Finn spread his palms open in a gesture that implied he was being honest; Faye doubted that he was telling her the full truth. He was a faerie king; faeries were not prone to truth, as a rule.

'Murias is the realm of emotion, of water, magic, what you humans call mysticism. Modron Morgan was a witch in life, though she never fully realised her powers, in the same way as you have not so far. She wanted the power of faerie. She learned it here.'

'What is the power of faerie?' Faye demanded, feeling her heart lift. *If Moddie learned it, then so can I.*

Finn frowned.

'It is secret. Not for humans.'

'I am not fully human,' she replied crisply. 'You taught Moddie.'

'I did not teach her. The faerie queens are the keepers of the magic.' Finn turned away from her, his voice peevish.

'Glitonea?' Faye continued to push him.

'In Murias – she is the Mistress of the Cup.' Finn was evasive.

'Will she teach me? I am half-fae,' Faye repeated. To have the faerie magic would give her the power she lacked in Murias. With it, perhaps Finn wouldn't be able to take advantage of her human weaknesses.

'No!' Finn shouted, turning to her. There was an uncomfortable silence. 'No, *sidhe-leth*,' he repeated. 'Your mother was a special case.

And she had passed from your realm already. We cannot teach the faerie magic to anyone that resides in the human world. It is forbidden.'

'Well then, will I see her again?' Faye's heart sank; she had made her peace with Moddie's death. *When we pass over, we are busy elsewhere,* Grandmother had taught her, though she had never specified where. *We can teach others on the inner planes; we can come into another body for another life; we can heal, we can spend time with our loved ones. All is possible once we have passed, but that person as you knew them, when they are gone from this world, they're gone for good.* But seeing Moddie again had thrown Faye completely – all those months and years of grief were unpicked, like wool being wound back from a blanket. Now, she longed for her mother, and it hurt.

'Murias is wide and far-reaching, Faye. Do not expect to see her again,' Finn's voice was soft, but she sensed the firmness of his resolve.

'Why not?' Her voice was quiet.

'She should not have appeared to you. There are rules,' Finn replied grimly.

Faye felt exhaustion take her over, and she crumpled on to the bed.

'I want to go home,' she whispered. 'I'm so tired.' It was a physical tiredness, but the revived grief for Moddie filled her with a heaviness she remembered all too well.

'You are free to go whenever you desire,' Finn motioned towards the heavy door. 'You are not my prisoner.' He caught her arm. 'But you must promise to love only me from now on, *sidhe-leth*. Otherwise the magic between us will decline. It will not be so easy for you to be here, in the faerie kingdom, without my love. I will treat you as a queen if you honour me as your king. But if my lover loves another, then I will punish him. And you too—' The threat against Rav was clear. Faye pulled her arm away from Finn's grasp.

'I can promise no such thing until you treat me as queens should be treated.' She turned to face him. 'Queens rule. They pass judgement. Queens understand the realm they command. How can I be your queen if I've done none of these things?'

His smile vanished and his fine-featured face took on a watchful look.

'I mean that I will treat you as a queen *should be treated*. I will adore you. With my lips, my hands, everything of myself,' he ran his finger up her arm, and she shivered at the electricity that flashed through her body at his touch. 'But I cannot wed you as you do in your world. Such a thing does not exist in Murias, or any of the faerie kingdoms. And you cannot ever be the real queen of this realm. Glitonea is High Queen of Murias, and there is no-one else who could be. You know this.'

'I don't want to be your bride,' Faye snapped. She was picking him up on his use of the word; but inwardly she was surprised at the suggestion. She also knew that if he touched her again, if his hands held her breasts, if his full, sulky lips found hers again, she might be submerged again in the erotic lassitude that had kept her here this long. 'I don't feel comfortable here any more. I need to leave. To think,' she insisted.

Finn picked up a golden vase and threw it against the wall, near to Faye; some of the tall reeds and white water lilies in it caught at her skin like a rebuke, and the water inside exploded on the wall.

'There is nothing to think about!' he roared; his eyes bulged in sudden fury, and Faye stepped back, her arms over her head as he kicked one of the delicate bedside tables over: it was made of crystal, and shattered on the floor. 'You have no idea! None! How fortunate you are, what I have done to bring you here! Do you think all this – the feasting, the celebrations, the fine clothes – do you think this is how every mortal woman is treated in Murias?' He strode over to her and caught at her hands, but she pulled them away.

'Don't touch me.' Faye was trying to keep her voice calm and controlled: she felt that if she shouted back, the situation would worsen. She felt as though she was trying to calm a wild horse. She was terrified, but the only way out of this was to pacify the faery king. *Moddie, Grandmother, give me strength, please help me,* she prayed silently, trying to regain her strength, to have something to protect her. She tried to visualise the shop, her safe place, but she couldn't concentrate.

'Time to think! You don't know what you are *thinking*, Faye Morgan. Few mortals are ever chosen to be the King's consort, to come and go with freedom from his kingdom. You are special, and I offered you more than anyone. I… I loved you. I love you.' Finn's eyes were desperate. *Does he really believe that he loves me?* Faye wondered, and, with the anger that arose in her belly – *how dare he threaten me, how dare he intimidate me like this* – some of the illusion that had kept her here fell away. She saw him for what he was under the cold, powerful, desirous facade: spoilt, insecure, unable to control his emotions.

'Go back to your realm. Think. I will be here, waiting. But I will not wait forever, *sidhe-leth*. I will not have my heart broken a second time.' Finn shrugged on his clothes and walked out, banging the door behind him.

The black thread that she had felt, weaving itself into the fabric of her awareness, was thick now, and woven with danger. Now that her head was clearer, she was worried for Rav. Even if she never kissed him again, even if nothing ever happened again between them, he was in danger. Finn was jealous, and she had seen the shadow under his golden magic.

Faye pulled on her own clothes. She unfastened the rose-gold cuffs that still circled her ankles and lay them on the bed. Last, she gazed at the ring on her thumb for a long moment before taking it off and placing it next to the cuffs.

As soon as she took it off, she felt a noticeable lessening of the faerie power on her. Was it some kind of magical tool by which Finn could influence her? She remembered the first time she had put it on; how, even when she was back in Abercolme after that first time in Murias, she was different. She shook her head, trying to clear it. She remembered that she hadn't had the ring on when she was with Rav, but then, when she had put it on again, she found herself in Finn's bedroom. It was clearly enchanted.

He wouldn't change: he couldn't. He was of the oceans, and every ocean held monsters. Finn's realm of water held the deepest, darkest places, where humans could never venture, just as much as sunlit bays where warm, transparent seas stretched over white sands. Finn Beatha was the King of Murias; he *was* Murias, and he was unable to be anything else.

Faye doubted that he knew what love was, at least, what humans considered love. She knew that when he said it, he meant the intense passion they'd shared. There was no doubt that making love with Finn had been unparalleled, otherworldly. But the illusion he had thrown over her, like a glamour, like a net over a fish, had shifted, and she knew she couldn't go back to him. She could follow the labyrinth back to the faerie road that ended on Black Sands Beach. She could go home.

Heart heavy, Faye walked out of Finn's bedroom; out of the castle, through the market and followed the labyrinth home. The way was open; no-one stopped her; nothing dallied her. And yet, as she made her way back to Abercolme, the grief at losing Moddie for the second time weighed heavy on her, and part of her longed to run back to Murias to search for her mother.

Chapter 26

Faye awoke in her own bed and sat up with a combined sense of disappointment and relief – as she had every morning in the two weeks since she had returned from Murias. She stretched out her arms and looked at them in the morning light that slanted through her normal, floral cotton curtains. No golden cuffs. No elaborate necklace and no ring on her thumb. If she went back to Murias now, it would be on her terms.

She had been busy since returning to Abercolme. It wasn't enough to have Finn's permission to be away, or enough that she had discarded the ring he had used to summon her. In the past week, with the waning of the moon, Faye had returned to Grandmother's grimoire. She had enchanted mirrors to turn away faerie enchantments, and drawn banishing sigils on their backs. Grateful for the pile of hagstones that she and Annie continually brought back from the beach, she strung them into companion charms for the one that Grandmother had hung by the door and hung them around the house. She smudged the house with smoking bundles of rosemary and rue for protection, and spritzed the corners and the doors liberally with blessing oils.

She swung her legs over the side of the bed. Though she had thought about Murias every day, she hadn't tried to go back. The risk was too great – for her and for Rav. Now that she was back and her head had cleared she realised how dangerous Finn was. And though much of her yearned for Murias, she remembered the pain in the eyes of Glitonea's lover and felt lucky that she had escaped.

It was Sunday, and the shop was closed. Faye wandered downstairs, thinking that she'd try to catch up on the accounts; being away in faerie meant she'd neglected the business. But, once she was downstairs, she found herself idling by the counter, reading Grandmother's grimoire from where she had left it the night before.

She hadn't been to the beach since she got back. She had heard from Aisha that Rav was away on business, and she'd been avoiding him as well as the faerie road. She didn't know how to explain to Rav that it was for his own good if she didn't see him. She couldn't put him in danger.

Faye looked up as some villagers passed by the shop, on their way to church. The sun made the shop windows glow, and a thick shaft of sunlight sliced across the dresser where she stacked tarot and oracle cards. She felt its warmth on her hair like a caress.

There was a thick page at the back of the grimoire that Faye hadn't noticed before; usually, when she had looked at it, Annie had been with her, and they had spent their time searching for spells they could do, or reading out funny passages about people in the village being cured of the pox or of loneliness or some kind of unusual disfigurement, laughing just like they had at Midwinter.

Faye rubbed the paper between her thumb and finger, and realised that two pages had got stuck together. In fact, as she inspected the pages closely, not wanting to damage the book, she realised that the pages had been purposefully stuck together; there was a light brown line of what might have been glue down one side of the paper.

Carefully, Faye separated the pages. The glue had long since lost its strength and the paper peeled apart. Inside, both pages were covered with Grandmother's small, crabbed handwriting.

But this section was something different. Rather than Grandmother's charms for love and fertility, or her record of various cures for ailments that beset the villagers, this was full of unfamiliar signs and symbols. Faye held it close to her eyes and read a section.

For the knowledge and conversation with High Queens of Faerie, Grandmother had written, _and to learn their magicks_.

Faye swore under her breath. So Grandmother _had_ known the faerie magic too. Why hadn't she taught Faye? Had Moddie known?

First, create the environment for the queen of your chosen element, Grandmother wrote.
To summon Her from her home element, you must create a ritual space of high vibration. Ideally, conduct the summoning as close to the right element as possible.

There was a note in parentheses which Faye had to bring close to her eyes to read; Grandmother had written:

High Queen of Murias = tideline
High Queen of Falias = sacred forest
High Queen of Gorias = mountain or storm
High Queen of Finias = ritual fire

Cast a circle. Summon in only the right element for the faerie queen in question. Dance or pace out the circle clockwise and then pace into the centre of the circle as if in a spiral. When at the centre of the circle, call out their full name three times. In Murias, She is called Glitonea, Mistress *of the Cup. In Falias, it is Moronoe, Mistress of the Stone. In Gorias, it is Tyronoe, Mistress of the Knife. And in Finias, it is Thetis, Mistress of the Staff. Your calling of the queen should be urgent and passionate, from the heart. Repeat this process, walking the spiral in and out and calling the names, three times.*

When you have called their name three times, entreat them to be with you as follows:

Beloved of the Fae, Queen of your Element, Mistress of Magic,
I seek communion with you; I seek knowledge of you and your realm,
Bestow your magic upon me, I am fain to know your secrets,
I am open; fill me with your blessings. (Name) I call on you
(Name) I beseech you, enter the space I have prepared for you
(Name) I would love you with my mind, my heart and my body
(Name) I summon you from your kingdom
I offer something of mine that I can give freely; this is the exchange
This is the promise between faerie and human
So mote it be

The promise between faerie and human, Faye mused, looking up from the book. What was that? And why was this hidden at the back of Grandmother's grimoire? The faerie realm was dangerous; she knew that. It was seductive and shadowy. But it was also bright and beautiful and full of wonder. Perhaps Grandmother and Moddie – if she had known about the hidden pages – had been waiting for the right time to share the knowledge with Faye.

Whatever they had thought, it was time now. Finn had been wrong about humans never learning the magic of the faerie realm. Faye's own magic might be enough for now to keep Finn away, but she couldn't be sure that it would be enough to protect her and Rav – and anyone else that needed it – forever. Here was a way for Faye to at least talk to Glitonea; she could appeal to her better instincts, beg her to teach her, if necessary.

Glitonea was a capricious, unsentimental faerie queen. But she was made of the same stuff as Finn, and if Finn could have his heart broken, then Glitonea might have some weakness, some glint of humanity within her, too.

At Black Sands, the moon was on its final waning quarter, and the night was dark. If Faye hadn't known the beach so well, she might well have fallen on a rock or a stray branch; as it was, she was careful, and took off her shoes and socks when she was on the sand, placing them on a nearby ledge.

She hadn't brought the grimoire with her, but had copied out the invocation on a piece of paper and had it in her pocket. It was still cold on the beach at night, though it was early summer, so she wore flowered leggings under her red-and-white polka-dot dress, with a green cardigan over the top; a mash-up of styles chosen mostly for warmth. Faye wore Moddie's pink coat over the top, fastened with its large round pink buttons.

She took a deep breath, nervous about what she was about to do. Grandmother had hidden this summoning magic for a reason; Faye knew that if Glitonea was anything like Finn, she would be powerful but unpredictable and vengeful if she perceived she was being wronged. The Fae were difficult and dangerous.

But, now that she was home, Faye had returned to the sobriety of the human world and realised that she needed both realms. She was a part of both, and she wanted to continue being in Murias. As intoxicating and incredible as it had been with Finn, she wanted more. She had seen glimpses of the power Finn had, something greater than witchcraft, and the truth was that she wanted it for herself.

And, she wanted to be able to protect herself and Rav. She knew Finn had meant it when he threatened them. Threatened Rav.

Faye traced a circle at the line of the tide, wide enough to contain her with her arms spread out and with ample room on either side. Her finger dug the shallow trench of the circle half in and half out of the sea; the water filled the gap on the sea side of the circle and smoothed it over with the tide as soon as she had done it. She didn't mind; a circle of half sea, half land was right for summoning a fae creature of the water to the land. Faye was meeting her halfway, in a space that belonged to neither of them; an in-between place, a place where magic could be made.

Clouds spread across the black sky, covering the stars that were visible until everything above Faye stretched into a blank unity of night. She swallowed nervously, then called out to the sea.

'Powers of the sea, of the ocean, of water, be with me! Fill my circle with your power!' She opened her arms as if to accept the power of water, and felt its energy crashing into her prepared space as forcefully as if she had been standing next to a waterfall.

She started to pace the circle clockwise, as Grandmother had instructed; then, making a spiral, she circled in a smaller and smaller circumference, feeling the energy in the circle compress as she reached the centre.

'Glitonea, Mistress of the Cup!' Faye shouted at the top of her voice, trying to imbue her voice with as much feeling as she could. She imagined Glitonea as she had seen her at the Faerie Ball, with roses in her golden hair, and her dress of silver and lilac.

Faye paced an unwinding spiral to the edge of the circle, and felt the energy loosen. She paced to the centre again and felt it contract, like a wave breaking and building. She called out to Glitonea again, feeling the energy rising in her and in the circle. The tide crashed on her feet and ankles as she stood in its shallows; slowly, it advanced into the circle. This was a much greater magic than she had done before, and Faye could feel its toll on her. The spiralling energy threatened to engluf her, growing in depth with every contraction; she fought with herself to stay in control.

Faye found the invocation from Grandmother's grimoire, inscribed on a page from her orders notebook in the shop; she flicked on a mini hand torch and read it aloud.

Beloved of the Fae, Queen of your Element, Mistress of Magic,
I seek communion with you; I seek knowledge of you and your realm,
Bestow your magic upon me, I am fain to know your secrets,
I am open; fill me with your blessings. Glitonea, Mistress of the
Cup, I call on you!

The tide was coming in, but it seemed to be coming faster than it usually would; rather than half of the circle being submerged, now three-quarters of it had been erased by the water. Faye steadied herself, breathing deeply and refusing the rising panic that wanted her to give up, to lose her focus. She pushed up the bottoms of her leggings and continued the call:

Glitonea, Mistress of the Cup, I beseech you, enter the space I have
prepared for you

Glitonea, Mistress of the Cup, I would love you with my mind, my heart and my body
Glitonea, Mistress of the Cup, I summon you from your kingdom
I offer something of mine that I can give freely; this is the exchange
This is the promise between faerie and human
So mote it be!

The tide was much higher now; a cold wave broke and soaked Faye to her thighs, flowing over the last of the circle she had traced with her finger in the sand. She still felt it there, energetically, but there was a shift; the power was no longer balanced between earth and water. The tide threw her off balance and she fell forward in the freezing salt water.

Gasping, she pushed herself up onto her hands and knees, the taste of salt in her mouth like blood. *Grandmother, you should have told me*, she thought. *You should have taught me. If you had, I would be stronger now.*

Glitonea stood before her in the water, a tall silver crown on her head, dressed in black robes that merged seamlessly with the waves.

'I am here as you request, Faye Morgan. Be assured that I do not take this summoning lightly,' she intoned, and her voice was like fracturing icebergs.

Chapter 27

Faye felt Glitonea's voice rather than heard it; despite its harsh quality, it was hypnotic like Finn's and drew her into a trance almost immediately.

'What is your part of the exchange?' Glitonea faced her across the waves which surged around them both. Faye stood up; she was up to her waist now in the water, and she struggled to stay upright, digging her toes ferociously into the wet sand under her.

'I... I... don't know.' Faye's teeth were chattering; she was wet through.

'You summoned me. You should have been better prepared.' Glitonea cast a cynical eye over Faye's soaked coat. 'Why bring me here? One of your kind has not done so for many years.'

'Grandmother? A– Al– Alice Morgan?' Faye tried to stop shivering but it was impossible.

'Yes,' Glitonea answered crisply. Faye noticed that her silver crown featured a crescent moon which curled upwards on her brow like horns. The rest of the points were made of crystal rather than silver, which reflected milky moonlight as the clouds parted and the waning crescent of the moon appeared in the sky above.

'I... I want to learn your magic. The magic of Murias. Of the realm of water,' Faye blurted.

Glitonea laughed.

'Do you, indeed? Unfortunately for you, it is not permitted. Congratulations on your power in summoning me here. But that is where this ends.' The faerie queen turned her back and began walking away, her dress merging with the water.

'Wait!' Faye shouted. She was losing the feeling in her legs; numbness from the cold was creeping up her body. 'I command you to wait!'

Glitonea stopped and turned slowly.

'You have no business commanding me to do anything, *sidhe-leth*. Just because my dear brother is enamoured with you does not mean I am, or that I will do anything for you,' she spat.

'I have something you want. I am willing to make the exchange,' Faye shouted over the waves, holding out her arms to steady herself, teeth knocking together so hard now that her head ached. Her clothes were heavy. A shadowy temptation to lie down in the water and never get up crept into her bones; whispered its seductive call in her ear.

'You have nothing I want,' the queen sneered. 'I have my choice of human lovers, Faye. You are not one of them.'

'I am Lyr's daughter!' Faye shouted with the last scraps of her strength.

Glitonea stared at her for a long moment, then laughed.

'I know that. Is that your great secret? We all know it. You have his look. Lyr is my cousin. I know his ways,' she laughed loudly, and turned away from Faye. 'If I see you again, *sidhe-leth*, it will be when you are naked and jewelled like a whore, on my brother's leash. That is where your kind belong,' she called out. 'If your parentage is all you have for an exchange, then you have nothing of interest to me.' Glitonea's voice was receding, and the waves were dropping. Faye felt herself slump, and pulled herself up as straight as she could. *No.* She had to fight.

'You are at war with Falias. If you teach me your magic, I can be a weapon against Lyr; I have no love for him. I have never known him!' She cried out. Moddie's throwaway phrase, all those years ago: *Almost killed me.* Her father had clearly tried to hurt Moddie, perhaps in anger at being expected to stay and look after her and Faye; or, perhaps, Moddie had told him to go when she realised he would be a terrible father. She had never known for sure but, ever since that night, the idea of her father as a violent man – a selfish and impatient one, like Finn – had stayed with her.

Faye called on all the strength she had; she reached for the anger she had always kept inside her, a private anger at being left by her father. And she reset her feet in the shifting, freezing sand, and pulled up all the energy she could from the earth below her and from the stars above. It was enough to steady her, but only that: Glitonea was so strong, so powerful. She was the tide: relentless, cold, violent.

If her father was a faerie king, then it was entirely likely that he was just as prone to violence as she thought; the fae were dangerous. Perhaps there had been another reason… but whatever it was, Faye didn't care about him now.

'I know that Finn made a bargain with Moddie, my mother. She gave him something – information, perhaps, that helped you in your war – in return for staying in Murias after death. She was Lyr's lover; Surely, as Lyr's child, you can make a bargain with me?' she added.

Faye coughed as a wave hit her chest and splashed hard into her face; her nose and mouth were filled with salt water again. *Beware the faeries,* Grandmother's voice echoed in her mind. *They are beautiful, but consorting with them is dangerous, ma darlin'. I wouldnae see ye enchanted. It's my job tae protect ye.* She hoped that it was enough; that she had offered Glitonea enough of a temptation. That she, Faye, was a big enough bait to catch the faerie queen of Murias.

The last thing Faye saw was Glitonea, tall and black as the waves themselves, advancing through the waves towards her. She closed her eyes as strong arms pulled her up out of the water, and let the dark take her. *Too late, Grandmother,* she thought before she passed out from the cold. *Much too late.*

Chapter 28

Glitonea, Faerie Queen of Murias, stood with her back to Faye and before a vast sphere of what looked like ice, suspended above a golden altar table. The light in the room was dim apart from where she stood, which was bathed in a diffuse goldenness, though Faye couldn't see the source of it.

'Where am I?'

Faye's voice echoed against the stone walls. Her feet, which she could now feel, were dry and warm in supple sky-blue leather boots which fitted her feet perfectly and were stitched with gold thread. She wore a long silky dress in a dark turquoise which fell to the floor; the top part of the dress left her arms bare, and the slippery material was plaited to make straps for the shoulders. At the front, the material wrapped over into a deep V to the waistband, exposing the curve of her breasts; she saw that a different necklace sat on her collarbone. This time it was a silver torc, with strands of the precious metal twisted in a circle that almost met at her throat; it shone against the blue shimmers in the dress's fabric which shifted in the light like a Mediterranean sea. Matching wrist cuffs again adorned her arms.

Faye swayed on her feet; she was exhausted.

'Take a moment to recover, *sidhe-leth*. You will find that being in Murias has a swift restorative power.' Unlike her voice as she stood in the sea which had been harsh and sharp, Glitonea spoke now in a voice that sang and flowed like a sweet river.

'You offered an acceptable exchange. I am fulfilling my part of the bargain.'

Faye nodded and sat heavily on a nearby chest, which was draped in luxurious fabrics. She felt the tiredness leave her bones, and strength return to her as if she had drunk some kind of magical draught.

'Thank you,' she answered wearily. This was what she wanted, but this was a realm of high magic: there was no going back. And though Glitonea was right, and her body felt refreshed and strong again, she was frightened, and tired of being watchful. 'I just… want to learn what you can teach me. So that I can protect myself from…' she trailed off and looked away. Finn's name hung between them, unsaid, a phantom.

Glitonea was fine-featured and golden like her brother, and tall and well-muscled; yet there was something more changeable about her, as if she could not be fully perceived. Faye had the sense that the edges of her were fluid like water; that she was everywhere and nowhere at once.

'I know what you wish,' the faerie queen replied, giving no indication of what she felt. Her loyalty would be to Finn, surely: he had told Faye again and again how he and Glitonea were the same, brother and sister, king and queen, the two halves of the kingdom. They were Murias.

Faye warmed herself by a great fire in a silver brazier to her left. Around the walls were lamps and silver censers, the censers billowing out fragranced smoke that smelled of lavender, rose and jasmine.

'Welcome to my quarters,' Glitonea smiled, and bowed slightly at the waist. She stood, looking closely at Faye's eyes. 'As I said, I can see Lyr's features in yours. Lyr, being the King of the Faerie Realm of Earth, has taken many human lovers, as humans are most aware of his element over them all, even though you drink our waters and breathe

the air and warm yourself in the fire of the sun. Without any of these things you would all die. But the mountains and the trees are the things you feel are the most real. Perhaps it is because you can cut them down and use their stones and logs to make your palaces of money.'

'I'm one person. You can hardly blame me for generations of industrialisation,' Faye argued back.

Glitonea remained impassive. 'I didn't bring you here to discuss such things.' She regarded Faye critically. 'This is what you wanted, wasn't it? To come to my private chambers to learn our magic?'

'Yes.' The blinding pain in her head and her lungs as the water had taken her over was gone, as was the feeling of heaviness in the water, of the shadowy sense of despair. She was alive. The summoning had worked, but only just. But she was determined not to appear afraid.

'So, do you remember our bargain?' Glitonea circled Faye slowly, her blue eyes looked almost black in the dimly lit room. 'You offered yourself as a weapon against Lyr. That is very serious, Faye. Before we begin, I must know that you are certain. Otherwise, our little arrangement will end.'

'I am.' Faye watched the faerie queen pace around her. 'He is no part of my life. I hate him. He broke my mother's heart.'

'But you don't know what that means. To be a weapon against him.' Glitonea delivered it as a statement, not a question. 'You would willingly make a bargain with me and not know the terms. That is rash, to say the least.'

'When you say a weapon, do you mean that it would hurt me in some way? Physically?' Faye cared nothing at all for a father she had never known, but it would be stupid of her to agree to anything that would bring harm to herself.

'No. You are half-fae and half-human. That gives you certain qualities we do not have; qualities we can use to build power in Murias. Also, Lyr is famously fond of his children. When he knows of you, he will want you with him. We will use that.'

'I don't want him. I don't want to know him at all,' Faye muttered.

'You will return to Murias. My brother has chosen you as his own,' Glitonea said, as if Faye's will was secondary to both kings, and as if Finn's appetites were unquestionable. *I will not,* Faye thought, but she said nothing. *Learning faerie magic is what will protect me from him.*

'I want power. I need power to be able to come here as an equal to your brother. I will not be his concubine,' she replied, thinking *and none of that is a lie. Only not in the way that you think.*

'Be careful what you wish for, Faye Morgan. Though you are named like a fae, and claim to be half like us, the ways of the fae are dangerous for humans.' Glitonea stared at her until Faye dropped her gaze.

'I am half fae; it's fair that I should learn its magic. That you should teach me,' Faye stilled the nerves in her stomach and steadied her voice, meeting Glitonea's gaze again. She couldn't show fear; she sensed that the faerie queen would use any weakness against her.

'I should do nothing other than send you back where you came from and let him use you as he wants,' Glitonea snapped. 'But your offer is interesting; the war with Falias goes badly for us, and we need whatever help we can get. However, the teaching of magic to mortals is forbidden, so no-one can know of our bargain. I will teach you here in my quarters; call me at the tideline and I will come for you. Is that agreed?'

'I agree,' Faye said, steeling herself. She had come too far now to go back, whatever the cost..

'I seal our agreement with my kiss,' she said. 'Now you kiss me and say the same thing.'

Faye repeated the promise.

'Finn must not know,' Glitonea said as Faye's lips touched her right cheek. 'He would not like me to be giving you our secret power. You are his lover, and faerie kings dislike their lovers to have much power at all,' she said in a low voice, as if someone might be listening. 'While you are with me, you must not leave this room unless I show you where to go or I am with you. He will not know you are here; my quarters are protected with my magic. But go anywhere else in the kingdom, and he will know. And, outside these rooms, you will feel the effects of his enchantment upon you. You know how that feels by now.' Glitonea's blue-black gaze was penetrating. 'Do you understand? Not even for a chance to win the war will my brother change his mind about you. I, fortunately, am clearer-headed,' she said, quietly. 'And, when you come back to be his lover,' she said, raising her eyebrows at Faye when she opened her mouth to disagree. 'When that happens, you must not lose your head and tell him the magic I have taught you.'

Faye nodded. 'I understand,'

She would not tell Glitonea the truth, that she would never go back to Finn. The faerie queen was being disloyal to her brother by teaching Faye magic. Perhaps she was so intent on masking her own betrayal from her brother that she did not detect Faye's duplicity.

'Then we will begin,' said the faerie queen, and the flames in the lamps around the walls glowed bright, filing the chamber with blinding incandescence.

Chapter 29

Glitonea took Faye's hand and led her to the golden table and the ice sphere. As well as the sphere which hung above the table, not tethered in any way that Faye could see, the table held a large golden chalice, the bowl of the cup easily a foot wide, and engraved with the familiar spirals that were everywhere in the castle. Yet on the chalice Faye recognised the alchemical symbol for water, the triangle with its point facing downwards. The cup was half-full of water which glinted silver in the odd light, and Faye saw a seven-pointed star engraved on its front. Alongside the large chalice, seaweed and shells were strewn on the table.

'This is the castle of Murias; the cup is its magical symbol and greatest treasure,' Glitonea said, watching Faye's face as she admired its beauty. 'This is where you will learn our magic,' she gestured to the altar table. We have made our bargain. I will teach you the magic. Whether or not you can wield the power is another thing.'

'I'm a quick learner,' Faye said, gazing into the golden chalice, where images formed and bled into each other as the candlelight flickered on the water. 'You'll only have to tell me something once.'

'Fine,' said Glitonea, and waved a censer of sweet-smelling incense over the top of the chalice. 'Then pay attention.'

As Faye gazed obediently into the chalice, and as Glitonea chanted strange words in an odd, ancient-sounding language, something shifted.

The perspective in the castle room changed, and she found herself either tiny, inside the chalice itself, or the chalice itself was suddenly impossibly large. It made Faye think of *Alice in Wonderland* for a moment.

Yet, as she looked around, the room was at normal proportions; it was the chalice that had grown, and she found herself inside it as if she was in a deep golden pool. The water was cold, but not freezing; with her feet on the bottom of the... cup? pool? she didn't know – the water covered her naked shoulders. Her dress and boots had disappeared.

Glitonea stood outside of the chalice and stretched into it, pulling a crystal wand over the surface of the water.

'*So is the test of water also the healing of it; so is the magic of water,*' she intoned, and drew a seven-pointed star on the top of the water. As she did so, the star lit up blue and Fay felt the temperature of the water change, warming to something more pleasant than the initial cold.

'See your power on the surface of the water,' Glitonea instructed, as images and sequences, symbols and faces came up as if from the bottom of the chalice, breaking onto the skin of the water like drowning faces fighting for air. Faye stepped back, horrified at the effect, but Glitonea held her shoulders and forced her to stay where she was.

'No,' she said, firm but not unkind. 'You must do this. To have the power of Murias you must accept your shadow and heal it. Our power is different to that you have been taught, but you must welcome it in. You must integrate your fae and human self to have the power you desire.'

Faye recoiled from the faces that were pushing through the water, but she took a deep breath and gave herself over to it.

On the surface now, the faces were becoming familiar. They were women's faces, and, Faye realised, they bore a common resemblance to hers. She watched as the features morphed from one woman to another:

sometimes a longer nose, sometimes the hair a different colour or style, but all of them somehow similar.

It wasn't until Grandmother's face blended into Moddie's and then hers that she realised she was seeing her ancestors; an unbroken line of Morgan women, stretching through the years like a ribbon unrolled. Her voice caught in her throat.

'Oh... I...' She didn't know what to say, and felt tears come.

'Don't fight it. This is your magic. Take it.' Glitonea's hands on her shoulders felt more like support rather than restriction now, and Faye was grateful for them.

In the water, the Morgan women clustered around Faye, wanting to be acknowledged. Wanting to give her something of themselves. Each one held out a gift, and she knew that she had to take them all, even the things she didn't want to receive.

Some of the women held out bones and skulls. Some held spheres of light or swirling darkness. Some gave her plants and flowers; some handed her crude figures that appeared to be crafted from mud and old pieces of cloth, or swatches from their dresses. Everything she took was made of water and disappeared as soon as she held it, but she had the sense that she retained all the gifts somehow; each was like a memory, firmly committed into her ancestry. She took it all, going around and around in the chalice until she had taken everything that the women had to give. And, at last, she stood at the centre with them around her, and they stepped forward, into her.

It was disorienting, terrifying and beautiful at the same time; Faye heard Glitonea's voice in the distance telling her to *accept, just accept this*. So she did, opening herself to her ancestors' spirits which didn't possess her as much as reconnect themselves with the traces of them that already existed in Faye. *We were always with you*, they said, the mothers and grandmothers that had helped shape every single part of who Faye was. Whose breath was in her lungs, whose blood ran in her veins, whose weaknesses and strengths were hers. They surrounded her in circles, four or five deep and radiating out, outside of the chalice and into the walls of the castle. Faye had the sense that the mothers went on forever, and that from now on they would always be watching over her, loving her, supporting her so she would never feel lonely or unsupported ever again.

She felt their embraces and closed her eyes, secure in the love of her grandmothers. It had always been there, waiting: Glitonea had merely shown her the way. And she was only dimly aware of Glitonea snapping her fingers, making the chalice shrink back to its ordinary size back on the altar, returning Faye back to normal, standing beside her in the faerie castle.

Chapter 30

'We are in Murias, Realm of Water. In the middle of the four faerie kingdoms, over the four crystal bridges stands the Crystal Castle of the Moon. That is where She who is the Highest Power resides,' Glitonea intoned, a week after her first lesson. There was no asking how Faye was; the faerie queen was patient with Faye, but there was a remoteness about her that had no conception of human niceties like small talk. As before, Faye had summoned her at the tideline, this time at the half moon, and Glitonea had transported her to Murias in a moment of swirling hyper-reality. It was nothing for her, a faerie queen, to transport Faye to her quarters. She was all-powerful, and Faye shuddered at the thought that Glitonea could summon any human to her whenever she wished, and keep them there for as long as she desired. She did not seem to need the help of any enchanted jewels or magical tools.

Not having had to fight so hard against Glitonea this time, as they had already made their bargain, the process was far less exhausting for Faye, but the summoning, with its spiralling, all-encompassing power, was as difficult as before.

The week in between had been tough. Faye was increasingly wary of Finn's threat to her and to Rav, who she was still avoiding, as well as yearning to learn more from Glitonea. But the faerie queen had forbidden her from doing so until at least a week had passed. The integration of her ancestors would take a long time to settle into her energy field, she said, and Faye had felt it. Every night she had vivid dreams that were sometimes nightmares; more than one night she dreamed of Grainne Morgan at the stake, making her escape into the sea. She was grateful for the mundanities of the shop; deliveries, customers, pricing and arranging the window display. It had made her feel almost normal.

'I thought there were four faerie realms. The four elemental kingdoms?' Faye said.

'There are four kingdoms. The Crystal Castle is not a kingdom. It is the centre of our realms. Morgana Le Fae herself; Mistress of Magic, my sister, the Faerie Queen of the Silver Moon, lives there,' Glitonea answered. Today her golden hair was loose and completely straight; she wore a silver circlet that dipped down in a point onto her forehead, and her gown was diaphanous and black, tethered only at the shoulders with clasps in the shape of crescent moons, jewelled with diamonds.

'She's… like an empress, then?' Faye was confused.

'No. She does not rule. She takes no side in war; our disagreements are nothing to her, and we do not involve her in our disputes. She is a neutral place of power. She is eternal.'

'Aren't you all… eternal?' Faye asked. Finn had told her he was much older than he looked, but she didn't know if that meant he was immortal.

'We do not die in the same way as you, but we can be replaced,' Glitonea answered. 'But our immortality is not of your concern. This is the next magic you will learn. You will speak with Morgana Le Fae and bring back whatever wisdom she bestows on you.'

'What will I do when I find her?' Faye asked. '*How* do I find her?'

Glitonea walked behind the altar table and drew aside one of the long curtains that hung on the walls as in the other castle rooms.

Behind the curtain Faye saw a tall door, enamelled with what looked like gleaming white shell. Glitonea unlocked the door and beckoned to Faye, who followed in wonder at what lay beyond.

'As you are half-fae, you can walk the crystal bridge.' Glitonea pointed out a glistening, silvery-white crystal bridge that stretched across a deep ravine. Below, Faye could hear the sea, but not see it. She shivered; the bridge was narrow and had no sides; it was barely the width of her body. She realised that the faerie queen had not answered her first question.

The bridge was lit with the glow of a vast crystal castle that sat on its own island in the distance. Faye could see its pink-blue sheen reflected in the glassy crystal near to her. It must have been a mile away, but she could see it clearly and she wondered how big it was, if its light shone this far.

'That's the… that's where Morgana Le Fae is?' she breathed, gazing across.

'The place of all magic,' Glitonea answered. 'I can teach you little else if you do not experience what awaits you there.'

Faye felt her resolve waver, but if this was her way to power, then she was going to take it. The faerie magic was so different to what she had learned from Moddie, or even from Grandmother, and it had changed her already, even in such a short space of time. It was subtle and full of strange delight. Glitonea's magic completed her. It sustained a part of her soul, and now that it had been fed, it hungered for more.

She stepped onto the crystal bridge, concentrated on putting one foot in front of the other, and didn't look back.

When she reached the other side, she looked behind but couldn't see whether Glitonea had left the door open or closed. She had no idea how long it had taken for her to walk over, either; time was elastic in the faerie realm. In the ordinary world, walking the bridge might have taken years.

As she set foot on the island, she heard singing. Faye closed her eyes and the strange rhythm of the song took her into a light trance; the tune was haunting, and yet it made Faye's heart soar.

Now that she was close to it, the castle was strangely small, considering that she had seen it from so far away. It had seven tall, twisting spires that glowed and pulsed gold, white, pink and blue under a vast moon that hung in the black sky, bigger than it could ever be in the ordinary world. The walls were high and contained no windows, and they jutted out in points to her right and left. She wondered if, from above, the castle was the shape of a seven-pointed star, and guessed that it was.

The mist melted away as she stepped forward and followed the path uphill. To her left, the path fell away into a sharp grey cliff that led down to the crashing blue-black sea. Faye felt no fear of it now, but stayed on the path nonetheless. There was a smell of sea spray and, underlying that, the sour tang of seaweed. It was a steep climb, but there were steps cut into the rough grass and she took them evenly.

When she reached the top, she looked down and saw that she was standing on a carpet of pink rose petals. The smell of rose captured her in its soft, sweet kiss.

Faye felt the sea breeze on her face and held out her arms in pleasure. The energy vibration was high here; it was like standing inside a rose quartz crystal, her favourite stone to use in meditation, in healing, magic, everything. She liked to have a big piece of it nearby when she made her incenses in the shop. She thought of it, her safe place, for a moment, but not because she needed to protect herself. More, that there was so much that she wanted to do there when she returned home: she was learning so much. She could *do* so much more.

As Faye smiled up at the castle, a golden door appeared in front of her where she couldn't have missed it before. A sudden breeze blew the rose petals up around her feet and cleared a path to the door; she laughed out loud. This was the way in, then.

She pushed the door and it opened easily, so she stepped inside.

Immediately, the sound of singing intensified. The space opened up to her as she walked in; a wide, circular palazzo, open to the elements; she could see the seven corners of the castle lead off the main centre. There did not seem to be any other rooms or floors.

The main courtyard was partly covered by a tiled roof, with a large circular opening in the middle, the roof held up with gold pillars. She walked to the centre, wondering what she should do.

As she stood in the centre of the palace, at the very middle of the circle, looking up at the moon above her which seemed to fill the whole space, three wide moonbeams bathed her in a silver glow. A figure emerged from the light; she coalesced from the moonlight, pulling her form from the stability of the stones and the hill. Faye could see silver blood under her black skin. The shape merged and drifted in the moonlight; first, she was a pre-Raphaelite maiden, then she changed, a crone's face, then a harpy that made Faye gasp a little.

She stood in front of Faye and held out both of her hands.

'My lady,' Faye murmured. 'Am I in the presence of the Faerie Queen of the Moon?'

The woman was more beautiful than any human could be; made of moonlight, she was pure luminescence.

'I am Morgana Le Fae, Mistress of Magic. Blessings on you.' The queen nodded gracefully.

'Blessings on you,' Faye echoed, filled with the overwhelming sense of peace she usually felt when doing magic back in Abercolme; but if that was a temporary sense of otherworldliness, this was total immersion.

'I can grant you a wish, and you can ask me a question,' Morgana said, the moonlight glowing through her silver hair.

What to ask? Faye wondered, then spoke. 'How can I step into my power as half-faerie? Glitonea is teaching me. But I...' Faye trailed off, holding Morgana's hands and feeling her power sing through to her. 'I want more,' she murmured, as the faerie queen's power encircled her like perfume, like lust.

'It is less about doing – not following a formula, not having the right things.'

Faye thought about the shop, full of equipment. It wasn't just witches that came to her for candles, incense, crystals and tarot cards. Busy mums bought meditation CDs and scented candles to encourage calm. University students asked her to order in books on shamanic journeying and yoga; she sold love potions to teenagers and citrine and black tourmaline crystals to businessmen who liked to carry them in their briefcases or flight bags for wealth, luck and protection. Whoever you were, there was a variety of *stuff* that was needed, one way or another, to subtly change one's consciousness, to learn a new skill, to understand a different culture.

Being in the realm of faerie and experiencing its heightened energy, Faye was starting to understand that magic in the ordinary world needed a little scaffolding, especially if one was practising it away from a natural place of power. She hadn't needed anything on the beach, because the sea and the sand had intense natural power. She probably wouldn't need anything other than sticks, leaves and flowers if she was to make magic in a forest. But in a block of flats, in a city, on a paved patio in a crowded town, people needed tools to help them focus on and raise energy. Here, in the Crystal Castle of the Moon, the power was so intense that Faye could feel it around her, touchable and pliant.

'The fae is in your heart; it is part of you. Relax and let it out. Feel your faerie heart. Hear its song,' Morgana whispered. For a moment Faye heard the singing again; it was louder, coming from the palace itself. 'You have power. Coming to my realm will help you see it. Navigate the shores and the hills of this place. We are at the heart of the power of the faerie kingdoms: Murias, Falias, Gorias, Finias. I am the Mistress of Magic at the centre of all things. Explore and regain your power, Faye Morgan. For it is not a coincidence your mother named you after me.'

'Thank you,' Faye whispered, feeling Morgana's power fill her; it began in her feet, travelled up her legs and exploded in her body with the power of a kiss, with the eroticism of Finn's mouth on her.

Morgana smiled, and where Glitonea's smile was cold, hers was fire.

'This is all you need. I am all, and you must let me in. Find yourself, Faye, remember your heritage, your ancestors, let them hold you. Let me fill you with my magic, Faye; and it will stay with you for ever.' She leaned forward and kissed Faye gently on the lips. Their mouths lingered together, and Faye felt the fire of Morgana's kiss consume her. Morgana's touch filled her soul with magic.

Morgana pulled away and traced Faye's lips with her fingertip.

'Get to know this place. This is the place of patterning.' she said. 'And, remember. I am here, for ever. You may visit me to refill your cup at any time.'

This is the place of patterning. Faye realised she was standing in what Moddie had called the astral plane; Faye had spent her whole life learning magic that began and ended here. This was where her carefully crafted poppet doll had taken its inspiration from, and this is where her instructions – her desires – had entered the ether as she sewed them into the doll. Inspiration flowed to the ordinary world from here; intention flowed upwards, to make patterns which were then transmuted into reality.

Faye nodded, and kissed Morgana's unnaturally long-fingered hands. She had no fingernails, Faye noticed, and her skin was formed of neatly overlapping black scales. When she met the queen of the moon's eyes, she was startled that they were not eyes at all, but the moonlight streamed through the place where eyes should have been as if through a slit in a black mask.

Morgana withdrew her hands and stepped back into the three shafts of moonlight, dissolving into them. Faye felt the loss of her keenly and as suddenly as her desire had appeared; she was dazed, aroused and yet fulfilled at once. Morgana had lit something in her soul, and she felt different, though she couldn't say how.

There was nothing to explore inside the crystal castle. Faye walked around the edges of the palazzo and in and out of the corners, but all there was were the walls made of their glowing crystalline material. A piece of it came away in her hand, and Faye held it up in wonder: it glowed like a lamp. Carefully, she put it in her pocket, feeling that if Morgana didn't want her to have it, it would not have come away so easily.

There were no other doors in or out except the one she had come in. Only the floor of the castle held any pattern at all, and that was the seven-pointed star of faerie, tiled in what looked like black glass or crystal against a pink-white stone.

Back outside the castle, she walked around it and approached the edge, and the wet grey cliffs fell away under her again.

She felt her breath catch. The drop was high and deep and she felt suddenly afraid, even though she hadn't before. But she took a breath and steadied herself, and let her gaze wander over the surface of the blue-black sea.

As she watched, something broke the surface of the water. She narrowed her eyes; perhaps it was a rock sitting under the water. Though she loved the sea, and her beach at Abercolme, she had always been terrified of deep water – both its power, of the storms that occasionally lashed Abercolme – and what was in it; of mysterious, leviathan-like beings that roamed in the deep oceans, in the dark. Beaches were in-between places, liminal, where water met earth. The deep water was something else.

The waves crashed over the shape again and Faye narrowed her eyes, watching it. Now that she was looking carefully at the water, she could see that it was full of life, though not in the normal way. Shapes drifted and formed, broke up again and re-formed in different patterns. Faye remembered the fairy stories she had listened to as a child, when Grandmother tucked her into bed or when Moddie sang old songs to her in the shop to keep her entertained. Seals that became women and married human men, creatures that were half-faerie, half-horse and dragged children to their death under the waves. Hags that lived in ponds and waterways, waiting to do similar. There were a lot of cautionary tales made up for children that had roamed a lot freer to rivers and lakes in their times, that was for sure. And yet a continuing thread held all the tales together; a life under the skin of the water that was its own realm and had its own rules.

But the rock was not a rock and, as Faye watched, a black head emerged from the waves, followed by a large black-scaled body. Her eyes widened.

The kelpie rose out of the sea; Faye stood on the edge of the cliff and watched it, her heart beating wildly. Here was her fear made flesh; a creature of darkness, emerging from the impenetrable black water. Scotland was full of myths of them: a black or white horse creature that drowned anyone that climbed on its back. They were said to reside around lochs and rivers, especially at night or at dusk. Like all Scottish children she had been told to beware of them, but had taken it for a cautionary tale to stop children drowning in dangerous water.

The kelpie pulled itself of the water and stood on the short beach, beneath. She had always imagined kelpies to be very like horses, but its eyes regarded her like marbles of the same blue-black water it had emerged from. It was a water elemental; a creature made from the dark sea that crashed and sang under her. A creature that knew the weight of the deep oceans; that had been birthed from the unrelenting crash of every tidal wave, and the soft gurgle of every trickling stream. It had the head and first half body of a vast horse, but its hindquarters were like a long black sea serpent.

It crawled up the cliff towards her; instinctively, she drew back, not knowing how it could make its way up rock, having no back legs. Dread panic overcame her and she began to run back towards the castle, but it followed.

When she reached the castle walls, Faye closed her eyes and tried to catch her breath. There was nowhere to go, and her lungs heaved with the effort of running. She tried to quiet herself, to tell herself that there was nothing to fear here, but she was lying to herself. The realms of faerie were perilous and full of danger; she had seen that already.

She sensed the kelpie approaching, and squeezed her eyes tight like a child would, hoping that the monster might disappear, her back pressed into the wall of the castle, her arms over her face. Even after all of her experiences in Murias, even knowing that she was half-faerie herself, her longstanding fear of the deep ocean and what lay within it almost overcame her. She cried out *no, no, no, please,* but the kelpie approached her: closer, closer.

No, I won't be afraid. Faye reached down into herself, remembering the ancestors that had appeared to her in the golden cup of Murias. Remembering their gifts, their wounds, their magics, she appealed to them for help, and something came.

It was like a memory, only it wasn't hers: a gesture of banishing, a knowing of the power of a witch's gaze, of the casting of a curse.

She opened her eyes, heart beating manically, her right hand formed into an instinctive pointing gesture, her eyes aflame with will. *Leave me!* the words were on her tongue, but the kelpie licked her hand, like a dog would.

Faye jumped, pulling her hand away.

The kelpie sat next to her, head bowed slightly; it made no move to get any closer to Faye.

She watched it, fearfully, expecting it to pounce, to move suddenly, to attack her. Yet, it sat next to her peacefully, panting slightly. The noise was somewhere between a dog and a horse after a run.

Cautiously, feeling her panic subside slightly, Faye laid her palm on the kelpie's nose, ready to pull her hand away at the smallest hint of danger. Yet, as soon as she made contact with it, she was overwhelmed by a sense of power that she couldn't pull her hand way from if she tried. The kelpie's energy was pure water, and Faye felt the joyful rush of a waterfall mixed with the furthest, darkest depths of the ocean; it was at once the brightness of a stream in a sun-dappled woodland and the insurmountable grey wall of a tsunami.

Pictures flashed in front of her eyes, and she opened them again in surprise when she saw what the images were, but it was too late; they came, like dreams, with her eyes open or closed. Faye saw her ancestor Grainne Morgan at the stake, and her heart clenched with sorrow. The intense fear of all the women who hung next to Grainne, lashed to stakes, awaiting their deaths, made her feel sick. She saw the little pouches of gunpowder tied around the necks of some of the other women and knew, instinctively, that their wealthier families had paid for the executioner to tie them there to provide a quicker death for the women. She wanted to take her hand away from the kelpie, to stop the stream of vision, but she took in a deep breath and knew that she drew power from the kelpie, too. She had asked for her ancestors' wisdom, and she was being given it.

And then, she saw further back, and the grief lessened. She saw Grainne's mother drying herbs in a room with a warm hearth fire that threw leaping shadows on its rough stone walls; she saw other women she could not name, but knew they were other Morgans, woman upon wise woman that came before her; she remembered their faces from when they had come to her in Glitonea's cup. She saw women in more and more historic dress, in petticoats and stays, in aprons and rough leather boots, trudging through the rain under slate-grey skies, looking for plants and remedies. And she saw some of them dancing, naked, under the moon, and her heart filled with joy at their freedom; in their lack of fear at practising their own magic.

Faye looked into the kelpie's unblinking stare and felt her fear melt away as it returned her gaze with its ageless seawater-and-glass eyes. Without thinking, she climbed up onto its black scaly back, and, as if it knew she would, it stretched up into the sky, and then dived back under the black water.

Faye held the image of Grainne Morgan at the stake in her mind as she gulped in one last breath of air, and went under willingly with the kelpie, just as Grainne had with the fae that had come to her aid. And, under the water, she released the last of her fear – fear of taking up space, of being herself, and of coming into her full power, which, perhaps, she had masked under a fear of the depths of water she could not navigate safely – in one long, ragged scream that the seawater swallowed as if it had never existed. Her ancestors had danced naked under the moon without fear; they had known their own power, and accepted the natural power of the moon and the sea and the earth into themselves with no qualms.

Faye felt the faerie part and the human part of her merge, and was filled with the power of both worlds. She plunged down into the deep darkness on the back of the kelpie, she found that she could breathe here too, and she was filled with a wild exultation. She screamed again, but this time, with unfettered joy, and the kelpie under her roared a jangling, unearthly rumble that made the rock shake and pulled all the other water elementals behind them, in its wake.

And when she finally returned to Glitonea, the faerie queen opened the door made of glistening shell. And Faye Morgan, who knew light and shadow, and who had gone below the waves and returned alive, slid off the black water kelpie and strode back into Murias with a piece of pink crystal in one pocket and three rose petals folded securely inside a single black kelpie's scale in the other.

Chapter 31

'Where've ye been, Faye? It's been three days and nae word,' Annie waved her spare shop keys in her friend's face. 'Just as well I had these, eh?'

Faye went to the kitchen to make herself a tea; she was freezing. In Glitonea's chamber she had walked in the rose-scented air in the diaphanous blue gown; she had dived into the blue-and-black sea on the back of a kelpie and felt nothing but comfortable. In Abercolme, she couldn't get warm, even with two jumpers, a thermal vest and thick socks under her jeans.

'Don't shout. I feel terrible enough,' she muttered, hugging herself to get warm. 'It's freezing in here. I'm going to put the electric heater on.'

'What're ye on about? It's almost June.' Annie frowned at her friend, clearly concerned. 'Are ye ill, sweetheart? Why didn't ye say? I rang and texted but there was no answer, I thought ye'd just left. Packed up and gone on holiday or something.'

'Oh… Yes, I was ill, that's right,' Faye grasped at the easy excuse. 'I'm so sorry, Annie. I was so out of it. Hallucinating.' It wasn't even that much of a lie. She'd been in the faerie kingdom; the most hallucinatory of places. She checked her phone; there was a text from Rav and a missed call. *Please, Faye. I want to talk. I miss you.* She sighed. She wanted to reply; her fingers hovered over the screen. But she thought of Finn and knew he was serious when he threatened her. If she wanted to keep Rav safe, she couldn't see him any more. The thought made her heart ache, but she knew she had to be strong – at least, until she had enough power to stand against Finn if she had to.

She pushed the phone away, picking up her tea instead, gulping it down in one go.

Annie watched her warily.

'Looks like ye haven't eaten for a few days either, sweetheart.'

Faye opened the cupboard where they kept the biscuits and took out a packet of digestives and two cereal bars. She was ravenous. She had tried not to look shocked when Annie had told her that her time in the crystal castle had taken her away so long. Glitonea hadn't said how long it had been, and when she had returned, had asked her nothing, merely nodding when Faye requested some time at home.

'No. Starving,' she replied between bites of the bars: vegan ones that Aisha brought in most weeks.

'Okay, well. Next time drop me a text. Or ring and just groan down the phone, eh? I'll know it's you. I'll come round with a takeaway or something.' Annie's tone softened, and Faye smiled apologetically at her friend. Next time she visited Glitonea, she would need to work out some better excuses for why she was away.

'Okay. Sorry. Love you,' she repeated, and reached for her friend's hand, covered in silver rings. She squeezed it affectionately. 'What would I do without you, eh?'

''I love ye too, lassie.' Annie squeezed back.

'What did I miss when I was away?'

'Oh, not much. Aisha did some work for Rav, bit of light emailing. Made him a contact database, apparently. She said the guy has no IT ability at all. Ye didn't see him, then?'

'No, I told you. I was ill.' Faye said, though the thought of Aisha and Rav made her heart ache a little. It made her sad, but she had made the choice not to see Rav — at least until she was sure she could protect him from Finn. Perhaps it wouldn't be too long now; she was already gaining power. Merging with her ancestors and letting go of her fear about her magic had been two huge steps; she felt transformed.

'Aye.' Annie gave her a funny look.

'What?' Faye snapped.

Annie looked away. 'Nothing. Got some news of my own, that's all.' She looked uncharacteristically shifty.

'What is it?'

'I got a job. Acting.' Annie was trying to hide a grin.

Faye's anger evaporated. 'You're joking! That's fantastic, Annie! Why didn't you say? I don't mind if you're going to be away a week or so. Aisha can cover.' Faye hugged her friend. 'What is it? The role?'

'Ah. That's the thing, see. It's in London, sweetheart. It's TV. A series.'

'A series? Wow!' Faye beamed. 'How many episodes are you going to be on?'

Annie sighed and pulled away from Faye.

'All o' them,' she said. 'It's a new show. They've put me in for six months and see how I go. Maybe permanent. I've got to move away, Faye. To London.'

Faye felt thunderstruck.

'London?'

'Aye. I'm sorry, sweetheart. I'm going to miss ye like crazy.'

'But why didn't you say before? That's where your audition was?'

'Aye, well, I didn't think I'd actually get it, did I? Outside chance, I thought, but I had an old girlfriend I wanted to call in on, an'... well. Here we are.'

Faye felt tears of shock well up in her.

'But what will I do without you, Annie?' she whispered, and Annie enveloped her in a hug again.

'Aw, now. Come on. Ye've got Rav now, aye? Though I didn't see him bringin' ye groceries and holdin' your hand while you were sick, mind ye,' she tutted. 'Still, I know ye'll be okay, sweetheart. An' I'll come home for weekends here and there. It's just that the filming's pretty intense, they said. Not many days off for a while, aye.'

What could Faye say? That she didn't really have Rav in the way that Annie thought? That she really needed her friend, even though she hadn't yet told Annie anything about Finn or Murias?

But as she looked into Annie's green eyes, she didn't have the heart to ruin this for her. She wouldn't say anything; she could do it on her own. She didn't need Annie looking out for her all the time any more. And this was the big break Annie had been waiting for.

'What show is it? One I've seen?'

'*Coven of Love*,' Annie shrugged. 'Stupid title, aye. But it's about these three modern witches that are looking for love in London. They said they liked my interest in the subject, and they wanted a Scottish witch as a character, so. Life imitates art, aye,' she winked at Faye. 'Tell me you're happy for me, lassie?' she asked, quietly.

Faye couldn't stop the tears coming, but she smiled through them.

'Of course I'm happy for you,' she said, but her face betrayed her, and she sobbed into her best friend's shoulder. 'I'll just miss you, that's all.'

Annie patted her on the shoulder. 'I'll miss you too, you daftie,' she said, but there was a tremble in her voice too.

'When do you leave?' Faye mumbled.

'Saturday. I'm going stay with the ex for a while, until I find a place of my own,' Annie's voice burred in Faye's ear.

'That's only three days away,' Faye felt her heart wrench further. 'Do you really have to go so soon?'

'Prep starts next week. That's the way of these things, Faye. They have to see me for wardrobe fittings, rehearsals, the lot.'

'Oh.' Her voice was small; she felt powerless, suddenly, like a child. Everything was changing too fast.

'Faye? Are you okay? Is there something you need to tell me?' Annie peered at Faye's tear-streaked face. 'Is it Rav? You'd tell me, aye? If there was something wrong?' She looked worried. 'I don't like to leave ye this upset, sweetheart.'

Faye shook her head hurriedly and wiped her eyes. This was Annie's big chance and she wasn't going to spoil it.

'I'm fine. Really.' She forced a smile onto her face. 'We can have a little party to send you on your way,' she added.

Annie nodded.

'Aye, why not. Say a proper goodbye. I'll miss Abercolme, the old place, aye. But I'll miss ye the most, Faye Morgan. I need to be blasted for the next two days to get through it.'

Faye laughed.

'I'm serious,' Annie insisted. 'Out of it.'

Chapter 32

'He's a nice guy.' Aisha poured hot water into mugs for them both, then splashed in milk and pressed the tea bags out firmly on the sides of the cups. 'Funny. And he let me borrow some of his vinyl. He's got a wicked collection.'

It was Saturday and Faye had a hangover. Annie had got up early for her flight to London; they'd said a final misty goodbye sometime in the early hours before Faye had passed out in her bed; unusually, compared to recent events, she'd stayed in it, alone, and woke up with a headache like a drill.

She had to open up, though; tourists were finding their way to Abercolme for the summer and Saturdays were her busiest day of the week. Already the shop was full of customers milling between the scented candles and the tarot card display, leafing through the book where Faye kept sample cards of each deck.

She'd purposefully asked Aisha about Rav after Annie mentioned her helping him out with the festival, wanting to hear some news of him, anything. He had texted again and she hadn't replied. She felt wretched not being able to reply, but it was for the best.

Faye felt hopeless, weighed down by the idea that Rav and Aisha might have been getting close; sharing laughs, talking about music, all the pleasant, normal things that she could have enjoyed with Rav if she had never got involved with Finn Beatha. Any number of opportunities could present themselves for them to accidentally bump heads, for their hands to touch, for them to share eye contact for one micro-second too long. Those things were all it needed. And there was no reason why they shouldn't.

'He really likes you, you know. You could be a wee bit nicer to him.' Aisha broke into Faye's thoughts; Faye noticed a blush rise on Aisha's cheeks.

'Does he?' Faye sighed. 'Well, I like him too. It's complicated.'

'Is it?' Aisha drank her tea and looked innocently at Faye. 'Why?'

'It just is,' Faye didn't want to explain – couldn't explain – about Finn. What could she say? That she was learning faerie magic so that if the jealous faerie king she had become involved with turned on Rav, she could stop him enacting whatever punishment he wanted on both of them? For a moment Faye reflected that she had never before in her life been involved with two men at once (although one wasn't technically a man). She smiled ruefully to herself. Wasn't this what witches were supposed to do? Enchant men and drive them mad with lust? Wasn't that what many innocent women were put to the stake for supposedly doing? Perhaps Grainne Morgan *had* been one of them.

Of course, the ones who were persecuted as witches in Grainne's time often weren't witches at all. Faye shuddered as she thought of the accounts she had read of the horrifying torture and deaths inflicted on innocent men and women who had often had the misfortune of arguing with the wrong person, or just being odd, disabled or poor enough to be blamed for the slightest of things – a sickly cow, a rash; or, you could have the other curse, of beauty: an attractive woman who refused the advances of men in her village could just as easily be put to the stake for 'enchanting' them.

Faye watched Aisha; her long-lashed eyes, her clear skin and shiny black hair. She imagined them – Aisha and Rav – laughing together. Talking about bands they liked. Listening to music together. Faye's stomach twisted with a secret jealousy and she was shocked at herself.

'Faye? You disappeared off there a minute. Away with the faeries. We're getting busy.'

'I'll be right there.' Faye looked at her phone. There wasn't a new message from Rav… but as she hadn't answered the previous ones, it wasn't that surprising. The bells near the shop door jangled as it opened, and she looked up, hopefully, wanting to see him, but it was only a couple of middle-aged women she didn't know.

She washed up her cup and pottered around in the little kitchenette. *No good can come of thinking about Rav*, she chastened herself. *You've made your decision: now, stick to it.* Leaving her phone in the kitchenette on purpose, she went out to help Aisha on the shop floor. She unpacked a box of different-coloured little silk bags, herbal resins in small pouches and some new crystals. The bags reminded Faye that she hadn't made any new incenses for a while, and the shelf where she usually stacked her pretty glass jars, labelled with her own brand, Mistress of Magic, was looking sparse.

'Might go for a forage later,' she mentioned to Aisha, who nodded. Faye made all her incenses with as many locally sourced herbs and plants as she could; there was no need for some of the strange and unusual ingredients she sometimes saw added to herbal remedies sold to burn or to drink. Plants worked best in magic when you used what was local to you, wherever you were in the world; different cultures had plants that essentially did the same things.

'Foraging's definitely a good idea. We're low on love incense in particular,' Aisha sighed. 'I could do with some of that.'

'Love spell not worked yet, then?' Faye said it lightly, but she watched Aisha closely; she couldn't help herself. To see whether there was a twinkle that meant she might have fallen for Rav, or not.

Aisha avoided her gaze and blushed.

'I dunno.' She muttered and turned away to help a woman who wanted to know which colour candle to buy for a protection spell. Faye waited for her to finish her conversation with the woman. Suspicion bloomed in her like a black rose.

'Aish. Are you *sure* you're not into someone?' Faye asked, her heart was beating hard. Aisha shook her head, but Faye wasn't convinced. It must be Rav; it *must* be. She knew it was for the best, but it tortured her nonetheless. 'Come on. You can tell me. Wallflowers' club, remember?'

She was being disingenuous, and she had betrayed Aisha in a sense – she was certainly no longer a wallflower – but she had to know. Faye had to stay away from Rav, but it would be so hard if he and Aisha started seeing each other. She knew she shouldn't ask; that the knowledge would be like sticking her finger in a cut. But she couldn't help herself.

Aisha smiled awkwardly and motioned Faye towards her.

'I can't say. It's… it's not the time,' she whispered. 'I think we need to talk. Later.' She gave Faye an odd smile and moved away from her, behind the counter to serve more customers that were waiting.

Faye turned away, saddened. She knew that Aisha and Rav had more in common than she and Rav did. Aisha was beautiful, intelligent, she loved music as much as Rav. Faye and Rav had been nothing more than a missed opportunity…

Faye's thoughts turned to Finn. She knew Finn was vain; but he had every right to be, as beautiful as he was. And if he was sulky and spoilt, like a child that had never been refused anything – he probably hadn't – well, he was a faerie king, and the fae realm wasn't like the human world.

Even so, there was a part of her that wondered how much she was excusing Finn's dark side; the way he made her feel when he touched her; when the veil of desire covered her so completely. She still wanted him; she could admit that to herself. But if anything else happened with Finn now, it had to be on her terms and not his.

She took in a deep breath as the familiar desire for Finn started dragging at the edge of her consciousness, a reflex to thinking of him. She reached out for something tangible; her hand grasped the wooden edge of the glass-fronted shop counter and she felt its solidity battle the pull of faerie which had woven itself deep into her blood now. *This is a real thing, this is wood, glass, hard things, old things that hold their shape,* she thought fiercely, forcing herself to focus back into the ordinary world. She had returned the ring; he could no longer summon her as and when he wished. She had stayed away on purpose to reduce his power over her until she could become more powerful herself; more able to resist the debauchery he had led her into, almost unconscious with desire. She did not want to be a helpless lover in Murias; she wanted mastery of it. But, she realised, she would also have to master the balance of faerie and human within herself.

She drew a breath, closed down her energy centres and imagined pulling the black cloak around herself again as she had done at the gig, when Finn had enchanted her open, naïve spirit into a half-place between faerie and the ordinary world. She was *sidhe-leth,* half-faerie. She wasn't like Aisha, and she wasn't like Finn either. She was something in between.

'Faye? Are you okay?' Aisha sounded concerned.

She let go of the solid wood in her hand and felt her faerie power mix and mingle with her breath. *I am faerie, I am human,* she repeated in her mind. The faerie power swirled a deep and seductive pink, with starbursts of black that spread and contracted like the making and unmaking of the universe. Her breath was steady: in, out, like the tide. *I am faerie, I am human, I am faerie, I am human.* And, as the power started to coalesce together, into one regular tide that sparkled cerise and black, and with the smell of roses and seawater at the edge of her senses, she repeated *I am faerie, I am human, I am sidhe-leth.*

She opened her eyes.

'I'm fine,' she sighed. Aisha took an instinctive step back.

'You look…' She frowned worriedly. 'Different.'

The queue of shoppers stared at Faye, but she accepted their gaze steadily.

'I am different,' she said. 'And I never knew how different, until now.'

Chapter 33

On her foraging walk, Faye avoided Rav's modern house by the sea, careful also to skirt the faerie path that ran alongside the house. That wasn't why she was here; she was staying in the ordinary world for now.

She was pretty certain there was no-one home anyway – the house looked deserted, so she followed her usual path down to the beach. Some things could be collected here: small shells to include in the readymade spell bags she sold alongside the Mistress of Magic incense; small spells that could still be remarkably effective. Feathers, too; she picked up a few small grey feathers belonging to sea birds, and one black crow's feather.

Walking along the land way to give a wide berth to the faerie path up the hill to the right, she filled a bag with sea buckthorn berries, intending to dry some for incense and make some into the tart jam she liked. She filled another half-bag with lovage and one with orache, which was better than spinach to eat. Pine was everywhere: she used it in incenses for purification and divination. Faye could never forage without remembering Grandmother; the way she taught Faye which plants could be eaten, which berries could be dried and burnt, like hawthorn and rosehip; which looked tasty but were poisonous, like the red yew berries that covered the trees in the churchyard so prettily every year. For an hour or more, Faye lost herself in her foraging, taking pleasure in the small finds along the familiar ways she had trod since girlhood.

As evening came, she turned and followed the coast path back to Black Sands. The pull of faerie was strong now; more insistent than it had been before. Faye recognised the familiar call in her blood as her gaze settled on the faerie pathway outside Rav's house again, and, clearer than before, she found she could see the fae twisting and running along it in their chaotic way.

In the old faerie stories, humans sometimes had their eyelids anointed with a faerie balm that meant they could see faeries in the ordinary world, but this seldom turned out to be a good thing. Faye remembered one story where a cunning woman had taken the balm and put it on her eyes herself rather than the faeries doing it. She had delighted in being able to see the faeries play their tricks on the unknowing humans, until the fae realised she could see what they were doing and struck her blind.

What did it mean if she was half-faerie and half-human? Would the fae take some kind of revenge on her for being able to go in and out of their kingdom at will? For being able to see them in the ordinary world? Or did it mean she was blessed in ways she was yet to discover?

'I thought you'd be at the shop,' Rav's voice broke into her stream of consciousness.

'Oh. Hi.' She felt the same sense of coming home when she looked at him as she had before; that there was some unarguable rightness about Rav that made her feel at ease, whatever the situation. Ease wasn't a feeling she associated with Finn, but she resolved not to think about him in Rav's presence. With Rav she was a real woman with a real life, and he desired her for who she was.

There was an uncomfortable silence.

'I'll leave you to it.' He turned away to walk back to his house.

'Rav… please. Don't go,' she pleaded, reaching for his hand.

'I didn't think you wanted to talk to me. See me. Return my messages?' Under his cold tone, he was hurt; Faye could feel it, and her heart twisted with sorrow.

'I do want to. It's just been…' she sighed, not knowing what to say.

'You don't have to explain,' he stopped walking, but refused to meet her eyes. 'I thought we had something, but I understand if you don't feel the same way.'

'We do. We did. There's a connection here, between us, Rav. But…' She bit her lip and looked away, unsure what to say.

There were some black clouds coming in, far off on the horizon. Rav nodded to them.

'Black horses coming. Better head in,' he said.

'That's a strange expression.' She was grateful for the change of subject; she sensed that he wanted to stay, to talk to her, and that was something.

'Oh. Is it? My mum used to say it about a storm. Like white horses in the sea.'

'I haven't heard it,' she laid her hand on his arm. 'Look. Can we talk?'

'Sure.' Rav met her eyes with a direct but kind stare; he didn't make any move to either remove her hand or put his own hand on top of hers.

'Okay. So… I'm sorry. About not answering your texts, about being distant. There is a reason, but it's… it's hard to explain.'

'So what are we going to talk about if you can't explain anything?' He shrugged and pulled his arm away from her hand. 'Seems to me that you think you want to talk, but maybe you just want to sleep with me and not call me after. It's cool. Whatever.'

'No! That's not it.' she said, firmly, and Rav raised an eyebrow.

'I mean to say, obviously, I did enjoy… that. I would like something with you, Rav. I just… I just… can't, right now.'

'Like I said, whatever.' He turned and started walking away. 'I'll see you round, Faye. Let me know when you've worked out what it is you want.'

The storm clouds were growing nearer; the air was changing. Now it had an electric smell like burnt ozone. Fear contracted Faye's body; she didn't want to lose Rav. Someone warm, funny, kind, who listened to her, who had wanted her, without conditions. Her heart ached, and suddenly she was sick of all her secrets. She knew she had to open up to Rav. To tell him everything.

She ran the few steps between them and made him turn around, back to her.

'Please. I will explain. Everything. Just listen.' She reached up to his face and touched his cheek. His eyes met hers again, and she dropped her hand.

'Faye, I don't know…' he muttered, and a distant thunder rumbled in the distance. 'I don't want to get involved if you're going to mess me around. I like you too much.'

She nodded.

'You're right. I'm sorry.' She turned to go. This was stupid; she hadn't planned to see Rav, and his presence was confusing. She liked being around him, but she knew that even speaking to him was dangerous. He deserved better than that.

He caught her arm.

'Don't go,' he murmured, turning her back to him and stepping close to her. He pulled her to him and stroked her cheek. 'Why does it have to be difficult? I like you and you like me. I think you do, anyway.'

'You know I do,' she confessed, her tone urgent. 'But I've got something to tell you. It's going to sound really strange. But I have to, I think.'

He pressed his finger softly to her lips.

'Tell me later. All I care about is that you like me.'

'I have to tell you, Rav. It's important. Please?' she insisted, fighting the desire to kiss him, to lose herself in him. It would be terribly dangerous, a kiss; the faeries had watched them make love on the beach before. This close to the faerie road, any number of Finn's spies might be watching, or even Finn himself.

'Fine.' His lips brushed hers, and Faye felt the heat between them build. 'But…'

He kissed her. It was a sweet yet rough and wanting kiss; his mouth was warm and she could feel her own deep yearning for him respond.

She closed her eyes and surrendered to it, unable to do anything else, despite the danger. His hands held the small of her back; his touch was at once intimate and gentlemanly, and she breathed in his warm, woody smell, remembering how he touched her, how cherished he had always made her feel, even in their short time of knowing each other.

The thunder had moved quickly, and the kiss brought on the rain, or so it seemed. The black sky rumbled ominously and lightning split it like slivers of moonlight, even though it shouldn't have been dark yet. Rav pulled away from the kiss; they both stared up at the storm for a brief moment, startled at its speed, and Faye felt a wave of unease clutch her heart.

'God. Come on, we'll get drenched,' he shouted over the thunder and guided her down the path towards the beach, but the rain came down hard and there was no escaping it.

Faye's gaze flickered to the faerie road alongside Rav's house: there was something odd happening. As she followed him, ducking her head under her arm in a vain attempt to keep off the rain, some of the black clouds had lowered to the path itself, disconnected from the sky, like a stray, angry storm-cloud, separated from the rest.

And at the same time, the seawater rose in tall waves and crashed onto the beach; when Faye looked into the waves, she saw the shapes of horses surging forward, relentless, driving the white sea spray in front of their glassy black manes. Her breath caught in her mouth. *No.*

She saw the power in their legs, which was the weight that drove the waves forward and rolled underneath them. Faye knew the power of the waves at Abercolme; knew from experience how, if you tried to wade out in a storm, they would throw you off your feet in seconds; how the cutting cold water would freeze your limbs in less than a minute, rendering you immobile; how the scorn of the water would choke you with salt and pummel your skin with sharp stones, taking your blood as a sacrifice in the water. And she knew what the horses were, and why they had come.

She could see the fae on the pathway, who seemed unbothered by the abrupt change in weather. But the black cloud, if that was what it was, pulsed in and out of sight around them; tall, bigger than most of the fae which varied in size as they had before.

Rav started running ahead. He turned back to wave something at her, but she couldn't make it out. He shouted something, but the wind took it away. He pointed to his house. She took it to mean he was going to open up so she could run straight in. She screamed at him, *run, run,* but he was too far away to hear her over the wind and the crashing waves.

Unlike her, Rav couldn't see the fae or the faerie road. He was completely ignorant of the strangeness ahead of him. And the cloudy blackness was so close to the house that Faye started running after him, a shout growing in her throat, *No, no, no*!

The shadow struggled and flailed as if it was caught; it darkened and lightened, coming in and out of focus. And Faye watched, aghast, as the black water horses – kelpies, like the one she had ridden under the water from the crystal castle back to Glitonea – rode out of the sea towards Rav with a white fire in their eyes.

She started running, then, but the kelpies were faster. They galloped towards where Rav was standing with his back to the sea, fumbling for his door keys. Their serpent tails powered them along, swishing side to side in the wet sand.

'Rav!' she shouted, but he couldn't hear her over the rolling of the thunder and a screaming sound that came with the wind and the rain. '*Rav!* No!'

He hadn't seen them; perhaps he couldn't.

Faye wanted to scream at him to run, run away as fast as he could from the kelpies, but she knew he would never be able to outrun them.

Rav turned around just at the moment that the kelpie reared up towards him; its webbed black hoof struck Rav at the side of the head, and he crumpled to the ground. The water horse gripped Rav's arm with its long teeth and swung him onto its back in one lithe, wet motion. As soon as Rav was on its back, black tethers of some kind lashed him to the horse's back; running, Faye watched as he struggled but failed to get free.

Faye screamed at the kelpies to free Rav, but they showed no evidence of having heard her. She felt the betrayal slap her in the face; she had ridden a kelpie, she had taken its leathery scale as a token of her communion with it, under the sea. And yet, that meant nothing now. She had had some power within faerie, but it seemed that was inconstant and fleeting.

'Rav!' Faye yelled again, panting with the effort of trying to catch up to the kelpie, but it was as though she was running on wet sand. Small butterfly-like faeries crowded her, trying to obscure her sight. *Mad Rav, sad Rav! Gone Rav, glad Rav! Bye, Rav! Bye, Rav!* they sang cruelly to her. She batted them away angrily.

'Leave me alone!' she shouted, but they ignored her, and the kelpie galloped away, along the faerie road and over the headland. The rain pelted her mercilessly; she was drenched already.

'Stop, please stop!' she shouted, trying to run, but no-one was listening to her, and the wet sand underfoot grabbed at her, refusing anything other than a fast walk. From the side of the road, tendrils crept out and wound around her ankles; grinning faces appeared on the buds and flowers of plants she could not identify. She shook them off, tearing at their leaves desperately as she tried to run, and failed.

By the time Faye had reached the headland and gone on to the gates to the labyrinth, Rav and the kelpie had disappeared.

Gasping for breath, she looked expectantly at the same two bearded gnomes that had let her in the first time.

'I need to enter the labyrinth,' she said, her breath ragged. 'My… my friend… has been taken,' she panted, trying to catch her breath and failing.

'She didn't say the magic word, did she?' the gnome on the left said to the one on the right.

'Nope,' said the gnome on the right. He looked up at her expectantly. 'Password,' he said, seriously.

'I don't have a password,' Faye snapped. 'I'm the king's lover. I am *sidhe-leth*, half-fae. I don't need one. Let me in, quickly. I command it!'

she said, feeling the now-familiar lassitude of being in Finn's kingdom cover her, but she fought against it and held on to her panic at Rav's abduction into faerie.

'Ooooh. She commands us!' the gnome on the left smirked.

'Password,' the other gnome said again. 'Orders from Up High. Even half-humans got to give the password or be locked out.'

'Well, I don't know the password!' Faye shouted. 'Just let me in! There must have been some mistake.'

'No need to shout,' said the gnome on the right, looking affronted.

'But… but I need to get in. That horse kidnapped my friend! My human friend. Please.' She knelt down in front of them and looked beseechingly at them both, but they avoided her gaze. 'Please. For me. I'll… I'll see you're richly rewarded.'

Faye had no idea what she was saying or indeed how she would be able to reward anything in the faerie kingdom, but she was desperate. The gnomes conferred between each other and the one on the left pointed to the silver pentagram ring she wore on her right hand; it had been Moddie's.

'We'll have that. Give us that and you can come in,' he said, stroking his beard. 'But you can't tell anyone we let you in. Say it was an accident. You just woke up in the labyrinth. They believe that sometimes.'

'It was my mother's,' Faye appealed to the gnomes. 'Have a heart.'

The gnome on the left pursed his lips.

'We want it, or you don't come in,' he repeated.

'Fine. Yes. Have it!' she pulled the silver ring off with some difficulty – she hadn't taken it off for years – and threw it on the ground between the gnomes. *Sorry, Moddie*, she thought. *I'll wear another one to remind me of you, I promise.*

'No need to be in such a hurry,' the slightly fatter gnome on the right bent down with some difficulty and retrieved it from the gravelly ground. 'Humans are so rude. I've never been to the human world and I don't want to, I'll tell you that for nothing,' he grumbled.

'Oh, whatever!' Faye muttered as both gnomes fumbled with a heavy lock on the labyrinth doors. 'Hurry up!'

The doors creaked open slowly, needing both gnomes to push them, and Faye barged through them. Yet, this time, the labyrinth loomed dark in front of her, reaching away into blackness. Faye stopped in her tracks.

'I can't see anything!' She turned to the gnomes, who were shutting the gates behind her; the last shards of the strange golden light of the entry to faerie narrowed to a crack, threatening to plunge her into oblivion. 'Please! Stop!' She ran back, putting her hands in the crack of the gate as it closed, trying to hold them apart. 'I can't see! I need light! Please, I'll be trapped in here!' she cried, but the doors closed and she had to pull her fingers out to avoid them being crushed. Faye heard the gnomes chuckling as the lock turned, and complete quiet and darkness suffocated her.

'No light for traitors, miss,' one of their voices called. 'King's orders.'

Chapter 34

Before, the labyrinth had opened to her like a rose; now, it clutched at her with branches and tendrils and refused to let her go.

Faye groped ahead of her in the dark, following only by instinct. Dead silence accompanied her concentration; the only sounds were her jagged breath and occasional cries of frustration as she met one dead end and then another. The stream of faeries of all sizes that had swarmed around her before, treading on her toes, singing, dancing, rolling and fighting, were gone. It was as though she was alone in the world.

'Help! Please, someone, help me!' she called out, but there was no reply. 'Finn! Finn, I command you to hear me!' she called in vain, but she knew there would be no answer. He had taken Rav, of that she was certain, and abandoned her here to the labyrinth; locked her in like any mortal woman. As a punishment; to stop her coming after him.

But she was *sidhe-leth*.

If I could come through before, then the only thing stopping me now is Finn, she thought. *So there's no point calling on him for help. He's angry… because Rav kissed me. Jealous.*

Faye stopped running and stood still in the labyrinth, gathering her thoughts and making herself steady her breathing. There was no point panicking.

She plunged both hands into her pockets while she thought and, as she did so, her fingers closed around the crystal in her pocket. She brought it out and held it up to her face; it still held a tiny amount of luminescence from the crystal castle where she had taken a little from one of the walls; she had kept it with her constantly since bringing it back with her.

Faye held the crystal up, but it made little difference to the dark. Yet she felt that it had more power, that she could use it to help her, if only she knew how. She racked her brain, trying to remember the crystalline singing that seemed to have come from the walls of the seven-pointed faerie castle in the centre of the faerie realm. It was the centre of all the magic of faerie.

She could remember the words, though she didn't know what they meant. She began to sing the words softly, and then louder as she gained confidence. She tried to replicate how it had sounded, standing in the centre of the multi-layered harmonies that had wanted to weave her into the sacred space.

Tar a thighearna… Tar a thi… She sang the harmony. And, as she did so, the crystal began to glow, lighting up the dark labyrinth. The pinkish light filled the pathway, shining into the overgrown high corners and the mud underfoot.

Faye looked around her; now, at least, she could see where she was, though she still had no idea where to go. It wasn't going to be an easy route through this time.

As she took some tentative steps forward, she heard a voice in the distance.

She listened hard; it was very, very distant, but Faye concentrated as hard as she could.

The voice grew a little louder; still, it was only the volume of a whisper, and it seemed to be passed leaf to leaf in the dark, a shushing noise that carried a word.

Faye, Faye, the leaves whispered, circling her like a net. *Faye.*

It was Moddie's voice. Faye turned around, trying to find the source of the whisper. She was sure it was her mother's voice. *Faye. Follow my voice.*

Holding the crystal in front of her for light, she followed twist after turn, sometimes feeling as though she was walking uphill, sometimes down. But try as she might, Faye couldn't get any closer to Moddie's faint call and, all the time, she kicked away reaching branches and trailing weeds that seemed bent on tripping her up and holding her back.

At the centre of a hedged-in square she found a large silver bowl of pink roses standing on a golden cube, which reminded her of the carpet of rose petals that had surrounded the crystal castle. As she stopped to smell them, she looked down and saw the letter M scratched in the dirt by her feet.

Moddie had been here; she was close by. Somehow, she was helping Faye through the maze. Faye still missed Moddie terribly; just the sight of someone with the same colour and length of hair or the same way of laughing or holding their head made her look twice, still desperate to see that familiar face one more time.

Faye took three of the roses and picked the petals off, scattering them behind her like the breadcrumbs in Hansel and Gretel; she would need to find her way back through the labyrinth, after all.

She followed another twist and another turn and, at the far end of the next pathway, Moddie stood waiting for her, wearing a gown made entirely of rose petals. She held out her hand to her daughter.

'Come on, darling. We don't have much time,' she said, and Faye ran to her, with tears burning her eyes.

Chapter 35

Faye ran through the labyrinth, holding her mother's hand.

'To the castle! We… must… get within the castle gates. We'll be safe there,' Moddie called over her shoulder, and Faye saw that there were tears in her mother's eyes too.

'I missed you,' Faye replied as they ran, dodging branches and stones along the way.

'The paths are closing!' Moddie shouted, and pulled Faye along faster. 'I missed you too, my darling.' She stopped briefly and hugged her daughter. 'There's so much I want to tell you, but there's no time. For now, we have to get out of here.'

Faye held the crystal up higher and saw that Moddie was right; the sides of the pathway were drawing together. Some way in front of them she could see the moonlight glinting on the castle. It didn't look that far, but to get just a little further might mean running miles from one side to the other in the labyrinth.

'I don't think we're going to make it in time!' Faye shouted in reply as the tendrils grasped for her more and more aggressively; she tore them away, but they caught her again and again, twisting up her legs and wrapping themselves around her wrists.

Moddie was the same, but different. She had not aged, because there was no ageing in spirit, and in fact she looked younger than she was when she died. And there were other differences, too. Moddie's hand in hers was light and insubstantial and, as they ran, it seemed that Moddie's feet didn't touch the ground.

'We'll make it,' Moddie said. Faye remembered that determined tone. When Moddie wanted something, she usually got it. 'Remember you're half-fae. Feel the faerie power as much as you can. You can use it here. Let it fill you.'

Faye focused on the swirling cerise energy of faerie; she called it in, surrendered to it, with as much of herself as she could whilst running. She felt the black stars swell and burst inside her chest; felt the power of faerie engulf her, thrill her body, sharpen her senses.

'That's right! More! Moddie shouted. Faye took in a deeper breath and felt the power unfurl from inside her at the same time it surrounded her; it grew thicker and flowed faster, faster, until she started to lose feeling in her hands and feet. 'I've got you!' Moddie yelled as Faye's feet hovered off the ground like hers did.

The faerie power lit up the labyrinth; the deep pink flashed on the dark hedges and holes opened up and closed again at random in the tall hedged sides of the labyrinth.

Moddie pulled her towards one, but it was too small for them to fit through.

'Can you make it bigger?' Moddie breathed, glancing around them as the labyrinth continued to tighten. 'When you focus on your fae magic you can disrupt the illusion of the labyrinth. Can you control it better?'

Faye tried, but it she didn't know how.

'Sorry.' She felt a failure and the memory of standing on stage as a child and forgetting her lines returned to haunt her for a moment. But Moddie shook her head impatiently.

'No time for sorry,' she said. 'You'll learn to use it here in time. But for now, we need something else. I can't get us through this on my own. He's too strong for me.'

'Finn?' A part of Faye somehow still hoped that it wasn't her lover doing this; that there was another presence scheming against her.

'Faerie kings are jealous, Faye,' Moddie chided. 'But it's my fault. I could have taught you about your true self, about your father, about faerie, but I wanted to protect you.' Moddie enveloped Faye in a hug and Faye felt the comfort of her mother's body envelop her. She gulped away tears; she had missed Moddie so much that it hurt to see her again now. It was an ache she had become accustomed to forgetting; seeing Moddie made her remember the pain of loss.

'It's okay. I've been learning faerie magic with the faerie queen, Glitonea. So that I can come and go freely in Murias without being so… bound to Finn. I can protect myself,' Faye said shyly.

'Faerie magic? With Glitonea? How?'

'The same as you. I made a bargain. On account of being Lyr's daughter.'

Moddie caught her shoulders.

'What? No, Faye. You can't… making a bargain with the fae is dangerous. You shouldn't have done that.'

'Well, I have, so it's too late now,' Faye snapped.

'What was the bargain?' Moddie asked, but the labyrinth seemed to have sensed their halt and wrapped vines around their legs. Faye kicked them off, and pulled her mother along the walkway.

'Come on. We have to keep moving. There's no time to talk about it now. I offered myself as a weapon of some kind against him, in this war they're having. Glitonea says Lyr is fond of his children. Maybe at some point they think they can… I don't know… send me to talk to him?'

They turned a corner into a walkway that they both had to turn sideways to get into at all. Faye felt a wave of oppression wash over her and she tried to take a deep, calming breath, but the denseness of the hedges reaching in choked her.

'No, Faye! That's not what they mean. You must not...' But Moddie didn't finish her sentence. Something in the hedge reached out, as if it had arms this time, and dragged Moddie back into it. She screamed and tore at the vegetation, but in seconds it had covered her body. Faye rushed to her mother and started pulling the leaves away, but it was too fast and replaced whatever she pulled off with twice as much.

'Mum!' she cried out, but the leaves and vines were too fast.

'Faye. You don't understand, about your father. I—'

'He tried to kill you. I don't care what happens to him!' Faye cried. Grief filled Moddie's features.

'No, Faye. That's not true... I—' Moddie choked and spat out the leaves snaking into her mouth.

'You said it. I was eight, I came down that time, you were drinking with that woman from the coven. You said he almost killed you.'

Moddie shook her head, confused.

'No. Faye... he didn't. That's not what I meant.' She coughed again. 'There's no time to explain, but you're wrong. Glitonea... did you visit the crystal castle?'

'Yes.' Faye felt branches pull at her clothes; vines wrapped around her leg. She felt them circle her left wrist; she pulled away, but they were too strong. Desperately, she stripped vegetation away from Moddie with her right hand. If Moddie didn't mean that her father, Lyr, had tried to kill her, what did she mean? It was so long ago, and Faye had been just a child. What had Moddie's *exact words* been? Whatever this meant, she couldn't think about it now.

'Did you bring back any of the rose petals? From Morgana's castle?' Moddie retched as the hedge reached the back of her throat. Faye nodded, horrified. 'Cast one on the ground. Hurry!' Moddie coughed as the vine disappeared into her mouth.

A leaf brushed Faye's own mouth; she suppressed a scream and reached into her pocket with her right hand, drawing out the black kelpie's scale which she had folded in half like a purse. Its tough, leathery hide had kept the three petals safe underwater, when she had ridden the kelpie and ever since.

The plants had both of her legs now and would twist into her mouth the next time she opened it; she knew. They would reach down inside her gullet, like they had with Moddie, spreading new roots inside her lungs and stomach, assimilating her into the labyrinth. She had a sudden vision of herself with leaves and stems sprouting from the corner of her eyes, pulling her eyelids open in an expression of permanent horror as they wove her flesh back into the verdant green.

Faye took out one of the rose petals and threw it into the ground between them. At the same time, Moddie shouted *Tar a thighearna… Tar a thi!*

A scream cut through the air. Faye's last vision, bathed in the light of the glowing crystal, was her mother's face, contorted with pain.

Chapter 36

When Faye opened her eyes she was standing behind a pillar in the great hall and the faerie ball was in full swing. She was alone.

She slumped behind the stone and wept, her tears sudden and bitter. To have her mother back so suddenly, after all that time, and have her taken away again so cruelly was shocking; it was nightmarish, a stab into a heart that had managed to order its grief, to manage it so that it no longer consumed her. She sobbed like a child, hugging her knees, wanting Moddie back. She whispered her mother's name between her tears, hoping to summon her, but the cacophony of dancers continued behind her, and Moddie did not come.

Faye peered out from behind the pillar at the whirling dancers. Around and around they went, faster and faster, while the faerie pipers and fiddlers played their jig. Faye was reminded of the fairy tale of the red shoes; of the mysterious gypsy dancer who would give her shoes to innocent girls but, once the shoes were on, they could never be taken off and would dance the wearer to death. This dance was underpinned with a similar strange kind of desperation. Faye saw more clearly now that many of the dancers were human, but emaciated, being pulled around unconscious like dolls, danced to the point of exhaustion.

She hadn't noticed before, when she was in the dance. Because she had been with Finn, and Finn's glamour covered over the things he didn't want her to see. She closed her eyes as a vision of Moddie's face covered in vines struck her like a sword. Was Moddie alive? Was she stuck there in the labyrinth for ever, as part of Finn's punishment for helping her daughter? She was in spirit already, and yet the hedge had held her fast. But nothing was as it seemed in Murias; it was a place of illusion, woven with terror and desire in equal measure.

A knot of dancers reeled dangerously close to the pillar; the faeries among them screeched with the wild joy of the dance. Faye closed her eyes and held her breath. If she was seen, she knew she would either be cast out of Murias, or punished in another way. Moddie had helped her get this far against Finn's wishes. But she owed it to her mother to save Rav.

The dance was slowing. Faye watched Finn Beatha enter the ballroom with Rav at his side. Rav's hands were bound with a golden rope; he stumbled as he walked, and Finn shoved him forward.

The faerie dance slowed to stare at its newest participant.

Faye watched Rav stumble. She wanted to go to him, to wrap him up in her arms, but she knew she couldn't.

Finn strode into the centre of the dance, pulling Rav behind him. The music stopped suddenly; the dancers halted. There was an expectant hush. Now that the dancers had stopped moving, some bodies fell to the floor; no-one made any move to pick them up.

'Be blessed, faeries of the dance, for you have a new dancer!' he cried, and the crowd cheered, though Faye could hear forced jollity in the throng. 'This foolish human sought to take my property from me. Perhaps you will all deign to teach him some manners!' he cried. There was a loud cry of approval from the crowd, but it rang hollow to Faye's ears.

Watching the dance from the edges, and no longer under Finn's enchantment, the great hall was darker and more shadowed than Faye remembered. The gold and silver lamps that had glowed so merrily were dirty, the glass smokily opaque; now they cast only a dim, dull orange light. The hammered gold bowls of candlelit water were dark; no light reflected off their surfaces. The walls of the castle were more soot-blackened than Faye remembered; the lush, velvety tapestry hangings that she remembered from the rest of the castle were here too, but on the one nearest her, she made out pornographic scenes embroidered into the muted blues and dull orange hues. She looked away, shocked at the explicit imagery and the tortured faces of the humans and faeries.

Finn pushed Rav into the centre of the dance and motioned to the band to start playing.

'Dance, dance!' he cried out as the crowd started its mad whirling once again. 'For you will never stop; the faerie reel is the power of the Kingdom of Murias! Were it to stop, our lights would go out. Our power would dim. So, dance! Faeries and mortals, dance and be merry. For the love of your king!' Finn clapped and danced through the crowd. Faye's heart beat fast in her panic. She had to get away, and take Rav with her. But how?

The music grew louder. Faye put her hand in her pocket distractedly, feeling the leathery kelpie's scale. She watched as Finn made his way through the crowd, kissing faeries, picking them up, spinning them around and putting the down again with a smile. Jealousy twisted in her belly, especially when he held the young pretty fae around their tiny waists and whispered in their ears. Faye watched as they blushed and giggled at whatever he said, and how they watched him as he danced away from them, to the edge of the circle. She watched Finn, in the dark hall, full of the depravity his enchantments had masked. His power still drew her to him; like the girl in the red shoes, she wanted to dance. The music was a siren call; she wanted to stop up her ears like the sailors had done in the old myth, to ignore the sirens' seductive song. But she had the start of an idea, and she gripped the kelpie's scale tight in her pocket.

Faye waited for a swell of dancers at the edge of the circle to reach where she was hiding, and she stepped into the dance just as Finn stepped out of it and watched as it spun around.

The pace had quickened already; the pipers were playing at full speed, and Faye felt out of breath almost immediately.

The shapes and beings passing her were so fast at times that they were only a blur, but sometimes the crowd slowed, seeming to take a temporary breath before it swung around in its endless dance. In those moments skeletal faces leered at her and strange faeries with cavernous bodies and upside-down heads and feet that were laced with bulbous veins, or, worse, covered in blood, pressed against her. She couldn't see Rav.

She felt as though she was dancing on glass; that if she had the red shoes from the fairy tale on her feet, now they were aflame.

The dance swung her around and around, closer to where Finn stood, surveying the dancers with a critical eye. Faye craned her neck to catch sight of Rav; she could see flashes of his black hair through the faeries at the centre of the circle who spun like dervishes, and she could hear his voice calling out for help. *Just stay there*, she willed him. *Don't do anything. I'm coming to get you.*

But she was being pushed closer and closer to Finn and Faye couldn't fight against the tide.

Don't look this way, she silently begged. A few more moments and Finn would see her; he'd know that she had broken through the labyrinth, despite his best efforts to keep Faye out.

Carefully, shielding the kelpie's scale with her body from the dancers, she reached into it and took out one of the rose petals from the faerie castle. She replaced the kelpie's scale in her pocket. A group of spiralling dancers caught her and pulled her into the centre of the circle.

Faye saw Rav's back and shouted his name, but the music was too loud. *Turn around, please turn around and see me*, she willed him, but Rav was utterly lost in the panic of the dance. Some kind of troll was laughing, pulling at Rav, trying to trip him up; on his other side, a bare-breasted faerie with beautiful blue wings and violet hair floated in front of him, laughing when Rav pulled away as she tried to kiss him.

She could no longer see Finn at all. She had no way of knowing whether he was still there, whether he had seen her, or if he had left the ball. She stopped, resisting the push and pull of the faeries around her, and craned her neck, looking for him. The rose petal was limp and hot in her hand, and she knew that if any of these creatures jostled her, she would drop it.

Suddenly, Faye thrust her hand up into the air and launched the petal as hard as she could, not expecting it to go any further than dropping on the floor, it was so light. And as she let the petal go, she shouted the words Moddie had just moments before in the labyrinth, hoping for the best. *Tar a thighearna... Tar a thi!*

The rose petal floated upwards, growing in size.

The music continued and the dance spun Faye around, but the petal spread wider and wider above them until it covered the whole dance, hanging above their heads like a silk barrage balloon. Some of the faeries stopped and looked up, but most were too lost in the dance, and the ones that had stopped were in danger of being trampled.

Tar a thighearna... Tar a thi! Faye shouted again, and the petal split into a million pieces, falling onto the dancers like rain.

The dance stopped, and every single faerie was frozen to the spot. Only the humans left among them moved; some cried out, but most of them slumped to the ground in exhaustion, their faerie captors no longer whirling them around. One girl, trapped in the frozen arms of her toad faerie suitor, screamed to be let go, but the man-sized toad's legs grasped at her greedily even under the enchantment.

At the other side of the hall Faye saw Finn, rooted to the spot, his gaze trained on her. She halted in fear for a moment, heart beating wildly. Finn's eyes watched her keenly but he didn't move. *He can see. He knows I'm here*, she thought. Faye remembered his anger, even though she knew he had masked its true force. She had betrayed and disobeyed him, and his eyes burnt with fury. *I have made my choice*, she thought, and met his gaze. The fury in his eyes was far from the adoration he had shown her before, and it awoke her like a sharp slap. She didn't love Finn; now that she could see him without being under his control, she knew it was not love. It had never been love, and he did not love her. Finn Beatha did not love anyone; he took who and what he wanted and used them until they had nothing left in them.

Faye pushed through the inert bodies, through the strange, gnarled limbs and the ripped wings, to Rav, who had dropped to his knees and was cradling his left arm. Pain was written across his face.

'Rav!' she cried, and knelt down in front of him, wanting to hold him. His eyes widened in disbelief.

'Faye? You're here? How?' he stammered. The sheen of faerie was in his eyes; his pupils were dilated and sweat was pouring off him. Faye could feel Finn's stare burning her back.

'Never mind. I'm going to get you home,' she said.

She helped him up. With Rav half-leaning on Faye, they staggered through the ballroom, edging past yellow-skinned goblins, diminutive flower faeries and beast-like creatures for which Faye had no name. She turned her eyes away from the humans that lay here and there; bodies that had slowly had the life trampled from them.

They passed a girl who was still alive; her skin was sunken, barely even covering her bones. Too weak to raise an arm, she made a pleading noise as they stumbled past.

'We can't leave them like this.' Faye stopped and held out a hand for the girl; the change in her stance tripped Rav, who stumbled and steadied himself on a pillar. Faye crouched close to the girl, cradling her head on her lap. Faye couldn't carry her as well as support Rav, and the girl was so frail, so thin, that Faye felt she would break if she touched her at all.

'What can I do?' she asked the girl softly, her heart breaking. She felt a rush of anger at Finn: *how could he do this to anyone?* And then she was angry at herself, too. For not seeing. Her feet might have trampled this girl as she danced with Finn, heedless of the horrors that lined the great hall. She had been seduced. She had been stupid and powerless. *No more*, she vowed to herself, angrily.

'Kill me,' the girl whispered, her voice a rasp of desperation. 'Please.'

'No! I can't leave you here. I'll find a way. Just stay with me, all right?' The girl's eyes fluttered closed; she was barely conscious. 'Stay with me! Come on,' Faye cried, but the girl whispered something; Faye had to put her ear to the girl's lips to make it out.

'It's too late,' she said. 'This is the kingdom of faerie. This is...' The girl coughed and Faye reached for her hand and held it, feeling powerless, hopeless. 'I stayed longer than I should...'

The girl coughed again, and Faye knew she was already too far away.

'I'll stay with you, then,' Faye said, but she could see some of the faeries beginning to break free of the magic she had cast. There were too many of them to be held off for long.

Faye remembered Grandmother telling her: *The fae have their own ways, and it's not for us to judge.* But it was impossible not to judge Murias as she looked at the bodies of humans, twisted and injured, around her. *I am part of this. I am half-faerie, half of these shadows are mine*, she thought, and she felt a terrifying guilt consume her. She hadn't brought any of these men and women here, and she hadn't tortured them. Yet the faerie blood beat in her veins, and she knew what it felt like to revel in the seductive cloak of magic. That made her an accomplice to their suffering.

Rav coughed and Faye looked up; he was pale and she knew he needed her.

'He will die if you keep him here much longer,' the girl said, opening her eyes slightly.

Faye took in a ragged breath.

'Leave me,' the girl repeated. 'There's nothing you can do.'

Faye still had the bag of herbs she had gathered at the coast slung across her body. She opened it and rummaged around, watching as the faeries started to move slowly.

'I'm sorry,' she said, getting up and placing the girl back on the floor as carefully as she could. She opened the girl's mouth and placed a few flowers onto her tongue.

'Swallow this. It will… ease your journey,' she said, feeling the tears roll down her cheeks.

'Faye, please, I…' Rav cried out in pain, and she turned away from the girl, her heart hollow.

Chapter 37

'Where are you going?'

The imperious voice filled the long hall, ornately covered in gold carvings, and Faye froze.

'You seem to have a human man with you, *sidhe-leth*.' The voice laughed lightly, and the echo resonated in the quiet. 'That stunt in the Great Hall – it seems that you have learned my magic all too well.'

Glitonea stepped forward from a dark doorway and dropped her cowled hood. She was wearing a dark blue robe which covered her almost entirely. She seemed unaffected by the spell, but, as the holder of the magic of Murias, Glitonea was most likely able to release herself from spells easier than anyone.

Faye felt relief that it wasn't Finn appearing as if from nowhere, but Glitonea was still a faerie queen, and loyal to her brother. And Faye was aware that they only had moments before her spell released all the faeries, and they would be caught.

'Your brother kidnapped this man and brought him here as a punishment. If he wishes to punish me for being unfaithful to him, then I will stand his punishment. But Rav is blameless,' she argued. Glitonea arched a dark eyebrow.

'What makes you think that I will let you go? What makes you dare to ask me to ignore my brother's wishes?' she intoned, and Faye felt the ice in her voice fill the hallway; the temperature dropped and Faye felt she could see icicles start to form at the edge of the windows, the glass frosting with an iridescent blue-white covering. Nevertheless, she refused to drop the faerie queen's gaze.

'You thought that because I have taught you, that I have begun to show you the ways of the faerie realm of water, that I am your friend,' she answered crisply. 'Do not make that mistake. I am not.'

'No, but—'

'My brother brought this one here for his own reasons. He will stay here until my brother sees fit to let him go.'

'Since when do you let your brother rule you?' Faye faced Glitonea, who returned her gaze steadily.

'Finn Beatha is Faerie King of Murias, just as I am Faerie Queen. I do not expect him to find fault in my actions, and so I do not criticise his.'

'We made a bargain. I am your weapon against Lyr, when you need it,' Faye countered, slightly panicked; Rav slumped against her.

'I do not see Lyr anywhere? And I have taught you magic in return,' Glitonea glared at Faye.

'Please.' Faye could hear movement in the great hall. 'I'll do anything. But I have to get Rav home.'

Glitonea looked away and pursed her lips.

'You love this man?'

'I care for him, and I don't want him to be tortured by Finn for something that isn't his fault.' Faye looked down the hall, at shadows flickering wildly in the dim light.

'If you have a great passion for this mortal man, then I do not hear it in your voice,' the faerie queen sneered. 'My mortal lovers look at me as a queen should be regarded; they love me more than their own beating hearts, as the woman above all women. Yet you do not even know if you love this one.' She nodded to Rav, who was slipping in and out of consciousness. Faye was holding him up now, and he was heavy and cumbersome. 'Why should I help you? Your bargains are for naught.'

'But you will let him die, eventually, your lover – the one I saw you with at the dance?' Faye argued.

'A faerie lover is worth dying for.' Glitonea smiled faintly, and Faye remembered the first time she had been at the faerie ball. It had looked so different when she had been in Finn's arms; the dresses were beautiful, the fae had been masked with glittering feathers and jewels. There were no starved, exhausted bodies swept along in the chaotic and relentless tide. And Glitonea had been dancing with a handsome young man. Faye remembered him well.

'Don't you love him?' Faye asked, desperately. 'He'll die if you keep him here.'

'The fae have a different way of loving than humans do,' the faerie queen said, dismissively. 'And I can keep him with me, alive, beyond his years. There are magics that can do that. Time can be manipulated here; it runs differently to your world.' The queen smiled. 'So you see, Faye Morgan, you have nothing to bargain with, and I will not allow you to leave. Unless...' Glitonea looked appraisingly at Faye and held out her hand. 'There might be something. But you will not like it.'

Rav slumped in Faye's arms; faerie soldiers pounded towards them.

'If this is the only way, then I'll do what has to be done,' Faye answered grimly. 'Will you help us get home? If I agree to your bargain?'

'Of course.' Glitonea's smile twinkled brightly.

'What is it? What do you want in return?' Faye took Glitonea's hand, and the queen waved her other hand at the soldiers; they slowed as if they were running in syrup.

'Something you can make but I cannot. A child.'

Faye frowned in disbelief.

'What? No! That's… inhuman.'

Glitonea laughed.

'I am not human,' she agreed.

'Why… a child?' Faye stammered.

'I would have a *sidhe-leth* heir of my own. I have observed you; the power you hold from both realms. It is full of potential, but it needs teaching from birth. Lyr has his by-blows, and they give him power. I would have the same.' Glitonea regarded Faye impassively. 'Or, I can wave my hand and they will take you. And they will put you and your lover in the darkest place in this castle and leave you to rot there. It is your choice,' she smiled icily. 'And believe me, *sidhe-leth*, the dungeons here are very dark and filled with horrors you cannot comprehend.'

'It's no choice!' Faye cried. 'Please don't ask this of me.'

'Another plea. You humans are full of wants, and yet when your pleas are answered, you do not like the solutions,' Glitonea snapped. 'You are human. You can have other babies; as many as you wish. You will not miss one. And I assure you that it will be well taken care of. It will live as a Prince or Princess of Murias.' There was no compassion in Glitonea's eyes; no understanding that a baby was anything other than a possession or a pet. 'Choose. Quickly.'

I managed to get Rav away from Finn, Faye reasoned. *So I can make this right, too. For now, this is what has to be done.*

Glitonea smiled.

'You will have to leave a different way than you came in,' she called over her shoulder as she hurried along, pulling her cloak around her. 'He is watching the labyrinth.' She stopped suddenly and opened a golden door in the wall where none had been.

'Through. Quickly,' she chided. Faye carried Rav's inert body over the bottom step of the golden door, and out onto the narrow ice walkway to the crystal castle.

Glitonea raised her arms over her head and called out something in the language of faerie.

There was a ripple on top of the blue-black water, and the head of the black kelpie Faye had only half believed was real emerged from the water. Though she had ridden it successfully once before, and felt her power merge with it, now the creature terrified Faye. It had taken Rav from her; it had been Finn's creature as easily as it had been hers.

'Now. There is no time,' Glitonea reprimanded. 'Do not be afraid. It will do as I command.' Full of misgiving, but knowing she had no other option, Faye climbed on the kelpie's back and pulled Rav on with her.

'Put the kelpie scale over the man's nose and mouth,' Glitonea called up to Faye. 'It will enable him to breathe underwater.'

'What about me?' Faye shouted down from the kelpie's back; it was rising up out of the water, readying to dive down in to the blackness again.

'You are a sea witch, *sidhe-leth*,' Glitonea replied, unsmiling. 'You will breathe without it.'

Chapter 38

The last of the midsummer sun caressed the stage, casting its twilight warmth onto the audience. Some in the crowd held up their palms to the shafts of twinkling softness that spread over their heads like a cast spell, stroking their fingers through its sparkle. They were chanting, waiting for the headlining band to come onstage: Dal Riada, Dal Riada...

Finn Beatha strode onto the stage, stripped to the waist; his swirling tattoos and the symbols on his warm honey skin were painted over with blue paint, like woad on Scottish warriors going into battle. The side of his face he wore his radio mic was painted in the same blue, from forehead to chin; on the other side the audience close to the stage could see a fierce twist to his mouth. Yet, as he bowed to them, the last rays of the setting sun landed on his dark blonde hair, giving him a kind of angelic aura.

The first ten rows closest to the stage erupted in a kind of madness: screaming, crying, reaching out for him. Several women sat atop their friends' shoulders, reaching for him; one tore off her t-shirt immediately and threw it at the stage, exposing her bare breasts. He took the shirt from the stage, straightened up, smiled at her and stroked the shirt over his chest, then threw it back. Two young men, probably in their early twenties, also sat on their friends' shoulders; WE LOVE YOU FINN was painted across from one's chest to the other. Finn blew them kisses which they grabbed excitedly from the air.

'Abercolme. Finally we meet!' Finn drawled as the rest of the band took their places alongside him. The crowd roared. 'We've waited so long to be here. And what finer evening to watch the sun set over the sea than at Midsummer?'

He walked from one side of the stage to the other, cupping both of his hands in front of his face, blowing something from them into the crowd. You had to be very close to see the glitter on his hands; the front row reached out for it.

'Blessings of faerie be upon you all!' Finn cried out, and the crowd laughed and cheered as the first fast riff began, and the music of Dal Riada reached out for them.

Aisha stood in the wings of the stage, her heart in her eyes. This was what she'd been waiting for, what would make all the spreadsheets and phone calls and social media promotion worthwhile. This close, she could see the gold glitter and the braids in Finn Beatha's hair; she could see the rough texture of dark interweaving checks in his kilt. She could hear his sweet, rough voice in the second before the mic picked it up, sense the easy strength in his languid pose; this close, he was wild, raw, otherworldly.

As she watched Dal Riada spin, scream and weave their first song for the crowd, Aisha felt the same hypnotic effect she always did when listening to them. It was like finding the lull between sleep and dream, where she was still in the real world but somehow the normal rules didn't apply. The familiar songs made images in her mind; of long, twisting paths through a forest, of gilded corridors, of a dance that went around and around without ever stopping. She closed her eyes and let the fast melody enchant her body. She was dancing now, around and around, spiralling deeper and deeper.

She felt her breasts swell, a strange sensation of them being full and aching for release; as she danced she opened her eyes and watched Finn, imagining kissing him and touching his warm skin. Her body filled with a deeper sweetness; she remembered every moment of making love to him, taking him inside her. It had been unlike anything else she had ever known; even though she was a virgin when she came to him for the first time, she knew it was different than anything she could expect from a mortal man.

They had slept together only once, but it had been months since then. Aisha was impatient with the dreams where he came and spoke to her and filled her with unresolved desire, but also came to her with messages and requests; things for her to do for him in the ordinary world. He had promised and promised: a world beyond this one, where she could merge herself into the fabric of all being. He would show her life at the atomic level. He had spoken to her in the terms she understood, had taken the fascination of her scientific work and woven it into the seductive treasure of his faerie domain. If only she would help him, just a little, here and there…

At first she had connected to Finn through his music. At the concert, before she had taken Faye outside, she too had been transported to a strange place: a room with a golden four-poster bed, a room hung with blue and green tapestries adorned with strange symbols. Finn Beatha had taken her hand and pulled her onto the bed without any preamble; she was naked, suddenly, and he was kissing her. His hand stroked her thigh, and she had wanted more, oh, so much more, when Faye had jolted her away from her reverie.

The next night, in a dream, he had told Aisha to take down the hagstone charm that Faye kept hanging by the shop door so that he could enter. And, in gratitude, he had made love to Aisha a week later on the sheepskin rug in front of the hearth, inside the shop, in the middle of the day; she had locked the door behind him, but had not even thought of being seen through the long windows of the shop. He filled her with an unruly, wild lust that made her not herself; she wasn't Aisha when his fingertips grazed her nipples and she cried out for more; she wasn't herself when he kissed her neck, her throat, when he made her strip naked and stand in front of him. She didn't think twice about obeying him when he commanded her to touch herself as he watched and then, when she was almost at climax, her belly hot and sweet, made her kneel on all fours. It didn't escape her that this was the same the rug she had, not long ago, sat on whilst she, Faye and Annie had conjured their love spell. And when he entered her, kneeling behind her, she had welcomed the deep pressure of him bringing her pleasure closer and closer until she ground against him, crying out, and he held her waist and then gripped her breasts as he climaxed.

Soon they would be together for ever. He would make her his queen. He had whispered to her in her increasingly hot and fervid dreams, *Midsummer, midsummer, midsummer delight; come to the faeries on midsummer night.* Something big was going to happen tonight. She had done what he asked her in the dreams. She was his faithful lover. She knew her reward was coming, and she ached for its sweetness.

At that moment, Finn Beatha looked directly at her and smiled.

Chapter 39

'Don't leave me,' Rav reached out weakly for her as she eased him into her bed. 'Please, Faye.'

'It's okay. You'll be all right,' she whispered as she pulled her old patchwork quilt over him and handed him a herbal tea – a sedative. Valerian and hops would make him sleep, and sleep was what he needed right now. In the distance, she could hear the thump and roar of the festival like a storm off the horizon.

She sat on the edge of the bed and held his hand, waiting for the tea to take effect. He was so feeble, already, after so little time in Faerie.

'I… what happened? I don't understand… what happened.' Rav yawned, and his eyes fluttered closed. 'Where was I, Faye? The dance… I… I can't remember how I got there…' Faye held his hand gently as he drank thirstily.

'Just sleep,' she whispered, and put her other hand on his brow. Rav sighed, and settled back into the pillows. She had walked him back to her house rather than take him anywhere close to his; that close to the faerie road felt like a risk: would Finn take him again? Glitonea had helped them escape, but Finn had seen them in the great hall. He was there, frozen, when she picked up Rav and carried him out.

Faye felt a stab of grief for Moddie, but she pushed it to one side in her heart. Moddie had died, and was still dead. Whether she remained in Murias in spirit or whether Finn would leave her imprisoned in the labyrinth, Faye couldn't guess. She resolved to one day return to free Moddie; she shivered as she remembered the leaves snaking down her mother's throat. She had seen the shadow in Murias, and it was terrifying.

Rav's breathing fell into a deep rhythm and she gently released her hand from his, waiting a few more minutes to make sure he was really knocked out. She looked out of the window; on the horizon the sun was setting over the ocean, making the island off the shore a brooding silhouette.

But it wasn't that easy. After her escape, she wouldn't be allowed back into Murias. She'd done the right thing, but at what cost? She had saved Rav, but agreed to an infernal bargain in the process; it was exactly like the old stories.

At Midwinter one of the faerie kingdoms of Murias, Falias, Gorias or Finias take a child, and at Midsummer, a willing woman. The child must be under a year old, so that it can be raised in the Glass Castle with no memory of its mortal parents, and the woman must be fair, and willing to join the Faerie Dance forever more. In thanks, the faerie king and faerie queen will bless the land and grant boons to the villagers of Abercolme for their generous offerings.

She remembered it from Grandmother's grimoire, but she had hardly believed it could be true. Thinking about it now, Faye shuddered. She had never thought much about having a child herself but, if she did, she would be damned before she gave it up to live in Murias.

Rav started to snore. Faye got up quietly and pulled the coat on properly, then padded downstairs in her socks. She would find a way out of the bargain with Glitonea when the time came; the important thing was that she had saved Rav. She had chosen him over Finn, and it felt right.

Downstairs in the shop the last of the day's light glanced through the plate-glass windows; it was late, past nine, but this was the longest day of the year, after all. Midsummer. And, in the distance, Faye could hear music thumping through the village.

She had to confront Finn. There was a reason Dal Riada were performing at Abercolme Rocks; Finn wasn't just there for the adulation, she was sure. Midsummer was the time the faeries abducted women, to nurse their faerie babies or to live as human lovers, never to return. Was this what Finn had in mind? Before, she would have dismissed the idea. But now, it seemed all too real. The men and women that lay unconscious on the floor of the great hall, imprisoned in Murias, had come from somewhere. And Faye had experienced Dal Riada's own special brand of enchantment for herself.

She looked around her at the shelves and then behind the counter, at the neatly labelled glass jars Moddie had arranged on the shelves and which Faye refilled as faithfully as her mother had. What could help her? What would count as strong enough magic against a faerie king who was able to entrance whole rooms of people with his enchantments? A faerie king who, whenever Faye was in his presence, made her forget everything except him and the deep desire that thrummed in every part of her body when he was near?

If she was to stop him, Faye had to resist his power.

She stared at the jars, feeling the pulse of the music in the ground under her feet, pulling her to the abandoned castle. *Not yet, not yet, I'm not ready*, she thought, trying to push against Finn's call, but her faerie blood was responding to his demand. She could feel that familiar lassitude begin to cover her; instinctively, her hands went to her throat, feeling the seductive ghost of the opals against her skin.

'No, no, NO!' she shouted aloud. Moddie had taught her, when she was older and could understand more about magic, sometimes the best way to banish energy was to just shout at it to *go away* or *be gone*, as loudly and definitely as you could. Whatever spell Finn was casting right now – and she had no doubt that he was – he wasn't going to weave her into it as neatly as he had before.

She took a sage bundle out of a bowl and put it in her pocket with a lighter and a small bottle of rue water. Both were good for banishing and cleansing bad energy, but she doubted that either would be enough to combat Finn. What else? There were poisons – henbane, belladonna, wolfsbane, digitalis – among her herbs, though they were only dangerous if they were used in the wrong quantities or the wrong way. But she couldn't exactly get Finn to drink a poisoned tea if he was onstage… and, anyway, she didn't want to kill him, only stop him taking any more men and women into Murias. After the show perhaps she could sneak backstage and offer him something. But her instinct was that if he was going to do something, it would be during the performance. After would be too late.

Her gaze alighted on the protective charm that hung over the door: a black ribbon onto which were tied nine hagstones: pebbles with naturally occurring holes through them. Both the charm and the bells that hung next to it and jangled every time someone came in kept bad intentions and bad doings away, Grandmother said. And, if you looked though the holes, you could see faeries and see through faerie enchantments. Faye unhooked it and took it down gently, putting it in her pocket. It felt wrong leaving the shop and Rav unguarded and taking the charm with her, but her instinct told her that this was the right thing to do, and Faye found that it was usually best to obey any instincts she had, especially when it came to magic.

She locked the door behind her and set off down the street, noting the minister in his garden opposite, stubbornly ignoring the music. The village was otherwise deserted; everyone was at the concert and that meant that everyone in Abercolme was currently under Finn Beatha's spell. She quickened her steps and broke into a run as the thump of the music grew louder and more insistent, and as the sun set over the ocean, covering Abercolme in darkness.

Chapter 40

Faye could hear Finn's voice over the PA system as she panted her way through the gates and showed her ticket; Rav had left her one. He was singing in that strange, otherworldly way he had, and a chill ran up her spine.

'Bit late, miss.' The older man on the gate nodded her through. 'They're almost finished for the night. You better hurry.'

'I will,' she gasped, and ran through the field where a number of food and drink stalls were packing up for the night; some people were chatting at the makeshift bar, and the occasional person too worse for wear was strewn on the grass. But apart from these, everyone was watching Dal Riada.

Faye felt a wave of fear wash over her in a way it never had before when thinking about Finn.

She was right at the back of the crowd, but there were two large screens, one on either side of the stage, that were showing the action onstage. As she looked over the shoulders of the thousand or more people in front of her, both screens focused in on Finn's face as he held the last note for a long moment. It was jarring to look at him; at the face she knew so well, at the high cheekbones she'd kissed, at the full lips she had bitten gently, had tasted so often. She felt a pang of fear; it was terrifying, how he had been able to seduce her. At the same moment, he opened his eyes and smiled into the camera that fed the screens, and right at her.

It was just a moment, one second, but she knew she had been seen. There was a flicker of displeasure in his eyes.

'Thank you, Abercolme!' he shouted, and bowed at the waist. The rest of the band came to the front of the stage amidst deafening cheering, clapping, catcalling. The crowd were beside themselves, in the same kind of hypnotised delirium she'd been in that first time, at the bar in Edinburgh.

She looked at the faces of the people standing around her, lit only by the florescent plastic bangles and necklaces they wore. Some of their faces were painted with rainbows and flowers, some wore glittery faerie wings that picked up the firelight from six tall iron cages that were packed with burning hay. The strange half-light gave them all a wild look she recognised all too well from the faerie ball. They were enchanted, and Finn Beatha had them right where he wanted them.

The band filed off the stage, but the stage lights stayed down, and the crowd started to cheer for an encore. Faye started to push through the crowd; she had the strong feeling that something was happening, but she didn't know what. She only knew that she had to get to the stage and stop Finn.

'More! More!' the crowd were screaming at the stage. Faye got through a few rows, but the gap she was following closed in front of her just like the labyrinth had, and she was hemmed in by a group of drunk girls – or, at least, they seemed drunk – who wouldn't let her through.

'Eh, stop pushing!' One pushed her back, and her friend shot her an evil, possessive look. 'Get back. We were here first.'

Faye looked around, but she couldn't see a way through. She was starting to panic when she saw Aisha walk onto the stage. Aisha was here! Yes. Of course, she had been so excited about the concert – Rav must have given her a backstage pass. If she could get her friend's attention, Aisha would help her. But Aisha was onstage, and Faye was still rows away from being able to make herself heard over the chaos.

Faye made her way to the side of the crowd and gestured to a St John's Ambulance man, who frowned at her but came over anyway.

'What is it? Concert's nearly over. If you want the ladies' room I can't let you through this way.'

'No, I… it's not that. I need to talk to my friend. On stage. It's urgent,' Faye replied as politely as she could, but her heart was pounding with urgency.

'Sorry, love. No can do.' He smiled at her.

'Please. It's that girl I want to speak to. With the dark hair, up there?' Faye pointed to the side of the stage where Aisha was watching Finn raptly. 'Please, it's urgent. She knows me.'

'Can't it wait, sweetheart? There's still the encore – ten minutes and they'll be finished, this lot. Not that it's my cup of tea.'

'No, really. I need to speak with her now,' Faye gripped the hagstone charm in her pocket. 'Please. It's a matter of life and death.' it wasn't necessarily a lie, she told herself, although she felt like she was being overly dramatic. Still, her instinct was shouting that something bad was about to happen, and she had to stop it.

The man sighed.

'Ah, all right. But don't tell your friends or they'll all want to get through.' He unhooked the security rope and let her through. 'I've got to search ye, I'm afraid.'

'Fine.' Faye opened her coat and turned out her pockets; the man took the sage bundle from her and sniffed it, then gave it back. 'Going to make some stuffing later, are ye?' he grinned, then frowned at the hagstone charm. 'What's this?'

'Oh, it's… a necklace,' Faye lied. The man scratched his beard and held up the stones on their ribbon to his eyes.

'It isn't a necklace, sweetheart. These are hagstones.' He met her eyes and stared into them for a long moment, then handed the charm back to her.

'I can go?' she asked, her eyes darting to the stage. The band were coming back onstage; she could hear the guitarist adjusting the tuning on his guitar before they started playing again.

'Aye. Right you are.' He pointed along a walkway that was delineated by traffic cones along the grass. 'That way should take you to the cabins, and the side of the stage.'

'Oh. Thank you!' Faye tried not to show her surprise, but the man nodded.

'I didn't recognise ye at first. You're Modron Morgan's daughter, aye?'

'That's right.' Faye didn't think she knew the man, but he smiled at her again.

'Fine woman, she was. I know better than to disrespect Moddie's kin. Not least anyone who carries those.' He pointed at the hagstones, which Faye returned to her pocket.

'Thank you.' She smiled this time, and pressed his hand. He blushed.

'Get away with ye. Urgent business, ye said.'

She nodded and ran up the walkway. There wasn't time for pleasantries.

Aisha was still standing at the side of the stage watching the band when Faye found her. She turned around when Faye tapped her on the shoulder.

'Faye! Where have you been? Where's Rav?' Aisha turned her eyes away from Finn reluctantly; Faye could see that whatever spell Finn had cast on the audience, Aisha was caught in it too.

'There's no time. Rav's safe.'

'*Safe*? I just thought the pressure got to him or something. When he didn't turn up—'

'No. He was...' Faye shook her head. 'I'll tell you later, okay? But we have to end the gig. Now. Before Finn can...' She broke off, because Aisha had turned away from her and was staring raptly at the stage. 'Aish! Please. We have to stop it. Put the curtain down. Put the lights up. Whatever we have to do to get the people to leave... I...' Faye exhaled in frustration. 'It's dangerous.'

'What? Why?' Aisha's brow furrowed. 'It's all run fine so far.'

'I don't know exactly,' Faye confessed.

'You don't know? Then why all the panic?' Aisha hissed. 'Faye. Please. It's the last song. Stop being a drama queen.'

Finn was playing the flute, and the quick trills of notes, up and down, had grown faster and faster. The drummer was playing so fast that the individual beats were hardly decipherable.

'But he's not what he seems. Finn Beatha. He's... Look, I know you won't believe me. But he's enchanting this whole crowd for some kind of nefarious purpose. He's a faerie king, Aisha. I know, I've been to the faerie realm. I've seen it. Please. I think he wants to take... a woman, maybe more than one, back to his kingdom. To be his lover. Trapped there for ever.' Faye pulled at her friend's arm to make her turn away from the stage and, as she did so, her hand slid down to Aisha's wrist, and she noticed the rose gold, opal ring on Aisha's index finger: the same as hers.

Her eyes widened in shock as Aisha pulled her hand away.

'No!' Aisha scowled at her. 'God, you've always got to be in control, haven't you? Got to be the top dog. Can't stand it that I have Finn Beatha now.'

On the stage, Finn was opening his arms wide as the rest of the band piped and drummed. Faye hadn't been listening to the tune as she'd been in such a panic to get to Aisha, but now she realised that it was familiar.

'You… and Finn?' Faye's heart felt like it stopped beating as she stared at her friend. She was dimly aware that the crowd had formed a huge circle and was dancing, running around it in exactly the same way as the dancers at the faerie ball in Murias. She stared out at their contorted faces and a dawning horror made her mute.

'Yes. Me and Finn.' Aisha turned her wide brown eyes to Finn, metres away, and he held his hand out to her. Below him, the crowd were no longer dancing; now it had turned into something else, something darker and more savage. They reeled and trampled each other; there was screaming, but Aisha couldn't hear it, Faye could tell: her face was beatific as she caught and returned Finn's gaze. 'It was the spell, Faye. It brought him to me,' she sighed and then, without warning, ran on to the stage towards the faerie king's open arms.

'Aisha! No!' Faye grabbed for her friend's hand, but Aisha's fingers slipped through hers. Faye ran after her, but it was too late. Finn Beatha picked Aisha up, and glared victoriously at Faye.

'You didn't want me, *sidhe-leth*. Don't blame me if someone else did,' his voice cut through the music as if there was a direct channel between them.

'You can't take her!' Faye shouted, but Finn cradled Aisha in one arm and thrust his other palm out towards her. Faye felt an invisible barrier rise in the space between them.

'You can't stop me,' he replied, smiling, and swept Aisha into his arms so that she lay in them like a child, bewitched. 'I will have my lovers, human or half-human; it is no matter to me. We need human blood to keep us strong. Worry not, Faye. I will keep your friend safe in my bed.' He cast a wry glance over the half-naked, cavorting crowd. 'Perhaps with some of these others, too. A faerie king does not like to be bored. And I need half-human heirs, and women ripe to nurse them when I am done with their mothers…'

Finn was no longer singing and so the drumming reached fever pitch; everyone in the crowd was leaping and screaming. Their faces were masks, and the sheen of humanity was slipping from them; they became more and more bestial with every second.

Faye felt horrified that she had ever desired Finn so deeply. She took out the hagstone charm from her pocket and tried to push through the energy barrier towards him. 'You will not take her!' Faye screamed, holding it up like a lamp in the darkness, but his power was too great and the barrier, whatever it was made of, choked her as if she was drowning.

In desperation, she threw it at him, but he caught it and jumped into the middle of the crowd, which ran to him like rivulets into a stream.

'Your charm cannot stop me,' he called as he jumped. 'It protects *you* from my kind like it always has, *sidhe-leth*. But none of these others are so protected.' Aisha clung to him, her arms around his neck, burying her face into his chest, kissing him. Finn threw the hagstone charm away to the far side of the stage.

'Aisha! Don't go!' Faye screamed, but she could see the enchantment in her friend's eyes; Aisha didn't even hear Faye. She knew what Aisha was feeling, and she felt a stab of shame at her own hypocrisy; no-one would have been able to call her back from Finn's arms when she had been the one in his favour. But Aisha was at Finn's mercy now; if she displeased him, she would have no defence against his power; she didn't have the magic that Glitonea had taught Faye; she was not half-faerie. Aisha might not survive the faerie reel if she was thrust into it by a faerie king who had grown tired of her. She scrabbled at the dirty stage floor for the charm, where it had landed among wires and electrical leads.

Faye watched as others in the crowd grabbed him and went to him willingly, for they all wanted him; they had all been enchanted in exactly the same way as she had.

'Farewell, *sidhe-leth*,' Finn's stormy eyes met hers and she felt grief pass through her: she still wanted him, even now; her heart and the deep passion he inspired didn't want him to take Aisha. She knew it was wrong, but she couldn't help it. She steeled herself against the power in his gaze. 'Until our lips meet again.'

'You will never have me again!' she screamed, making her eyes meet his with as much power in them as she could muster. *Resist him, resist*, she told herself, but his power was strong. If she had not had the hagstones' burning heat in her palm, anchoring her to the ordinary world, she felt that she would have followed him. *But Rav needs me*, she thought, desperately: she made herself repeat his name. *Rav. The man who loves you. Who you could love, if this madness was removed from your life…*

Finn laughed, and she knew that he was reading her thoughts.

'As you will. Go back to your mortal man. But you will always yearn for me,' he smiled, and there was no kindness in his expression, but instead the calculating look of an eagle weighing up its prey. 'And since you have betrayed me three times now: by loving the mortal, by rescuing him from my realm, and for trying to thwart me tonight, I will bar you from entering Murias by any means from now on.'

'I am half-faerie. It's my right to be there if I choose,' Faye retorted, but dread twisted her stomach. Murias was Finn's world, and she knew he could do whatever he wanted. He could keep her out. There was no way to stop him, no way she could help Aisha if he took her there.

Finn called out something in Gaelic to the band, still playing onstage; as if following an order, they finished the song, dropped their instruments and jumped into the crowd, grabbing people at random.

'Please! I'm begging you. Please.' Faye fell to her knees as an unnatural golden witchlight flashed in the crowd for a moment, on and off. The sudden darkness interspersed with light caught the jerking and flailing movements of the crowd in strange, monstrous angles and shadows. Faye blinked, shielding her eyes as bodies writhed and thrusted.

'Take me! Take me instead of them and I'll be loyal to you. Forever!' Perhaps it wasn't too late to trick him into taking her instead? As half-faerie, she would survive and perhaps be able to find a way back. If he took the villagers, they would most likely end up in the faerie reel when Finn and the rest of the fae tired of them: a slow and horrible death.

'Too late, Faye Morgan,' Finn smiled.

The golden light lit the whole crowd for one brief moment. A many-voiced scream, a chorus of the crowd's violent, insane lust ripped through Abercolme, and then, just as suddenly, a dark and dead hush followed it, which was far, far worse.

Chapter 41

Faye ran down the steps of the stage into the crowd. The villagers who were left looked around them as if they were waking up from a dream. She had to try to re-enter the faerie realm and rescue whoever had been taken.

She started to try and push her way through the crowd, but they were confused and disoriented; in many cases they were hurt: people sat on the ground, holding arms that might be broken and with cuts and grazes to their faces, legs, anywhere with exposed skin.

Faye had some basic first-aid knowledge; she'd taken a course years ago when she took over the running of the shop. *You never know when someone might faint on the premises, or worse*, Moddie had warned, *it's smart to be prepared.* She wished Annie was with her; Annie would shoulder her way through the crowd and lead Faye through; or, she would put her hand on Faye's shoulder, look into her eyes and say *sweetheart, let it go for now. These people need you. Let's focus on the wounded first.*

She looked around in desperation. Every second that Finn was gone it felt like it would be harder to go after them – to save the ones they had taken with them. She had to get down to the beach and find the faerie road; it was the only way into Murias that she knew... Feeling that she was doing the wrong thing, she started making her way out, but there was nowhere she could get through easily now, and the confusion was starting to turn into alarm. People were running around, screaming.

Faye saw the same group of women she had tried to push past on her way in wandering around, looking for a friend they'd lost; Faye suspected they wouldn't take it well if she explained to them that their friend was most likely on her way to the realm of faerie, or already there, naked and willingly pleasuring Finn and his faerie court. *Or, unwillingly, but enchanted*, Faye thought grimly.

But then, Grandmother's voice spoke in her ear, as if she was suddenly next to her. *Don't judge them for the things they don't understand, Faye*, she said. Faye felt that if she turned around she'd see Grandmother there, short and round with her hair still long and twined up in a grey bun and the ghosts of a life of wisdom and kindness etched into her face. *It is your job to help the people, Faye. Never forget that*, Grandmother's voice said.

'But I have to help them. The ones that were taken by Finn,' she protested.

Aye, and ye will. Grandmother's voice seemed to come from all around her; she was in the wind, in the night, in the moonlight that bathed the chaos around her. *But first things first.*

Grandmother was always right; Faye had known better than to question her when she was alive, and she certainly wasn't going to argue with Grandmother in spirit. For a moment, she closed her eyes and breathed in; in a half-second she felt Grandmother's hand in hers, like Annie's that first day at school.

Faye cast one last desperate gaze at the beach below and turned back to the people that needed her.

❦

There were burns. After Finn and the rest of Dal Riada had jumped off the stage into the throng, the burning haystacks had hit tents and stands, falling on people who were too dazed to get out of the way. Without any useful equipment or medicines, she made do with what she had.

She managed to herd most people away from the fires and persuade some of them to help her find the worst wounded; even if they did nothing other than sit with them, it was something. She kept listening for sirens over the shouting and the crying, but there was nothing.

What use is it being half-fae if I can't help these people somehow? she berated herself.

In her mind's eye, she was taken back for a brief second to her immersion in the golden chalice. She remembered all her ancestors merging with her; giving her their gifts. She had what they had, now; she contained all the power of the Morgans. Their knowledge, their skills with herbs and magic; their loves and losses. It was like possessing a vast library she had not yet read. *I might have all that within me now,* she thought, opening her eyes in desperation, *but I don't know how to wield it.*

And yet the memory was persistent. She let the faces come, until one face smiled at her, up through the water. Without having ever seen her face, she knew it was Grainne Morgan. And in a sudden rush of knowledge, Grainne spoke to her and told her what to do.

Faye left the woman she had just propped up against a stone wall and asked a nearby man to keep an eye on her. Then she made her way back through the chaos and onto the stage.

She picked up the microphone stand that had fallen over when Finn had jumped off the stage and adjusted it to her height.

The words were alien to her, but she sang them anyway. She knew they made up the song that Grainne had sung to the faeries in her last hour; the song that had brought her familiars, the water fae, to take her home.

Faye felt self-conscious, but she persevered, pronouncing the strange words and following the simple lilting melody which was at once familiar, like a half-remembered lullaby, and as strange as the realm of Murias itself. The PA system was still on, and she heard her voice echoed back to her over the noise of the people below.

And as she sang, she saw them coming; the host of water, surging over the black sea.

And they covered the crowd, the servants of Murias; the servants of the high queen, who Faye had promised her first-born child. Faye sang, knowing the horror of the debt that she deepened with Glitonea, but unable to stop; had Grainne Morgan made a similar bargain? Was that why the fae had rescued her? Faye felt as though reality turned back like a tide and she saw the bare ocean floor, littered with wrecks and bones. *There is knowledge in you now*, said Grainne's voice in her ear. *But it comes at a price.*

And as Faye continued singing, the water faeries, in all their strange and unknown forms – many-legged, gilled, scaled, wraith-like – healed the wounded, brushing their burns and cuts away as if they had never been. They swam over the fires and extinguished them, babbling to each other like mobile streams. She watched as the crowd quieted; as they came back to consciousness, as their pain left them and a flat calm covered the castle grounds.

There was no sense of time; Faye only knew that she must keep singing until the fae had finished their work, for it was Grainne's song that kept them with her. But it was Faye's power that amplified it, and called them so quickly. She felt it deep within her; a waterfall, a depth of flowing, pounding water that couldn't – and shouldn't – be stopped. It was Faye's bargain with the faerie queen that meant these people could be saved. One small life for so many. But as the song spilled out of her, as she felt the power come, she cried at what she had to sacrifice for it.

Finally Faye stopped singing, and felt the power that had filled her quieten.

For one moment, Glitonea appeared before her on a sleigh of water, pulled by two black kelpies.

'I have helped you again, Daughter of Light and Shadows,' she smiled coldly. 'Remember our bargain.' The faerie queen clapped her hands, and she and the faerie host disappeared.

In the distance, Faye heard sirens approaching.

Chapter 42

It was a few weeks later and Faye and Rav lay in Faye's bed, their legs entwined.

'If you go, I'll make you a cup of tea every day for a week,' Faye offered.

'Make me one today then.' Rav snuggled next to her. 'I don't want to get up. It's too nice in here.'

'If you make it, I'll bring you cake with your tea every day for a week,' she counter-offered. 'Please, Rav. Go on.' She pulled the duvet off his side of the bed. 'See, you're cold now anyway. Might as well get up.'

'Oh, fine.' Rav got up and pulled on a hoodie over his boxers. 'Only because you might turn me into some reptile or something.'

'Shut up,' she said, then, after a second, called after him. 'An otter. I could turn you into an otter, that would be a sufficiently cute replacement.'

Faye's smile faded as she stared out through the window at her late summer herb garden. She hadn't had the time to tend it much. Soon it would be time to harvest and dry everything for the winter; the rose hips dried for incenses, made into a vitamin-rich syrup for coughs and colds. The lavender had to be dried, the nettles dried for tea or made into healing tinctures. The apples would be made into apple jam, apple chutney; for a few weeks in the late summer she would fill boxes of the sweet, red fruit and put them outside the shop for anyone to take. The irony of witches giving away free apples wasn't lost on her, but otherwise they would waste.

Rav was recovering slowly. After the concert they'd shut themselves away in Faye's house. She'd closed the shop – not permanently, but until she felt ready to reopen it. She didn't care that news of what happened at the concert – the mysterious disappearances of eight people – had made Abercolme into a media circus. She could have opened the shop and talked to all the journalists that had, initially, waited on her doorstep, like they had all the local businesses, wanting a scoop, an insight, some secret that the people of Abercolme were keeping to themselves. She could have made a fortune, selling to all the curious that streamed into the village, determined to uncover the truth behind the rumours. That aliens had abducted the men and women. That they had been kidnapped for ransom by a secret sect within the village. Worst of all, that Abercolme was the centre of a black magic community that had sacrificed all eight to the Devil. Faye wondered how the minister felt about that; she doubted he was pleased about the village being associated with devil worship. Perhaps now he would – they all would – understand how Grainne Morgan felt, all those years ago.

But Faye kept her mouth shut. Nobody talked to the press; not Muriel in the bakery, not Mrs Kennedy, not the minister or anyone else. They kept themselves to themselves, and, slowly, the press began to leave.

Rav had been left weakened by his abduction into faerie; Faye was shocked at how little energy he had for weeks afterwards, and the deep burns on his legs and arms that were only now starting to subside with her repeated treatment of comfrey salve. Faye could only imagine that the burns came from being lashed to the black kelpie that had taken him to Murias. He had hardly any appetite for the first week, and had gone in and out of consciousness for days until she brought him round, finally, by making him eat some soup.

Faye couldn't heal him with the faerie magic as she had done to the crowd at the concert; she couldn't ask any more of Glitonea. Despite the terrible exchange Glitonea demanded, the water fae that had swarmed over the sea had taken away every injury from the people that were left, confused and hurt, after Dal Riada had disappeared, taking their sacrifices with them. *Midsummer sacrifices.* Finn had spoken of it; Grandmother had warned her, in her way.

A familiar stab of guilt wrenched Faye's stomach; ever since the concert, after she had limped home in exhaustion, unable to do anything more than slump into her bed, beside Rav, she had felt it. Had she known what was going to happen, would she have been Finn's willing sacrifice? Should she have gone, so that he didn't have to look elsewhere, and find Aisha and the rest of them? At least Faye could survive in Murias and, perhaps, have time to plot her escape as she had done before...

She had been back to Black Sands, but the faerie road had vanished. At least, it had for her. She knew that Finn had revoked her access to Murias, and Aisha and the others would eventually die if they stayed there. She doubted she had anything left that she could offer Glitonea in exchange for Aisha's release, and a dungeon awaited Faye if she managed to find her way back.

She heard Rav's footsteps on the stairs and sat up in bed, chasing the dark thoughts away for now. Though they were both recovering in their own separate ways, their time together had been sweet. It was just them, eating the food she had in her larder and the freezer, and the ripe fruit and vegetables from the garden. Faye hardly slept, racked with worry for Aisha; whenever she thought about her friend – even though she had gone willingly with Finn – she felt shadow overtake her. Rav found it hard to get through to her at those times. But, nonetheless, she and Rav were talking, sharing themselves with each other. And that, in itself, was a healing. She resolved to get Aisha back somehow.

Faye had told Rav everything that had happened with Finn, even though it was hard to talk about; she had betrayed Rav. *She* was the reason he had been taken, endangered. *But you're also the reason I'm alive now*, he'd replied, holding her shaking hands when she confessed. How she had been seduced by Finn; how she was half-faerie, and how that had blinded her to the darkness of the faerie realm. But there was also something in the shadow part of her that loved faerie and always would. On the nights after Rav had fallen asleep and she sat up in bed, hugging her knees and watching the moon, she worried about Finn. It wasn't over; he had more or less said so. But she wanted it to be. She wanted a normal life.

You can't be anything other than who you truly are, Rav had sighed. *And, now that I know all of it, I can make the choice to be with you or not. Problem is, I can't help loving you. It's not a choice. It just is.*

He set a tray with two of Grandmother's old china cups with faded roses painted on them, a teapot and a packet of biscuits on the white-painted wood table by the bed.

'I checked the post.' He handed Faye a sheaf of envelopes and papers. She made a face at a couple of handwritten notes from journalists with their business cards attached and screwed them up.

'No thanks,' she muttered. There were a couple of bills to pay, and one handwritten envelope without a stamp. 'More press?' She showed it to Rav who got back into bed next to her and poured the tea. He made a face and took a biscuit from the packet.

Faye opened the envelope and read what was inside, then made a yelping noise. Rav spilled his tea on the duvet and swore mildly.

'What's up?' he asked, dabbing at the cotton where the tea had stained it.

'It's from the minister. He says they had the vote for the statue versus memorial. I completely forgot that was planned for the week after the concert.' She stared at the letter in disbelief, and then at Rav. 'Oh my God.'

'What? Don't be upset, Faye. It's something we can sort out another time. Don't worry about it for now.' He put his cup down on the tray and put his arm around her.

'They voted for Grainne. For the memorial,' Faye whispered.

Rav stared at her in amazement.

'Abercolme village voted for a memorial to dead witches over James the First? Are you serious?' He grabbed the plain piece of notebook paper from Faye and read it for himself.

People saw what you did. Whatever you did, Miss Morgan, you were the one that helped the wounded at the castle. Without you, some may have died. The village recognises its debt to you.

'Oh my God,' he repeated, a grin spreading over his face. 'I can't believe it! This place of all places...'

Faye realised she was crying. The stress of the last months was still with her, always near the surface. It could break through at any time, and often did. She pulled her knees into her chest and hugged them, sobbing.

'Oh, Faye. Don't be sad. This is a good thing!' Rav rubbed her back as she let the tears come; after a minute, she could talk again.

'I am happy. I'm so happy, for Grainne and the rest. They'll finally be remembered like they should be. But…'

'But what?' Rav's warm hand made slow circles on her back.

'I don't feel like they should have a debt to me. I didn't do a good thing. It was wrong of me to have a relationship with Finn. I think it made him stronger here, somehow, having me, and… Aisha… loving him, reinforcing his power. I think Grandmother and Moddie didn't tell me about faerie because they were afraid. And now he's gone and taken those people and I don't know how to get them back.'

Faye got out of bed and went to stand at the window; she stared out at her garden, bathed in the rich gold sun of early August. She opened the window and leaned out to breathe in the air; the smell of the wild roses, the raspberry leaf and lavender scenting the soft air.

'There's a card from Annie, too.' Faye felt her heart lift; she missed her best friend terribly. She let out a short laugh when she looked at the photo, which was a London Beefeater mooning the camera; the caption said: *Having a ball in London!*

'Typical Annie.' She showed Rav, who rolled his eyes affectionately. *Dear Faye*, Annie had written in her rounded script.

Hope you're okay. I tried calling a few times but I couldn't get hold of you. I hope you got my emails and letters. I'd come up and check on you but the filming schedule down here is mad…

Faye hadn't had it in her to reply much to any of Annie's emails yet, except to say that she was all right, that she and Rav were taking it easy together, and that she'd catch Annie up with everything when she was up to it.

Anyway, it's fun. Coven of Love *is kind of cheesy but I do get to wear great outfits. Plus things are going well with Suze. Will fill you in more when I see you – come down and see me when you're feeling up to it, maybe. There's room for you here if you want. Thinking of you and love you always, sweetheart. Annie xxx*

Faye smiled and handed the card to Rav, then stared back out at the garden. Roses would always mean faerie to her now; the crystal castle of magic where they were underfoot, the petals she had taken and used, wrapped in a piece of kelpie's scale. It had been the smell of rose in the air when she had first made love to Rav at the beach, almost upon the faerie road. But the wild white and yellow roses that had grown in this garden all her life were a different smell, and they reminded her of Grandmother and Moddie, and playing at witches with Annie in the summers long before Faye knew anything of love.

If she drew power from the realm of faerie, then she also drew it from this house, this garden, and her ancestors, the Morgans. She had absorbed the powers of all of them that had come before, and, over time, she would unwrap every piece of knowledge, and know what they had known; feel what they had felt and seen and heard.

'You'll put this right. I know you will.' Rav stood behind her. His arms circled her waist, and she turned around to kiss him. There was electricity between them like there always had been, and there was kindness and warmth, too. For the first time in her life Faye felt known. And she knew that, in part, that was because she had begun to know herself for the first time, and accept the shadow as the continuing legacy of the light.

To be continued…

A Letter from Anna

Thank you so much for reading *Daughter of Light and Shadows*. I hope you enjoyed it as much as I liked writing it. If you'd like to keep up-to-date with all of my latest releases, you can sign up at the following link. Your email address will never be shared, and you can unsubscribe at any time.

www.bookouture.com/anna-mckerrow

I came up with the idea for this book when I was visiting family in Scotland. My uncle, husband and son had gone to find the beach in the lovely village we had gone to for the day, and my aunt wanted to show me a shop on the high street which she said she knew I'd love. Sure enough, I did, and I started thinking about a story that centred around a homely but magical shop that had always belonged to a family of witches.

At the same time, I was reading a lot about Scottish faerie lore and was fascinated with the real-life accounts of men and women that claimed to have spent time 'away with the faeries' – and the Seelie Court, a grand place where the Scottish faeries feasted and danced and liked to ride out on grand horses. I started wondering how intoxicating it must be to spend time in such a place – and what would compel a man or woman not to want to leave…

If you have time, I'd love it if you were able to write a review of *Daughter of Light and Shadows*. Feedback is really useful and also makes a huge difference in helping new readers discover one of my books for the first time.

Alternatively, if you'd like to contact me personally, you can reach me via my website, Facebook page, Twitter or Instagram. I love hearing from readers, and always reply.

Again, thank you so much for deciding to spend some time reading *Daughter of Light and Shadows*. I'm looking forward to sharing my next book with you very soon.

With all best wishes,
Anna

 www.annamckerrow.com

annamckerrowauthor

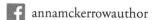 @AnnaMckerrow

 @annamckerrow

9 781786 814654